DANGER ZONE

Also available from MIRA Books and
SHIRLEY PALMER

A VEILED JOURNEY

And published under the pseudonym
NELL BRIEN

LIONESS

DANGER ZONE

SHIRLEY PALMER

MIRA®

ISBN 1-55166-943-9

DANGER ZONE

Visit us at www.mirabooks.com

Printed in U.S.A.

First Printing: October 2002
10 9 8 7 6 5 4 3 2 1

For my son
Dan Saxon Palmer, Jr.
With love

ACKNOWLEDGMENTS

While writing this book, I called upon the expertise of many people who gave generously of their time and patience.

My thanks go particularly to Special Agent (ret.) John Hoos of the FBI; Special Agent (ret.) Mario Fontana, Bureau of Alcohol, Tobacco and Firearms; Chief P.A. Specialist Randy Midget of the U.S. Coast Guard; and to David Watkins, expert in boats, helicopters, armaments, ordnance, explosives and general mayhem, whose wizardry regularly astonishes us in the world of movies. Of course, any errors are entirely mine.

Ken Atchity, of AEI Los Angeles, continues to be a good friend, as well as a brilliant agent. Thanks, Ken.

The people at MIRA have been, as usual, wonderful. No writer could ask for more support and enthusiasm than I have received from Editorial Director Dianne Moggy, editor extraordinaire Amy Moore-Benson and the entire team that has brought *Danger Zone* to life.

PROLOGUE

They were waiting as he knew they would be. He'd placed the call himself on Friday, a less than sixty-second conversation that couldn't be traced but he'd used a voice scrambler anyway to make sure.

Their Cherokee was slowing, just nosing through the gates of the private terminal at New Orleans International. He looked at the Jamaican impatiently.

"Come on, let's go." He pointed to the Learjet two hundred yards away, the only aircraft fired up, poised for flight. At the bottom of the steps a man dragged on a cigarette and kept his eyes on the Cherokee. "That's it."

The Jamaican tapped the steering wheel, eyes roaming, examining the perimeter of the airport. There was no one at the gate, no visible security of any kind. The Jamaican did not move.

"You crazy, mon? How you know the cops or the army or someone ain't sittin' around out there someplace playin' with theirselves, just waitin' to take us down?"

"I don't." And it didn't matter. Nothing did. Hadn't since before Bear Mountain. Six days before, to be exact. He dragged his mind back to the present, to the Jamaican sitting next to him reeking of *ganja* and some shit smelling island hair oil, to the stink of cordite from the weapons and urine from the kid lying across the seat behind them in soaked pajamas, mercifully silent now, unconscious from the shot he'd given him.

He nudged the Jamaican's arm. "You took the pay. The job's not finished. Go."

The driver eased the Cherokee through the gates, down the line of small tethered aircraft, their wheels chocked. He stopped a few feet from the Learjet. The man at the bottom of the steps was still, a hand in one pocket, eyes watchful. He dropped the cigarette, ground it under his shoe. A moment passed. Nothing moved.

Satisfied, he looked at the Jamaican. "Okay. Get the kid. And take this stuff." He handed the Jamaican the syringe and Ketamine.

The man got out, opened the rear door, dragged the damp boy across the seat.

He looked at the tousled head falling back over the Jamaican's arm, the soft childish limbs dangling like the limbs on a rag doll. His own boy had once looked like that, sweet and innocent. He turned his eyes away.

"If he wakes, tell them to give him another shot. Only one, otherwise they'll have a dead kid on their hands. He has to stay alive for the next few days. Tell them someone will be in touch."

The transfer took seconds. By the time the Cherokee was at the exit gate, the jet was battened and had started to move out onto the runway.

He looked at his watch and saw that it was still only 9:15.

A bright Sunday morning in Louisiana.

ONE

October 3rd

Sam Cady tightened his arms around his wife and Maggie wriggled her shoulders in response, burrowing her back deeper into his chest. A light breeze off the lake ruffled her hair, blowing strands like silk across his face. Sam bent his head, breathing in the rose scent she used. The picnic had wound down to the marshmallow-roasting and guitar-strumming stage, but earlier Jimmy's triumphant grin when he slid into home plate had been a sight to see. A milestone for them both, their first father/son softball game.

Sam took another moment to listen to the end-of-day sounds: the chorus of bullfrogs and cicadas, Petey Le Pont's guitar riffs from the other side of the fire as he noodled his way into a tune, the murmur of sleepy kids, the soothing voices of their mothers.

It didn't get much better than this. But it was time to leave. He put his lips against Maggie's ear. "Honey, I've got to go, but you and Jimmy stay. You can get a ride later with Petey and Elle."

"No, we'll come with you. It's been a big day. He should be in bed." Maggie shifted Jimmy's little boy weight in her lap. "And he's too big for me to carry now."

The four-year-old protested as Sam lifted his son from Maggie's lap. "I can walk, Dad."

"Okay, buddy." Sam set him on his feet, met Maggie's eyes and they both grinned as Jimmy took a few sleepy steps. Lately Jimmy had been doing his best to copy his father's swagger, but at four he was still having difficulty with a loose-hipped stride.

"Just because that man of yours has to go to his high-payin' job, don't mean you have to leave, no," Petey called. "Plenty poor policemen here love to see you home, *cher.*"

Sam placed a possessive arm across Maggie's shoulders. "Think I trust my wife to you guys?" he called back. "Know you too well, yeah." Sam imitated the exaggerated Cajun accent his former partner liked to sport on social occasions. "See you next Sunday, Pierre. If the weather holds, the brim will be jumpin' sure."

Maggie blew a farewell kiss to Elle, who was leaning contentedly against her enormous husband, their son, Yves, asleep in her arms. "Best party yet, Elle."

"You say that every year, *cher,* but I do love hearing it. Let's talk later in the week. We'll go shopping, spend some real money while these two go fishing, okay?"

The remnants of the potluck picnic were packed up on the trestle table under the oak trees, and Maggie sorted through to find her own dishes and the slices of the anniversary cake Elle had wrapped for them. Above the table a banner, "Elle and Petey Happy Tenth Anniversary," sagged in the moist evening air. They answered the chorus of goodbyes from the other guests, Sam responding in kind to the good-natured ribbing about his high-paying job from cops he had served with in his twenty years on the New Orleans Police Department.

The ride home was quiet. In spite of early protests that he wasn't tired, Jimmy fell asleep the minute he was strapped into his child's seat in the back; and Sam and Maggie were content to drive in companionable silence. It had been a long day.

As usual Max was waiting in the hallway as the front door opened, giving small whimpering sounds of welcome, his big body twisting as he wagged a vestigial tail. Sam had argued for a hunting dog, a tick hound, a redbone, even a Lab, but Maggie had got the Rottweiler she'd wanted. She rubbed Max's ears, let him out into the garden while Sam carried Jimmy up to bed. She filled the percolator for coffee, smiling as she listened to the murmur of voices upstairs.

Sam wrestled Jimmy out of his clothes, thrusting limbs that suddenly had the resilience of overcooked spaghetti into the sleeves and legs of his baseball jammies. In the bathroom, he made a pass at Jimmy's face with a damp washcloth, loaded his son's toothbrush with paste, watched Jimmy's hit-and-miss motions with the brush.

"I don't have to pee, Daddy."

"Yeah, you do. Come on." Sam stood behind his son over the toilet. "We can stand here all night if we have to, buddy."

The bathroom ritual finished, Jimmy knelt by the side of his bed.

"God bless Mama. God bless Daddy. God bless Max. God bless my baseball mitt. God bless the oak trees. God bless the redbirds..."

Sam grinned as Jimmy glanced at him through the cracks of his fingers over his eyes. "Okay, Tiger, how about God bless the world, and then into bed?"

"Okay. God bless the world. Can I have a drink of water, Dad?" Jimmy scrambled under the covers.

"One."

With Jimmy finally settled, Sam crossed the wide hall to the master bedroom. Maggie had insisted on remodeling when they bought the house so that the room spanned the width of the building at the end of the hall, with views onto the street in front and the garden in back. He checked the front windows first, stood for a moment admiring the quiet cul-de-sac, the way the golden light from the streetlamps drifted through the trees. He crossed the room, opened the double doors onto the gallery overlooking the garden, examined the locks then shot home the bolts before shedding the jeans and sweatshirt he'd worn to the party.

"Did you check both doors, Sam?" Maggie asked from the doorway. She put the tray she carried on the table in front of the fireplace.

"Yup. Before we left, and again a moment ago." Sam took the cup of coffee Maggie handed him.

Maggie poured her own coffee then settled herself against the headboard to watch him change. "You're looking good, Cady, for a man your age." At forty-four, he was fourteen years older than she. But he carried his 180 pounds easily on a six-foot frame and worked hard to keep his body in the same shape it had been in when he'd joined the police department straight out of Tulane. He worried about it, but she thought the way his dark hair was silvering made him look sexier than ever. It was as thick as it had ever been, and the silver emphasized the gray of his eyes.

"If I had more time, babe," Sam said, "I'd be happy to show you how age just sweetens the wine. But duty calls."

"Maybe later, then." Maggie fluttered her eyelashes at him over the rim of her cup.

"You can bet on it, darlin'." Sam sat beside her on the bed, slipped a hand inside her bra as he leaned forward to kiss her.

Maggie felt as if her flesh was melting under his touch. He'd had that effect on her from the moment he'd walked into her grade-school classroom over five years ago. Her cup tipped dangerously and she managed to put it on the bedside table before it spilled. "Don't start anything you don't mean to finish, Cady. I have to get some sleep tonight while you're flying that chopper." She took a shaky breath. "Be careful, won't you?"

"I'm always careful, babe. That's why I've got the job. Is it my imagination or has Elle gained a mite of weight around the middle?"

Maggie nodded, aware that he was changing the subject. He'd thought long and hard before leaving the department, but the offer had been too good to turn down. Now, instead of flying for the New Orleans PD, he flew for Louisiana Power and Light, and took great care not to let her know just how difficult and dangerous the job was.

"She's pregnant. After the miscarriages, she didn't want to say anything until she was safely through the first trimester."

"That's great. Old Petey must be feeling like a dog with two tails." Sam kissed her neck.

"Mmm." Maggie closed her eyes, turned her head so that his lips could move more easily over her skin, losing herself to the feel of him. She wound her arms around him, pulled him down until he fell across her and she could slip a hand under his belt.

Sam's voice was hoarse. "I gotta go, babe."

"Take a minute."

Her body still flushed, Maggie went to the window to watch Sam back out of the driveway, following the Explorer with her eyes until he turned onto Magnolia Avenue. Then she slipped on her robe, went quietly downstairs, Max at her heels, checked again the locks on the doors and windows she had checked before they left that afternoon. Satisfied, she returned, stood for a moment in the doorway of Jimmy's room, content just to watch him breathe. She directed Max to his bed on the floor by Jimmy's side, kissed her son again, then went back to the master bedroom. She picked up her book, settled back against the pillows although it would be hours before she would be able to sleep. Sam didn't know she couldn't sleep when he worked at night. He didn't know, either, that she knew exactly how dangerous his job was.

But there was so much that Sam didn't know.

TWO

Sam kept the blades turning just above stalling speed, his eyes moving from one side of the chopper to the other as he judged the distance from the whipping limbs of the cypress trees thrusting up from the swamp thirty feet below. Daz Robbins had to be kept steady on the end of the cable, above the water and weed tossing in the chop. Dawn was breaking, and for this kind of flying Sam needed all the light he could get. It was a tradeoff, leaving this section until the end of their shift. He rotated his shoulders, knowing Daz had to be as tired as he was. Suspended from a chopper above miles of swamp checking transmission lines was no job for the fainthearted. Doing it with only a spotlight stabbing the blackness was asking too much of their nerves when he had to fly this close to the trees. The cypresses were dense on this section of the line, taller, crowding together as they reached for the sun. One small error of judgment, and goodbye chopper. Anything left of the two of them would be groceries for 'gators and water moccasins.

Sparks sprayed in a fountain of gold against the darkness of the water below, outlining the suspended figure. Something had touched the live cable, and Sam quickly took the chopper up another five feet, hovering steadily. A voice spoke in his ear.

"That's it for me. Beam me up, Scottie. Our night's work is about done."

Heart rate dropping back to normal at the sound of the lineman's drawl, Sam threw the switch on the winch, the grind of the cable joining the whomp of the rotors. He fought to keep the chopper steady as Daz's weight caught a gust of wind and he began swinging like a pendulum below the hovering bird. Slowly the arcs lessened, and looking like a character in an old science fiction movie, the lineman hoisted himself into the cockpit. He unzipped his insulated suit, shrugged it off his shoulders.

"Bubba, there's gotta be an easier way to make an honest buck."

"Yeah, but where else we gonna have this much fun?" Sam swung the helicopter toward home.

For fifteen minutes he flew just above the treetops, watching heron rise from the branches of the cypresses, skim across the open ponds in the swamp as the helicopter passed overhead. There seemed to be more of them this year; maybe the swamp was starting to recover from the toxic mess made by the chemical and oil industries. More heron meant more brim, more redfish. Another couple of years and the fishing would be really good again. Maggie insisted Jimmy was too young yet, but as soon as Jimmy was five he'd get serious with her about taking him on his first overnight fishing trip. Elle allowed Petey to take their only child out when Yves was four but Maggie still wouldn't let Jimmy out of her sight. Petey thought it was because Maggie came from up north. Sam smiled to himself. As far as Petey was concerned, anyone not born in Louisiana might just as well be from another planet.

Sam settled onto the pad, switched off the double Rolls-Royce engines. Daz gathered up his gear and the two men walked into the flight building, called a greeting to the ground staff. Sam poured himself a cup of ancient chicory coffee from the pot that, rumor had it, never went off the boil, and settled at a desk to complete his flight log.

"Tell 'em we want a raise," Daz said over his shoulder as he disappeared toward his locker.

"Yeah, sure, they always listen to me. See you, buddy."

Ten minutes later, Sam stepped back out into a fresh untouched day. The streets were empty of traffic and the air smelled of moss and orange blossom. He drove leisurely, appreciating the Sunday morning quiet, the anticipation of the next two days off duty. On Lacrosse Street, he stopped at Pellie's for fresh beignets.

"Just two minutes old, these," Aunt Pellie Brown said. "Couple dozen for you this morning, Sam?" Aunt Pellie had been saying the same thing every Sunday and Wednesday morning since they moved into the neighborhood the year Jimmy was born.

"Even dozen will do it this morning, Pellie." Sam patted his flat belly. "Got a few pounds settling in here."

"You lookin' good, honey. That pretty wife of yours complain, you just come knocking at my door any time."

"Only if you make sure Horace ain't around. Don't aim to mess with no jealous husbands, me."

Pellie laughed, a rich comfortable sound. Pellie wouldn't see sixty again, and Horace was ten years older. "You let me manage that man." While talking Pellie had packed the beignets into a pastry box, added a couple more. "These for the boy. You tell him they're from Aunt Pellie, you hear?"

"Sure thing. Thanks, Pellie. See you Wednesday." As he left, Sam waved a greeting to the regulars sitting at the counter, dipping beignets into the coffee Pellie blended herself, just the right amount of chicory. Pellie's coffee and beignets were famous in the neighborhood, and had even been mentioned by the food critic in the *Times Picayune*.

A few minutes later, he turned into his own still sleeping cul-de-sac, enjoying the magnolia tree-lined street, the sight of his two-storey clapboard house at the far end, his own poincianas throwing a pattern of sunlight and shade across the white wood. He'd been satisfied enough with his bachelor life before he met Maggie. Now he knew that contentment had been an illusion born of ignorance about what life really could be.

Before he brought the Explorer to a full stop in the drive, Max was out of the kitchen door, through the carport, doing his best to plant a wet tongue on any exposed flesh he could reach as Sam climbed out. Laughing, Sam fought off the huge body, holding the pastry box high so that the beignets would not get damaged as they tussled. Max raced for the kitchen door, waited for Sam so that they could play out the last scene of their morning game—who could get through the door first. They hustled through, fighting for space, with Max, as usual, winning by a nose.

"Shh, you two. Jimmy's still sleeping."

Maggie wore a deep red suit, her dark wavy hair was swept up, fastened by combs, her makeup in place. Sam dropped the pastry box on the counter, grabbed her. Laughing, she held her face away from him.

"Sam! Stop! Your whiskers are like sandpaper."

"Thought we had a date this morning, darlin'." Sam tried to back her through the kitchen toward the stairs in the hall. "After that little hors d'oeuvre, only thing that kept me going through a long dark night was thinkin' of your tender body waitin' for me."

"I'm going to the eight o'clock mass, then we'll have the whole day." Maggie leaned back against his encircling arms. "You baby-sit this morning while Jimmy's asleep, then after lunch, you take him to a birthday party at Gillie's house. Gillie's mama's doing a puppet show, so that means we have two hours alone in our house before I pick him up." She raised her eyebrows at him. "Better than a quickie with your son asleep across the hall, right, big man?"

"How about a little preview now, and *three* hours alone later?"

"How about we save ourselves for the main event?" Maggie

kissed him, then slipped from his grasp. "Coffee's made. And don't let Jimmy have more than one beignet, and then only when he's finished his egg." She blew him another kiss. "Fried chicken for lunch if you and James behave yourselves while I'm at church." She closed the kitchen door behind her.

Sam poured a mug of coffee, bit into a beignet, dropped a chunk to Max. Maggie never missed mass on Sunday, something he found totally endearing. He even liked it that she usually insisted he go with her. Today, though, Jimmy's regular Sunday school teacher was away sick, so he was off the hook. Maggie never left Jimmy with someone she didn't know well. Carrying his coffee, Sam went upstairs to check on his son.

Jimmy lay on his back, his hair tousled into curls, flushed with sleep. Sam resisted the urge to wake him just to see the slow smile spread across his face as he saw his dad. Instead he drew the covers up to Jimmy's chin. Yesterday had been a big day for the little guy. Couple of extra hours would be good for him.

At the end of the cul-de-sac Maggie turned left onto Magnolia. The streets were still empty of traffic, the only sign of life a few people in bathrobes scrabbling to retrieve Sunday papers lodged in assorted bushes.

Ahead of her, a couple of kids were skateboarding across the street, and she pressed her foot gently on the brake, giving them time to reach the curb. Out of nowhere it seemed, a dark SUV in the oncoming lane roared down on them, making no attempt to slow. Skateboards skittering out of control, the two boys leapt to safety, tangling arms and legs in an untidy heap in the gutter. Outraged, Maggie stared at the vehicle as it passed her, catching a flashing glimpse of the driver, the blur of another man in the passenger seat.

Strangers.

Heart pounding, Maggie forced herself to relax her grip on the steering wheel of her Taurus. Of course, strangers. She didn't know everyone for a twenty-block radius from home. The neighborhood was full of strangers. She watched the SUV receding in her rearview mirror, resisting the impulse to make a U-turn and race home. She took a breath, forced herself to continue on toward Our Lady, Queen of Heaven.

Showered, dressed in old NOPD sweats, Sam poured more coffee, took the plate of beignets into the family room. He settled into his chair, dragged the ottoman toward him with his feet, clicked on the television, cruised the channels until he found a replay of the Saints/Atlanta game. Max stretched out beside him, chin on paws, accepting without question Sam's comments on every pass, how he'd make the play if he were the quarterback.

Sam glanced out of the window, his attention attracted by a vehicle, a stranger on the street. Cruising the cul-de-sac. He got up for a closer look. Ford Cherokee, dark green. License plate obscured by mud. Odd. It had been dry for a week. But not his business, he was no longer law enforcement. He turned away. Jesus, he thought, he had to watch himself. He was catching Maggie's anxieties. Jimmy had to have at least one parent who did not overreact to every mildly unusual event that happened.

Sam settled himself back into his chair and tried to concentrate on the game. The Cherokee had made a circuit of the cul-de-sac, and was doubling back. Maybe looking for a street address.

Maybe not.

Max got to his feet, head up, ears alert. He padded into the kitchen, and Sam heard the slap of the dog door as he went outside.

Then instinct honed from twenty years of police work kicked in. Sam hit the floor.

At the same instant the windows shattered, the room filled with down erupting from the exploding sofa. The walls shuddered under the thud of gunfire raking the front of the house.

Assault weapons.

More than one gunman.

And Jimmy upstairs. *Stay there, son, for God's sake, don't move.*

Sam crawled on his belly through the broken glass littering the floor, thrust his hand through the splintered wood of the cabinet opposite the window, fumbled for the weapon he kept locked inside. Of course the goddamn thing was unloaded. Cursing, he rummaged around in an old silver ice bucket where Maggie hid the clips. The firing from outside was diminishing. Sons of bitches were going to get away before he could get off a shot. He loaded, crawled through the hall to the shattered front door. He rose to his feet, jumped outside. The squeal of tires was clear in the sudden silence. The Cherokee careened toward the end of the cul-de-sac, taking the turn onto Magnolia on two wheels. The whole thing had taken only minutes.

He got a shot off, but as he fired, Sam knew it was useless. Max was lying on the driveway in a pool of his own blood, alive or dead, Sam couldn't take time to check. He raced through the glass-strewn foyer, threw himself up the stairs.

"It's all right, Jimmy. I'm here, son. Dad's here, honey."

THREE

Maggie started her turn into the parking lot of Our Lady, Queen of Heaven Catholic Church, then slowed almost to a stop and waved to Olive Benson, driving her mother to early mass as usual, to go ahead of her. In the far distance she heard the faint *whoop* of police sirens above the peal of the church bells. They seemed to be gaining, in volume, in number. But this was a big city, she told herself, they had nothing to do with her. Nothing to do with Jimmy.

Without conscious decision, she swung into a U-turn, catching a glimpse of Olive's shocked face as she was forced to run her old Dodge up onto the sidewalk to avoid collision.

It was early, still not much traffic. Not that it would have made any difference. Maggie ignored stop signs, tore without slowing through both red lights, retracing her route home. She skidded into a turn, straightened, narrowly missing a dark SUV driving fast in the other direction. She wrestled for control of her Taurus, and it was gone before she could get a look at the driver. Was it the same dark face, the same vehicle? The same pale passenger?

Maggie felt as if she were somewhere outside her body, watching herself grip the steering wheel, listening to her own voice saying over and over, "It's all right. It's all right. It's all right." Not believing for one moment that it was.

The police sirens were deafening, it seemed every black-and-white in the parish was converging on her neighborhood. She turned into her street, saw that the end of the cul-de-sac was crowded with police vehicles, lights flashing, radios crackling.

Maggie slammed to a stop, found she was shaking too hard to grasp the handle of the door. She reached for it with both hands, then, somehow, she was out of the car, running as if in a nightmare, in slow motion, mud dragging at her feet. A police-woman stepped into her path. The woman's lips were moving so Maggie knew she was speaking, but she could hear nothing but the pounding of her own heart, the shriek of terror in her head.

"Where is my son?" The shriek produced a strangled whisper. "Where's Jimmy?" Maggie reached to grab the woman's arms, to shake out an answer. Then her eyes went to the mangled heap lying in the driveway, and her legs gave way.

Sam raced out of the shattered front door, caught hold of her hanging on to the policewoman's jacket, her eyes riveted on the pile of flesh and bloody fur.

His arms wrapped around his wife, Sam motioned to the policewoman to cover Max's body.

"Jimmy. He's gone. He's gone, isn't he?" The words struggled from Maggie's throat.

"We'll get him back, honey." Sam's voice wobbled. "They can't get out of the city. I promise we'll get him back."

Maggie's eyes stayed on Max until a policeman gently covered him with a blue-and-green patchwork quilt from the family room. Elle should have made it larger, Maggie thought, it was too small to hide him, he was such a big, strong dog. She could still see his torn body, his blood pooled on the driveway. Gently, Sam turned her away, urged her toward the house.

She took only a few steps, then stopped. Jimmy's purple bike, with its gaily colored streamers on the handlebars, the yellow training wheels he had helped his father attach only days ago, had somehow escaped the bullets that had ravaged the house. Undamaged, it leaned against a banana tree.

Maggie slipped from Sam's grasp, fell to her knees. She wrapped her arms around her body as if to protect soft internal organs and rocked back and forth. Her gut-deep wail of utter despair rose and fell as if her heart was being ripped from her chest.

Sam knelt beside her. He attempted to put his arms around her, but she fought him off like a wild creature terrified of capture. Helplessly, Sam hovered over her.

Lt. Deke Washington of the New Orleans Police Department came out of the house, crossed the drive and knelt on the other side of her.

Sam looked at him over Maggie's head, and shook his head, a silent warning not to interfere. Washington stood, brushing a large thumb across each eye. He glanced at his crew, tough cops avoiding each other's eyes, shuffling their feet and staring at the ground in front of them.

Finally, Maggie's voice faded in exhaustion and Sam put a tentative arm around her. She leaned against him, and did not resist when he lifted her to her feet. Washington stood aside, and Sam slid an arm under her knees and carried her into the house, Washington close behind as Sam went toward the stairs. Maggie was silent now, and limp.

"Give us a few minutes, Deke, okay?" Sam said over his shoulder.

"Sure, but I have to talk to her as soon as possible, Sam, you know that."

"Just a few minutes."

Sam mounted the stairs, shouldered open their bedroom door. A panel in one of the doors leading to the gallery overlooking the garden and the outside steps was smashed, the splintered white painted wood strewn across the pale blue carpet. Otherwise the room was as Maggie had left it, untouched by the hail of gunfire that had destroyed the family room. He lowered Maggie to the bed as if reluctant to relinquish his hold, as if carrying her gave him the illusion that he could protect her. He sat on the edge of the bed, clutching Maggie's hand.

"I'll call Bill Deshotels—"

"I don't need a doctor, Sam, I need Jimmy, I need my son." She struggled to form words through the pain pounding at her chest and throat. "What happened? What happened? Did you see them?"

Sam shook his head as if unable to trust his voice. "Jimmy was asleep upstairs, I was watching a football game, then suddenly the house was being attacked. Automatic weapons. I just ran outside to try to... They were gone. Max was..." His breath caught and broke. "I raced up to get Jimmy... They'd come up the back stairs."

Maggie stared at the shattered door. "Through our bedroom. Oh, Sam, why did we buy this house? I thought he'd be safe at the end of a cul-de-sac."

"Honey, it wasn't the house—"

"Yes, it was, it was. The balcony doors, we should have built a wall there, made it solid—"

Sam put his arms around her, pulled her against him. "Honey, honey, shhhh. It wasn't the house. Don't." He rocked her gently, his tears mingling with hers. "They won't get far, sweetheart. He'll be okay."

A knock at the door was accompanied by Deke Washington's baritone. "Sam. Sorry to disturb you..."

"A minute, Deke—"

"You go on down," Maggie said. "Go talk to him."

"He can wait—"

"I'm all right, Sam. Really, I'm all right. I want to be by myself for a minute."

"No, honey, I'll stay with you."

"It's okay, Sam. Go talk to Deke."

"You sure?"

Her face creased with pain, she nodded.

"Okay," Sam said. "You come down when you want, sweetheart. You don't need to talk to Washington or anyone else until you're good and ready."

Looking up at him, Maggie nodded again. Sam went into the bathroom, moistened a face cloth, handed it to her. Maggie clutched the cloth in both hands, stared down at it as if she had never seen such a thing before. Gently, Sam lifted her chin, dabbed at the mascara streaking her cheeks, tossed the cloth into the bathroom sink before he left.

Maggie listened to the voices outside the room, Sam insisting that she be given a few more minutes before talking to the police, Deke protesting. But he and Sam had known each other for years, and Deke had a reputation of being a toffee-covered marshmallow, a hard shell covering a soft center.

As soon as she heard the two men descending the stairs, Maggie got to her feet. She opened the door, crossed the wide hallway to Jimmy's room. In a few minutes the police would come to turn this little boy's sanctuary into a crime scene, dusting for prints she knew they wouldn't find.

She knelt by the bed, lowered her head to press her face against the rumpled sheets, breathing in the sweetness of her son still lingering there. For a long moment, she stayed on her knees, grasping the baseball quilt that had covered him.

When she rose to her feet, the tears were gone.

FOUR

Maggie left her son's room, started down the stairs. The kitchen was empty but for Sam and the policewoman from outside. Through the kitchen window, Maggie could see Lt. Washington in the carport talking to several officers.

Sam was at the kitchen table, the telephone in front of him. He got to his feet when she came in, pulled out a chair for her and indicated the policewoman. "This is Pam Weston, honey."

Weston handed her a mug of coffee. "Unless you'd like something stronger, Mrs. Cady?"

"No, thank you. This is fine." Maggie raised the mug to her lips, but the thought of anything entering her stomach revolted her. She put the mug on the table without drinking.

In the living room, technicians were setting up equipment.

"They'll call," Weston said. "Sooner or later, someone's going to call."

Maggie nodded. She looked at Sam. "I'm going over to see Father Cobin, Sam."

Weston shook her head. "I'm sorry, Mrs. Cady. It's better if you don't leave the house just yet."

"I want to see my priest."

"I'll call Father Cobin, sugar," Sam said. "He'll come here to see you. You shouldn't go out—"

"No, I want to be in the church."

Weston spoke as if soothing a child. "Mrs. Cady, I'm sorry. I know how you feel, but that's not possible right now."

Maggie turned deep, dry eyes on her. "You know how I feel? How is that, Officer Weston? How do I feel?"

Weston looked down, then back at Maggie. "Well, I guess I mean..." Her voice tapered off.

Sam threw Weston a hard look, then said, "Mags, why don't I get Father Cobin to come over? It's best if you don't go out, sweetheart. We don't know who's out there. It's not safe."

"I have to be in the church, Sam. Inside the church. I need to be there." Maggie heard her voice rising. "I need my church, Sam."

Weston chose that moment to say, "Sam, she can't leave the house."

Sam turned on her. "Knock it off, Weston. If my wife wants the comfort of her church, who's going to stop her?"

"I'd say Lt. Washington has a good shot—" Weston stopped in midsentence, then said, "I'm sorry, that sounded terrible. I better get the lieutenant in here." She brushed past them.

Maggie pulled Sam's head down, pressed her cheek against his.

"I'll be back in an hour."

"I'm coming with you."

"No. You have to stay by the phone, Sam." Her voice was rising, a hint of panic creeping in. "They may call. Someone has to be here."

"Maggie. Maggie, sweetheart, you can't—"

Maggie put her fingers to his mouth, silencing him. "I'm

going." She kissed his cheek then turned and walked quickly to the front door. Sam was still protesting, torn, but she knew he would wait in case a phone call came in from whoever had taken his son.

Outside, she noted the changes that mattered. Jimmy's bike was gone, and his baseball bat from where it had leaned into the white camellia bush by the carport. Max's body was gone, too, though his blood would be there until someone hosed it away. Yellow crime scene tape was everywhere. Her car was still parked as she had left it. She walked down the driveway, and tried the car door, found it unlocked. As she'd expected, the keys she had left in the ignition were gone. Maggie slid behind the wheel, turned on the engine with the spare key she had brought with her and backed out of the drive. She had a blurred sense of her neighbors clustered in knots, coffee cups in hand, an air of shocked excitement hovering over them. A number of cops stared after her, but Washington was nowhere to be seen. He was probably in the back of the house talking to Weston about whether or not she should be allowed to leave. No one tried to stop her.

At the end of the cul-de-sac, she turned right onto Magnolia Avenue and hoped Sam was not watching out of the smashed windows of the den—he knew she would turn left to get to Our Lady, Queen of Heaven. She passed several gas stations, dismissed each with a glance, then turned into the Magnolia Shopping Plaza. The public phone booth outside Poinciana Drugs was still there, not yet replaced by a metal shell hung on the wall. A parking space opened up and she slipped into it, beating out a white pickup.

Maggie entered the booth, pulled the door closed behind her, punched out a number, waited for an answering voice.

FIVE

"What were you thinking, Sam, letting Maggie go off like that? Church or no church, it's not safe until we know what the hell we're dealing with here." Washington walked over to the coffeepot, filled a mug, cooling it with a generous amount of cream before taking a long pull. "All you had to do was wait a few minutes until Weston got hold of me and I would have sent someone with her. We don't know who's still out there."

"Have you ever tried to stop a woman when she's hell-bent on something? I couldn't stop her, for Christ's sake." Sam looked out of the kitchen window. The banana trees needed a trim, a job he and Jimmy had been planning to do together after school tomorrow. Jimmy's job was to drag the fronds he cut, pile them up for disposal, with Maggie supplying discreet help along with the lemonade and cookies. "Did you send a car after her?"

"Yeah," Washington said. "And I told them to keep out of her way in the church as you asked."

"Thanks. Have you talked to the feds yet?"

"Sam, we don't know if they've taken Jimmy across the Louisiana state line, or—" Washington stopped, avoiding Sam's eyes.

Sam rubbed a shaking hand over his forehead, knowing Washington couldn't bring himself to give voice to the unthinkable: If a sex crime was committed, then it would automatically become a federal case. If he was taken across the state line or a ransom demand was made, it would be federal. Until then it was Washington's call.

"Deke, he's four years old, man," Sam said. "Get the feds in now. They've got resources you don't have. Please. Don't wait."

"Why would anyone do this, Sam? You got any ideas?"

Sam looked into the living room on the other side of the hall. The techies had put their gear in place. If a mosquito farted, with that much equipment it would sound like Gabriel's horn. Sam shook his head. "I don't know. Flying for the power company's a good living, but it's not serious money."

"Okay. So you put away a lot of scumbags in your twenty years on the job. Anyone you can think of might be getting out about now?"

Sam shook his head. "There was more than one guy involved here, Deke," he said. "Someone shooting up the house while another guy was getting through the fence, into the backyard, up the back stairs. That takes some planning, some coordination. And they knew the house. Where to go to get to Jimmy. Right up the back steps, through our bedroom, across the hall to his room. They were in and out in a couple of minutes." He stopped.

Washington put a hand on his shoulder. "Let's go over it again, okay?"

"Yeah, sure, but I think I've told you everything I know."

"So humor me. Tell me again. From the top."

When he'd finished, Sam looked at the lieutenant, meeting blank eyes that gave back nothing. A cop's eyes.

Washington grunted. "Okay. Now, I want you to come on

down to the station house, go through some old files, see if you can get a bead on someone who might still have a hard-on for you and is bright enough to pull something like this. Give us something to turn over to the feds if we have to."

"I'm not leaving Maggie alone here just so you can look good to the feds—"

Washington cut him off. "What the hell are you saying, looking good? Get hold of yourself, man, and think. You can help this girl of yours avoid a whole lot of grief if you talk to the feds yourself first." Washington leaned closer. "You want Maggie dealing with tightass FBI agents she's never met before? Anyway, she won't be alone here." He gestured to the technicians fiddling with the equipment in the living room. "Weston will hang close, too, keep an eye out for her. She's new on the job, but she's okay. Sensitive."

"Yeah, I noticed." Sam looked at the cigar in Washington's mouth. Right now, he could taste the tobacco on his tongue, feel the craving in his lungs as if he'd never quit.

Washington caught his look, reached into his top pocket, handed Sam a cigar. Sam shook his head. "Okay. As soon as Maggie gets back from church, I'll come down. Get Petey Le Pont in, we made most of our collars together."

"Petey's off duty, but he's been notified. He was going to tear his ass over here, but I told him to go on to the station house. He'll meet us there. Anyway, I still got to speak to Maggie myself, remember?"

Officer Jerome Theriot thrust a shoulder at the door of the Blue Bird Coffee Shop, juggling a container of coffee in each hand, a bag of donuts clutched between his teeth. Automatically, his eyes swept the parking lot, then came back to rest on the telephone booth outside the drugstore.

He walked over to the patrol car, handed one of the containers to his partner, took the bag of donuts from between his teeth. He leaned into the window.

"Packey, tell me I'm seeing things. Isn't that Maggie Cady?" Officer Picard Gilette stared at the woman in the phone booth. He shook his head. "No. Could be her double, but no way would Maggie Cady be here with her kid missing." They'd been told to keep their eyes open for a dark green Ford Cherokee, mud obscuring the license plates. "Sam would never let her out of his sight, not with this shit going down. He's crazy about that woman."

Theriot settled himself into the shotgun seat. "Well, that's one pissed-off lady." They could see her fist punching the air as she spoke. He took a swig of his coffee. "Let's take a little swing by that phone booth. Wouldn't hurt to take a closer look."

Maggie smashed the phone into its cradle. Suddenly, the stink of the enclosed space—stale cigarette smoke, weed, damp unnamable swamp odors—grabbed at her, and she retched, leaning weakly against the glass wall of the booth. She wrenched at the door until it opened and she could fill her lungs with fresh air. She rubbed shaky fingers over her lips to stop the trembling, glanced up and caught sight of the police cruiser three lanes over moving slowly in her direction. Maggie lowered her head, walked rapidly back to her car, patting her pockets as if searching for her keys. She adjusted her rearview mirror to keep the cruiser in sight as she left the parking lot, half expecting it to follow her. It did not, and she breathed easier.

Fewer police cars jammed the end of the cul-de-sac. Maggie stopped just short of the yellow crime scene tape that now extended across the crushed shell driveway. They must have done that after she left. She got out of her Taurus, ducked under the tape, went to the carport and unwound the green hose from the wheel hanging on the wall. She turned on the faucet, directed the stream onto the dark pool of Max's blood, watched it turn pink as it mingled with the water and drain into the street. The water fell off to a trickle, and she stared at it numbly, trying to figure out what she should do to get it going again. It seemed a task beyond her capability. A large dark hand took the hose from her.

"We'll do this later, Maggie, don't worry," Lt. Washington said gently. "My people are not finished here yet. I'd like to ask you a few questions now, if you're up to it?" The words were soft, politely couched, but it was clear that no choice was being offered.

Maggie nodded. Washington escorted her the few yards to the splintered front door, held it open, and Maggie preceded him into the kitchen. Sam started toward her as she entered.

"Are you okay?"

Maggie looked at him, his face etched with pain, the lines from nose to mouth deeper, the laughter creases around his eyes now creases of anguish, and knew what he was really saying with those banal words was, "I love you. I would lay down my life for you and for Jimmy. And I'm terrified you think I've failed you."

Maggie went to him, put her arms around him, her head on his chest. "I'm all right," she said. "I forgot. Father Cobin was busy—it's Christening Sunday. A lot of people and babies." She stopped, unable to continue with the lie. She felt Sam's hand on the back of her head as he held her against him. She pressed deeper, trying to absorb his strength, all that he was, into her own being. "The church was filled with people, Sam. I couldn't stay."

Washington cleared his throat, reminding them of his presence. Maggie moved from the protection of her husband's arms, but held on to Sam's hand as he led her to the kitchen table.

"Have you had any phone calls lately, Maggie?" Washington asked. "Any hangups?"

She shook her head.

"Any strange cars around, anything unusual?"

"No. Nothing like that."

"Salesmen at the door, people you don't know?"

"No. Nothing."

"Did Jimmy mention anything about seeing strangers at school?"

Again she shook her head.

"Well, have you done anything out of the ordinary lately? Think about it—"

"No, nothing—"

"Wait a minute," Sam said. "That conference in Memphis, could there have been anyone there—"

"At a teachers' conference? I met second-grade teachers, Sam. They don't go around kidnapping babies."

"Honey, no, I know, but we have to think of everything."

"When was this?" Deke said.

"In August, about six weeks ago, the week before school started. I went on a Thursday morning, came back Friday night."

"Anything out of the ordinary happen?" Deke said.

Maggie shook her head. Beneath the table, she rubbed her damp hands over her skirt. She knew she had to stop this, and stop it now. She relaxed the aching muscles that were only just holding her upright, allowed herself to sag forward, cradled her head in her arms. The sobs she had been fighting rose in her chest until she thought they would tear her apart.

Sam crouched beside her, pulled her against him, crooned wordlessly against her hair. As soon as her sobs subsided, he smoothed damp hair from her burning face. "Shh, honey. It's all right. We'll get him back, I promise you." He reached for a tissue from a box on the table, dabbed her face. "But what I have to do right now, sweetheart, is go with Deke to the station house to look through some old files. I'll get Elle to come over and stay with you."

"No, don't do that, Sam. I'd rather be alone."

"My people will have to be here with you, Maggie," Washington said.

She nodded. The sound of the tech staff in the next room, the men outside calling to each other, the crowd of people moving about suddenly seemed louder, invading the kitchen.

"Maggie," Washington said, "we can continue this later if you like. But while Sam and I are gone, I want you to write down every event in the last six weeks. Start with the conference, go on from there. Look in your calendar to jog your memory. Who was where, and when. Every appointment you had, everywhere you and Jimmy went. Who you saw. Who has been to the house. Include everyone, even the Maytag man." His attempt to lighten the moment fell flat. "Every detail you can think of. Nothing is unimportant. If you're quiet here, things will come back to you. The key to this could be anything. Information we can use might just float to the surface of your mind. If you'd do that it would be helpful."

Maggie nodded. Washington motioned Weston to follow him, touched Sam's shoulder as he passed. "We'll be outside, Sam."

As soon as they'd gone, Sam said, "Babe, I'll be back as soon as I can. If you need me, call me at the station house. Even if you don't need me, call."

"I'll be all right." Maggie clung to him, fearing she would never see him again.

Sam rose, dropped a kiss onto the top of her head. She did not look up to see him leave. She heard footsteps, then Weston's voice as the policewoman entered the kitchen. "Washington's a good cop, he'll do everything that can be done. Nothing gets past him." Weston poured yet another cup of coffee, put it on the table in front of Maggie.

Maggie nodded, got to her feet, picked up the mug. "I'll drink this upstairs."

"I'll come with you."

"I'd like to take a shower if that's okay."

"Oh, sure. Sure. Whatever you want, if it'll make you feel better. I'm here to help you, so give me a call if I can do anything. I'll check in on you in half an hour, how's that?"

"Yes, okay. Thanks."

Maggie went upstairs, past Jimmy's open door, a crime scene now, no longer his safe, little boy's haven. She went into the room next to Jimmy's, a home office and activities room, littered with projects, plastic airplane kits, a train set on the floor, as much Sam's as it was Jimmy's. She opened a cupboard, took down the heavy-duty brown paper she and Jimmy used for artwork, a roll of wide sticky tape, a ball of string.

Then she caught the sound of voices, footsteps on the stairs, and she stopped breathing, willing them to go away.

A male voice called from below, "Hey, Weston, you got a minute here?"

Weston answered from the kitchen and the footsteps stopped, started back down.

Maggie cracked the door, saw that she was still alone, and sped across the wide hall to the master bedroom. She closed the door behind her, locked it, tossed the brown paper and string onto the bed as she crossed to the bathroom. She turned the shower on to full then returned to burrow into the recesses of her walk-in closet. She pulled out a box labeled "satin shoes" from behind the skirt of her lone evening dress, opened it and removed the black velvet evening pouch inside. She loosened the cords of the pouch, and took out a silk-wrapped package.

The smell of gun oil rose to her nostrils, familiar, evocative, becoming stronger as she unwound a series of silk scarves. The final bright red scarf fell away and Maggie looked at the weapon—snub-nosed, dark and ugly, only four inches long, but it could drop a man in his tracks. Unloaded now, it fit snugly in her hand—it had been custom fitted for her grip—but even loaded with an eight-round clip, it would not be heavy.

She checked its condition, although she knew it was well oiled. She cleaned it regularly so that it was always ready. Reassured, she rewrapped the gun in its silk and velvet camouflage, then ran her eyes over the line of boxes on the shelf above her clothes. She took down the sturdy corrugated box in which she kept the small steam iron she used in the bedroom for touching up the odd crease in a skirt or collar, and removed the iron. She wrapped the Beretta in a length of polyfilm from the dry cleaner, put it in the box, wedged tissue paper and more polyfilm into the remaining space so that it would not shift around in transit.

She reached for the round hatbox on the shelf above the short ivory silk dress she'd worn for her wedding, took out the froth of pale pink silk roses Sam had not been able to believe was meant to go on her head. Carefully, Maggie put the hat aside— she had no desire today to admire it, try it on, remember the look on Sam's face when she walked toward him in the church that day, as if he couldn't believe she was real and about to marry him—then she pried out the bottom of the hatbox and removed the spare ammunition for the Beretta, six clips, eight rounds each. She fitted the false bottom back in place, replaced the hat, shoved the hatbox back onto the shelf. Then she tipped out the handkerchiefs from a fancy red-and-gold box that had once held a Christmas special of perfume and body lotion—a gift from Elle—put in the clips, packed in extra tissue and polyfilm.

Working quickly, she wrapped each box in the heavy-duty brown paper, reinforced them with the sticky tape and string. Satisfied, she addressed each package, using a fictitious name and a phony address for sender. Then she shoved the roll of paper and the string and tape under the bed.

In a few minutes she had changed into jeans and a white T-shirt, put on the black leather bomber jacket Sam had bought her for her thirtieth birthday, far too expensive, but he loved her in it, called it her biker-chick look. She thrust another pair of jeans, a couple of extra T-shirts and some panties into her small leather backpack, stuffed her hair under a baseball cap. From a cupboard in the bathroom, she took out a box of tampons, and removed the five thousand dollars she kept hidden there. She had refused to accept more, only had this because her mother insisted she had to have emergency cash, another secret from Sam.

Over the sound of the shower, she heard footsteps crossing the bare wooden floor of the hall, then a loud knock at the bedroom door.

"Mrs. Cady? Maggie, are you okay?" Weston's voice. Then the door handle turned, found resistance. "Maggie?" The voice became insistent, an edge to it. "Maggie, are you all right?"

Maggie held her breath. The footsteps recrossed the bare oak floor, descended the stairs. Quickly, Maggie turned off the shower, hoping Weston would hear the change in the plumbing downstairs in the kitchen, one of the idiosyncrasies of the house, and be reassured.

Maggie sat on Sam's side of the bed, ran her hand over his pillow. But she couldn't allow herself to think beyond the moment, so she pulled the pad of paper they kept by the phone toward her and wrote swiftly.

Sam, I love you. I have gone to get Jimmy. Don't follow me, Sam, please. I can't tell you more, so please, please trust me. I know what I'm doing. I'll call you as soon as I can. I'll be okay. Don't worry.

She read it over. It didn't say what she meant but it would have to do, she couldn't take the time to rewrite it. She signed it, "Your Maggie," and put it on his pillow.

Then she picked up the packages, opened the broken door that led to the balcony, slipped out. She was down the wooden stairs in seconds. Into the garden. Into the lush enclosing growth.

And away.

SIX

"Lieutenant." A head appeared around the door of the filing room. "You got a minute?"

Irritated, Washington looked up from where he sat with Sam and Petey Le Pont, going through old case files, working back to their first years on the job. "Jonesy, don't diddle around in the doorway, man, come on in. You know Sam Cady."

"Rather you come out, Lieutenant."

Sam felt the blood drain from his body. He stood and was aware that Petey was on his feet beside him.

"What you got, you?" Petey asked.

"You've heard something." Sam braced himself with both hands flat on the table.

"No, Sam. No, no. Nothing about your boy." Sergeant Jones looked at Washington, gestured sharply with his head. "Lieutenant."

Washington got to his feet. "You get on here, both of you. Be just a minute."

Sam took a breath, felt his heart rate ease off. He lifted another set of files, a mass of paperwork, details of arrests, disposition of cases. His instinct told him he would find no answers.

"There ain't nothing here." Sounding disgusted, Petey echoed his thoughts. "We oughta be on the street, slam a few heads—"

"What?" The sound of Washington's voice blasted through the door. "Get that cruiser back here. Sam, you gotta hear this."

He came back into the room, Sergeant Jones behind him. "Tell him, Jonesy."

Jones's eyes met Sam's briefly, then slid away.

"Sam, one of our cruisers reported your wife had a phone conversation from a pay phone outside the Poinciana Drug Store an hour or so after your boy was reported missing."

Sam shook his head, raised a hand to stop him. "No, no, that can't be. She wasn't at the Poinciana Drug Store—"

"No, she was in the church and the car we sent missed her. That's what she said, right? In church. Jesus." Washington fumbled in his pocket for a stogie, thrust it into his mouth without lighting it. "Poinciana Drug Store. That's right close to your house, isn't it, Sam? Didn't she say she came back because the church was full?"

"That's right, so it wasn't Maggie. They made a mistake."

Petey's eyes shifted from one face to the other. He looked as if someone had hit him in the head. "What you saying, you?" Shoulders bunched, he started to move around the table.

Washington held him with a glance. "They're good boys, Theriot and Gilette, not given to jumping the gun. Are you sure that church was full?"

"Sure I am. It's Christening Sunday." Sam picked up the phone. "I'll call her."

Washington put out a thick finger and cut the connection. "Let's just go see Maggie ourselves, let her explain in person. Petey, you stay here, keep on with those files. And talk to Theriot and Gilette when they get in. You squeeze out every detail. They're running the plates of the car they saw, so call me the minute the number comes through. They could be wrong about this. You got the license number of Maggie's car, Sam?"

Sam gave him the number of the Taurus. Petey slammed a file onto the table, muttering a mixture of fractured French and English under his breath. Washington threw him a look, then strode rapidly through the office, Sam on his heels. Neither man spoke until the driver of the unmarked police car had turned the vehicle out of the parking lot onto Lake Street.

"So, what do you think, Sam?" Washington asked. "Why would your wife tell you she's going to church—" He stopped. "You do go to Queen of Heaven, right?"

Sam nodded silently.

"Yeah, I thought so," Washington said. "So why did she go to a public phone in the other goddamn direction?"

Sam shook his head. Washington sounded as confused as he was. He felt as if he'd been slammed in the gut with a two-by-four. There had to be a rational explanation. *Maggie would never lie to him.*

"It's simple. It wasn't Maggie," Sam said. "The guys saw someone who looks like her."

"It's not like she made a sudden decision to make a phone call on her way to church," Washington said as if Sam had not spoken. "That drugstore's in a completely different direction. No, she went there deliberately."

Sam didn't answer. There was nothing to say.

"How long you known Maggie, Sam?"

"Five and a half years. Married for five."

"Where y'all meet?"

"At the school where she was teaching."

He'd been on light duty after a drug bust on a cargo ship off the coast had gone bad, a joint operation with an alphabet soup of feds: FBI, BATF, DEA. CIA for all he knew. The Colombians had grenade launchers no one suspected they had and his chopper had taken a hit. After a stint in the hospital, he'd been assigned to community outreach—senior citizens' groups, neighborhood watch, schools. He'd thought it would drive him crazy, did nothing but bitch and moan about getting back to chopper duty, sending paperwork up the chain of command, making himself a general pain in the ass. Then Maggie Jameson entered his life and nothing else mattered.

When he'd first seen her, she was surrounded by small children awestruck at the sight of his uniform. A cloud of dark hair framed her face, and with her enormous black eyes and ivory skin, the luscious curve of her mouth, he'd thought she was Creole. He'd been stunned at the sight of her, couldn't believe his luck when he found out that she felt the same about him.

"Where was that, Sam? What school?"

Suddenly wary, Sam turned to look at him. These were a cop's questions, not friendly conversation to help him keep his mind from what was happening. A protest came and died unspoken. Jimmy was gone. That was at the core of every question, every suspicion. It was all that mattered.

"The parish school. She still teaches second grade there on the days when Jimmy... He's in preschool—" Sam's voice caught in his throat, and he turned the sound into a cough.

Washington gave him a minute, then said, "What sort of folks are her people?"

"Her people?" Sam took a minute to order his thoughts. In Louisiana, family ties were everything. Without them, no one knew where they fit.

"Goddamn it, this is like drawing teeth. Her people, man. Where does she come from? What parish?"

"She comes from Ohio, Deke. They don't have parishes there."

"Jesus, I know that, Sam. I just didn't know she came from Ohio. So what sort of family she got? Parents still living, brothers, sisters? What?"

"Her parents were killed in a car crash." Sam felt Washington's eyes boring into him. "She's only got Jimmy and me. There is no one else."

A couple of seconds passed in silence, then Washington grunted. "Well, I hope she's got a reason for making a telephone call from a drugstore instead of going to church." He leaned forward, tapped his driver on the shoulder. "Put your foot down, man. At this rate we'll never get there." He chewed on the unlit cigar.

"You want lights and siren, Lieutenant?"

Washington sighed, heavily patient. "Haven't we got enough noise in this town, Robbie? Just try not to fall asleep at the wheel."

Sam kept his eyes on the passing scene, thinking of Maggie's constant need to check locks, her fear of letting Jimmy ride with anyone but herself or Sam, her panic if he was out of her sight for a minute, her reluctance to let him even go to birthday parties until Sam had stepped in, insisting she loosen her hold, that Jimmy had to be allowed to have a kid's life. Still there were the constant phone calls to check on him. And then this morning—what had she said when she came home without going to mass? Not, "what happened?" But, "Jimmy's gone."

The thought that had been hovering in the back of his mind all day jumped to the forefront.

Maggie had known Jimmy was gone before he'd had a chance to tell her.

SEVEN

Maggie paid off the cab that had picked her up at the Mobil station on Magnolia. She'd waited in the women's toilet, dashed out when it arrived, made herself small in the back seat.

The airport was busy, but she kept her head down, her face hidden by the baseball cap, and slipped unobtrusively through the crowd, avoiding airport police just in case Sam had already been home and found her missing. Security had eased up in the last few months, the National Guard was no longer around. She ran her eyes over the departures board, found what she was looking for, made her way to the American Airlines counter.

"Can I still get on the flight to Chicago?"

The ground attendant smiled brightly. "Not if you have any luggage."

"I don't. Just this." Maggie lifted her backpack so that the woman could see it.

"Okay. You'll have to hurry."

Maggie put her credit card, the one in the name she shared with Sam, on the counter. "Return on Saturday, please."

Ticket in hand, she walked away from the counter, heard the ground attendant's voice. "Mrs. Cady, you really will have to hurry. Security may take some time."

Maggie waved her thanks, picked up her pace until she was out of sight of the counter, then turned toward the FedEx drop box. She filled in the airbills. Overnight delivery, steam iron valued at fifty dollars in one, books valued at fifty dollars in the other, shipping charge to be paid by recipient. Then she sealed the Beretta and ammunition into the respectability of separate FedEx cartons and put them in the drop box. Chances were against them being caught by security, even if they did a spot check. If they were, she'd have to buy a weapon when she arrived. She could only handle so much here in New Orleans.

At the United counter, she booked a flight to Kennedy using her single name and identification and paid cash.

She went through the security check without challenge, boarded, found her seat. The plane left on time. Maggie looked out of the window at the city below. A small private jet turning onto a runway ready for takeoff; Interstate 10, the freeway that ran from Miami to Los Angeles, crowded as usual; Lake Pontchartrain, cypress-fringed, polluted and so lovely. She wondered if she would ever see it again. Or Sam. She couldn't let herself think about Jimmy. She had to stay strong.

EIGHT

"Gone? What do you mean, gone?" Washington yelled.

Sam raced up the stairs while Washington continued to bark at Weston. "I want an APB. Margaret Cady, aka Maggie. Age 30. Caucasian. 5'2", 105 pounds. Dark hair, dark eyes. Wearing... What the hell she wearing, Sam?"

Sam took in the bedroom at a glance, saw the note that the sensitive Weston had somehow managed to miss—in all fairness easy to do—the small square of paper was the same color as the pillow. She must have rushed in, found Maggie gone, and rushed out in a panic. He picked it up, had time to run his eyes quickly over what Maggie had written before he had to shove it into his pocket as heavy footsteps pounded the wooden floor of the up-stairs hall.

"She pack for an extended visit?" Washington came through the door.

Sam stepped into Maggie's closet, breathed in the rose scent that seemed so much the essence of her. *Trust me,* she'd written. He ran his eyes quickly over her clothes, mostly slacks and jeans and shirts, some skirts. Her two good suits were hanging up, the red suit she'd worn to church that morning—Christ, was it really only that morning?—was discarded on the floor with a small heap of the fancy handkerchiefs she used on special occasions. He came back to the empty hanger where her black leather jacket usually hung. On the shelf above it, a hatbox had been moved, pushed hurriedly back into place. *Don't follow,* she'd said.

He pushed the red suit out of sight with his foot, closed the closet door. Whatever she was up to, his instinct was to protect her, give her time to call to explain. Failing that, he'd find her himself before the police did.

"She must be wearing the same thing. Red suit."

Washington shouted the information down to Weston, then moved toward the balcony doors and bent to examine the smashed locks. The doors had been dusted for prints, but still he was careful not to touch them.

"You got enough locks on these doors, Sam. You expecting what happened here?"

"What the hell does that mean? Maggie was nervous. I work a lot of nights."

Washington held his eyes for a moment, then nodded. He pushed open a door, stepped outside. "She left down these stairs, through the trees. Does this garden lead anywhere, except to the neighbors?"

"If you go through backyards, sure. Eventually you'll get out on Magnolia."

"Okay. So that's what she did. Otherwise my people would have seen her. Now what we need to know is why she did it. Why she went, and where she's gone." Washington removed the cigar from his mouth, regarded its soggy end with disgust. He looked over the balcony railing.

Sam eyed the cigar. "Don't even think about it. This is Maggie's garden. It's not an ash can."

Washington held the cigar delicately between his finger and thumb. "Maggie's running, Sam. So it looks like this is not the brainstorm of some scumbag from your past." He thought a moment, then said, "Petey Le Pont better keep on the files, anyway. Every collar you made, he made. If there's anything to find, he'll find it. So, Sam, help me out here, man. You got any idea why she left?"

"I'd tell you if I had."

"You got marital troubles? She plan to take your boy away, and did it the hard way to get at you?"

Sam held his voice steady. "She's not involved in this, Lieutenant. She wouldn't do such a thing. Jesus, you saw her on that driveway. And Max. She loved that dog."

"Don't kid yourself, Sam. She's involved. Weston said she was hysterical to get out of the house when you tried to stop her this morning. Goddamn it, man, open your eyes—"

"No. No way. She's got to be in some real danger herself to do this."

"Or she's being blackmailed."

Sam kept his eyes carefully away from the policeman. Deke Washington was giving voice to his own thoughts. Sam shook his head. "You know Maggie. She taught second grade, for Christ's sake. What's to blackmail?"

"Where in Ohio was she brought up?" Washington asked.

"Dayville, small town couple hundred miles south of Columbus." Sam put his hand in his pocket, felt the crinkle of Maggie's note. He stepped back into the room, stood by the door until Washington took the hint and followed. He walked the lieutenant toward the door to the hall. "There's a convent there. Benedictines. Nuns brought her up after her people were killed. She still goes back there couple times a year for a visit. Parents left a small trust for her education and the nuns sent her to Swarthmore."

Washington grunted. "Jog my memory. What was her single name?"

"Jameson. You can check it all out."

"You can count on it." Washington stopped in the doorway. "If you think I haven't figured you're hustling me out of here, Sam, forget it. We've got to search this room."

"Can you give me a few minutes alone first, Deke? Just a couple of minutes."

Washington slid a glance at the antique lowboy dresser against the wall opposite the bed and looked uncomfortable. "You don't have to worry, Sam. I'll have Weston go through her things, not one of the guys."

Sam pressed on Washington's discomfort. "Deke, come on, man. You know Maggie, she's not some stranger."

Washington expelled a heavy breath, then said, "Shit. Take a few minutes." He put a hand briefly on Sam's shoulder.

Washington left the door open behind him and Sam closed it when he heard the lieutenant's feet on the stairs. He took Maggie's note from his pocket, read it again slowly.

Don't follow, she'd written. *Not you or the police.* She knew better than to ask that of him. He thought like a cop, acted like one. More than that, he was the man who loved her, and loved Jimmy, more than life.

He went back to Maggie's closet, took down the hatbox he'd noticed out of place, lifted out the froth of silk roses she'd worn for their wedding. He'd never forget how she looked that day, the ivory silk-and-chiffon dress she'd worn just skimming her knees, the confection of silk flowers on her dark hair. She had taken his breath away. He started to replace the lid, then lowered his face, sniffed. Too faint to name, maybe a cleaner of some kind, out of place in the rose-covered hatbox. He put the box aside for later.

Then he pulled every hanger, every article of clothing off the racks, threw them onto the bed. He opened handbags, tipped shoe boxes, thrust his fingers into the recesses of every shoe. The box that should have contained her evening shoes was empty.

As he started to toss it into the corner with the others he caught a familiar smell and instead raised it to his nose.

Christ!

He tore it apart, examined every inch, then scrabbled through the clothes on the bed, found the hatbox, ripped off the lid. Barely discernible, but he'd been right. An alien smell for a bunch of roses on a wedding hat.

Gun oil.

He pulled out the lining of the box, then tore through the cardboard beneath. In a matter of seconds, the box was a pile of rose-patterned shreds.

In the top drawer of the bureau, he found the cotton panties she wore daily, tipped them onto the bed. Bras, panty hose followed. Half slips she wore on church days. Scarves. Sorting through the bottom drawer his fingers felt thick and clumsy, his skin catching on the delicate silk-and-lace lingerie she kept there. He held up the red lace thong he'd bought for her last Valentine's Day, its matching scrap of lace bra. Foamy black teddies. Stuff she wore only for him.

Nothing. Nothing secreted among the silks except rose-scented sachets, nothing under the lining of the drawers.

He pulled the drawers out of her dressing table, examined each, turned them over, tapped his fingers over the bottoms. In the bathroom, he tipped cosmetics into the sink, white powder rising in a scented cloud from the fancy box of talc he emptied into the toilet.

Back in the bedroom, he sat in the little chair, a slipper chair Maggie called it. He thought of the way she pulled on silk stockings as she sat there, leg raised, toe pointed, lingering over the moment, fastening a garter, teasing him, enjoying the game as much as he did. His eyes roved the chaotic room, sweet smelling from the powders he had spilled. What had he missed? Somewhere there was something to give him a lead, something to tell him who this hidden Maggie Cady was—a woman who hated guns yet apparently kept a weapon concealed in a shoe box. There had to be something to give him a clue to why she'd run, and where. And what the connection was to their son.

The dark rectangle left by the dressing table drawer he'd removed stared at him like an empty eye socket. He rose from the chair, knelt, reached inside the rectangular space, and ran his hand over the underside of the dressing tabletop.

His fingers touched something, maybe an envelope, taped to the wood.

"Sam, you finished here?" Washington entered without knocking, stopped on the threshold, looked around. "Jesus, what the hell do you think you're doing? This place looks like Sherman just marched through Georgia."

Sam left the envelope in place, rose to his feet, his back to the dressing table. He followed Washington's gaze around the chaos he had created.

The lieutenant's face was dark with anger. "I figured you wanted to get some things that are no one's business but yours and Maggie's. That did not give you license to tear this place apart."

"Deke, I was a cop for twenty years. I know what I'm doing. I didn't want anyone pawing through her underwear—"

"I said I'd have Weston do it, for Christ's sake." Fuming, Washington studied the room. "This is not just underwear. Christ Almighty, Sam!"

Sam was silent, waiting for the storm to pass. Washington crossed to the bathroom, peered in at the mess. "So, all this effort turn up anything?"

"No."

"Shit. Well, come on down, the feds are here. You got to talk to them."

"You called the FBI?"

"Isn't that what you asked for?" Washington glared at him from beneath lowered brows. "Last I heard you figured some ego bullshit stopped me getting the feds in fast enough." He nodded at the chaotic room. "Now you listen to me, and listen good. From here on in, you stand back, you let us do our job, you hear me? Enough of this bullshit." He exhaled a deep breath and his voice softened. "We'll get them back, Sam."

But as he said the words, Washington looked away, and Sam knew what he was thinking. If they found Jimmy at all, it was likely to be his lifeless body. That was the grim reality in child kidnapping cases.

Sam nodded, his lungs barely able to take a breath. A moment passed, then Washington spoke again, filling the silence. "Now, I'm going to have Weston finish up here—"

"She won't find anything." Sam picked up the dressing table drawer, replaced it, covering the envelope. "I've gone through it all. But you want to waste your manpower checking again, go ahead."

Washington stared at him with hard eyes. "You are getting close to the edge here, Sam. Man loses track of his wife and son on the same day, I cut him some slack. But right about now, you're pushing the line. You got me on this?"

Sam took a breath. He was hammering the wrong guy because there was no one else to hammer. Washington had been a good friend.

He nodded. "Yeah, Lieutenant. I got you. Sorry."

Washington nodded. "Okay. Come on down now, talk to these tightasses."

The cluster of dark suits turned as Sam and Washington entered the kitchen.

"Sam, you know Special Agent Wilson of the New Orleans Field Office," Washington said.

Wilson reached out a hand. "Sam, I'm really sorry about all this."

"Terry." Sam nodded, shook the proffered hand. He and Wilson had worked a few cases together. Wilson had been at the New Orleans Field Office for as long as he could remember, had to be looking at retirement by now. Washington introduced the other two men. "Agent Jake Jimenez. Special Agent Stephen Adashek from New York City."

New York? Puzzled, Sam shot Adashek a look.

Adashek caught it and said, "Just happened to be in town, Mr. Cady, and tagged along." He held out a hand.

Sam nodded. Adashek's grip was firm, his dark eyes steady. The guy was muscular and fit, mid-fifties, but could be five years either way, pushing toward the end of his career, or still driving hard. A different type altogether from Wilson. He looked as if he'd be a good friend and a deadly enemy. Sam studied each FBI agent in turn, assessing the men who would chase down Maggie. Find Maggie and they'd find Jimmy—that was how it was going to play. Trouble was the feds had built a rep for shooting first, sorting it out later. Waco, Ruby Ridge, other disasters every cop knew about but that had been played down—they all roiled around in Sam's mind.

The feeling of dread in his gut was becoming stronger by the minute. He had to find her before they did.

"Sorry about all this, Sam. It's a bad business." Wilson spoke for the group of agents. "Why don't you start from the beginning. What can you tell us about the attack?"

Sam pulled out a chair from the kitchen table, gestured to the FBI men and Washington to sit. He opened a cupboard, took down five mugs, put them on a tray. He poured coffee, set the tray on the table while they scraped chairs, got themselves settled. His own coffee mug in hand, he leaned his back against the kitchen counter, looked down at the seated men. His NOPD experience had kicked in without any thought—when dealing with the feds, grab any advantage you can.

"Maggie left the house about 7:30 for the eight o'clock mass at Our Lady, Queen of Heaven—"

"That the church over on Marsden?" Wilson asked.

"Yeah."

"She always go to that mass?"

"Yeah. Every Sunday morning."

"Then the attacker could have been watching for her to leave," Wilson said.

"Sure, could have been," Sam said. "But the Cherokee circled the cul-de-sac a couple of times before it stopped in front of the house."

"But he must have known the house, the layout. Looked like he was counting on you to react the way you did, Sam," Wilson said. "Almost as if he knew you'd be busy returning fire and that would give him the time he needed to get someone up the back stairs."

Sam stared at Wilson. He couldn't answer. The fed was right, he'd been suckered. He'd gone over that scenario a thousand times in the last few hours, wishing he'd just run upstairs to Jimmy at the first volley of shots. He looked into his coffee cup without speaking.

Adashek got up, reached for the pot, went through the motion of topping up his almost untouched mug. He leaned against the counter, coffee mug to his lips, eye to eye with Sam. "Why don't you tell us what happened step by step, Mr. Cady. We'll hold the questions until you're finished."

Wilson flushed, fiddled with his notebook, but kept silent.

Sam went over it again, seeing each detail in his mind. He repeated the line of questioning already covered by Washington. When he'd finished, the young agent, Jimenez, glanced at Wilson, received an imperceptible nod of permission to proceed. He flipped back through his notes.

"What about this school conference?" Jimenez asked. "Where was it held?"

"Memphis. I thought I said."

"I meant the exact location. Hotel, conference center?"

"The Sheraton, downtown."

Wilson leaned forward. "Jake, get a complete list, names, addresses of the people who attended," he said to the younger man. "Hotel staff and anyone employed just for that event, hotel, clerical, whatever." He turned back to Sam. "Anything you can tell us about the folks living on this street?"

Sam gave them a rundown of everyone—good people, friendly, no one too close. Good fences made good neighbors, something his old man had taught him.

Wilson gestured to Jimenez and the young man rose, laid a sympathetic hand on Sam's shoulder as he left.

Sam acknowledged the gesture with a nod of thanks, but he knew that, for now, he was their prime suspect. Jimenez would undoubtedly run a check on him as well as Maggie. They'd check with the nuns who'd raised her, fan out through her life, ferret out every fact. And they'd talk to his old man in Jefferson Parish. They'd find out the date his mother died, get the military police to interview his brother at his air base in Germany. They'd widen the net to include the rest of his family, friends, former colleagues at NOPD, his professors at Tulane, back through the years to the guys on his high school wrestling team. Standard police procedure was to first rule out family involvement.

The shriek of a phone tore through the kitchen. Before the first ring ended, Sam was racing to the living room, Washington and the two agents close behind. A technician held up a hand, waited until the phone had rung five times, then nodded at Sam. He picked up the receiver.

"Sam Cady," he said. His hands were shaking and he tightened his grip.

"Oh, hi, Sam." A woman's voice. "Is Maggie there?"

"Who's this?"

"Oh," the woman gave a little giggle. "Sorry. This is Kelsie Mae? Kelsie Mae Odom? Gillie's mama? Jimmy's going to be at Gillie's birthday party this afternoon, we're all going to make puppets and put on a puppet show and I wondered if y'all could pick up little Sally Ferchay when you bring Jimmy? Sally's mama's having a baby, and her daddy's at the hospital and..."

Sam broke into the flow of words. "Kelsie Mae, sorry..." Wilson shook his head, but it was unnecessary, Sam knew better than to tell her what was happening. He started over. "Jimmy won't be coming, and we won't be able to bring... Sorry." He hung up.

The silence hung heavy, then Wilson said to Adashek, "Steve, you got anything you want to add here before we leave?"

Adashek shook his head, said to Sam, "I know this is hard for you but keep the faith. We move faster than you can imagine on this sort of kidnapping. Child of tender years, we pull out all the stops."

Sam nodded. "Yeah. Thanks." He looked into Adashek's hard face and knew that he had to be with Maggie when the FBI found her. And they *would* find her. Sooner or later.

Wilson patted his shoulder as he passed. "I'll check back with you, Sam. Deke, we'll meet again at five this afternoon here, that all right with you?"

Washington nodded, walked out with the two FBI agents. Through the window, Sam watched the three men stop, stand talking on the driveway just at the edge of the pool of Max's blood, dry now. No one had finished washing it away.

The FBI men left. For a moment, he thought Washington was going to return to the house, but he had a word with one of the uniforms, then went to his own vehicle and climbed in. Sam held his breath, silently urging him to leave. The unmarked car drew away from the curb.

Sam went back into the kitchen. He opened one of the cabinets, reached into the cookie jar where they kept the emergency money, a couple of hundred dollars, expecting to find the jar empty. But the bills were still there. She'd left with only the cash in her purse.

The technicians in the living room on the other side of the

foyer were intent on their equipment; no one looked up as he crossed the hall. The smashed front door let in the sound of Weston's voice raised in a question, and a deeper voice answering her. Sam climbed the stairs, closed the bedroom door silently behind him.

The room looked as chaotic as when he'd left it. Weston had not yet got around to the search. He opened the drawer in Maggie's dressing table, detached the hidden envelope, opened it, felt inside.

It contained one photograph. He peered inside the envelope. That was it. One photograph.

It was of two young men, both laughing, one with his arm draped over the shoulder of the other—a priest in a black cassock. They stood on what appeared to be the steps of an old church—a metal-studded wooden door behind them was half open.

He'd never seen either of them before.

The familiar room felt suddenly distant, a wide, empty space, and he sat abruptly on the edge of the bed he'd shared with her, surrounded by her things. These were men from Maggie's life. His mind seemed to move very slowly. Sure, he knew he wasn't the first man she'd ever known—a woman of twenty-five when they'd met, in this day and age, he'd have been worried if he had been. There had been a couple of guys before him, no one serious. But here was a photograph of men she'd valued enough to hide from him.

He studied the picture again, trying to comprehend the incomprehensible. Maggie had secrets, a past she had kept from him.

At the left of the picture, behind the young men, was the edge of one of those carved wooden signs found outside old churches, giving the name of the church, the times services were held. The board was black, with only the end of a word visible, Gothic letters, probably in gold, curved across the top right. MER. He turned the photograph over. Nothing to indicate who, where, when. Only one faded blue ink stamp at the bottom, *QwikFoto,* and the number 322.

Moments passed, then the room came back into focus. Sam rose, crossed the room, cracked the door and listened. He could hear a hum of voices, nothing clear. He closed the door, went into his own walk-in closet, fumbled around on the top shelf until he found the backup he'd kept from his police days, a little .22 still in the ankle holster. He strapped it on. He pocketed some extra clips for the Sig Sauer he'd shoved into his belt at the small of his back earlier in the day. Then he opened the door, stepped out onto the balcony, ran down the outside steps, through the grove of banana and mimosa trees at the edge of their property. He vaulted the fence, keeping to the underbrush, following the route Maggie must have taken. The traffic noise became audible the closer he got to Magnolia, but still pretty light, and he remembered it was a Sunday. The longest Sunday of his life.

He walked briskly up Magnolia, turned into the gas station he used, a small independent where a bunch of guys could still hang out, borrow tools, bitch and scratch as they couldn't at home. He ducked into the repair bay at the back of the office, spotted the owner deep under the hood of a stock car.

"Hey, T," he called. "Be okay if I use the phone in your office?"

"Sure thing." T'bird Johnson straightened, wiped his hands on a piece of cotton waste, glanced at Sam briefly, then returned to the engine.

He'd banked on T'bird's lack of interest in anything that couldn't be tinkered with or raced on the stock car circuit. He was right. T seemed totally unaware of the activity of police cars, probably hadn't even heard the sirens. Sam picked up the phone in the gritty little office, tapped out the number.

"Petey Le Pont," he said to the operator when she answered. "You'll find him in the file room."

Petey, sounding pissed off, yelled his name into the telephone, and Sam said, "Don't say who this is, *cher.* I'm calling from T's place, my own phone's tied up and I don't trust the cell phone so close to the equipment in my living room. What do you hear?"

There was a pause, then Petey said softly, "The license plate checked out, Sam. It was Maggie's car all right, registered to her, your address. Washington doesn't know it yet, I sat on it until I could talk to you. What the hell's going on?"

Sam struggled to take a breath. "I don't know, Petey. Maybe she's been kidnapped, too." The silence on the other end told him that Petey wasn't buying it. He didn't, either. That note wasn't written under duress. Maggie had left under her own steam. "Can you get me the numbers called from the public phone at the Poinciana Drug Store between the hours of nine and ten this morning before anyone else gets hold of them? And the matching addresses?"

"Sure thing."

"Don't get your tail burned, Petey."

"Nah. What's the number there?"

"I'll call you, say ten minutes?"

Petey grunted, hung up the phone. Sam dialed information, asked for the 800 number of the corporate office of QwikFoto, glanced out the door while he waited, found T still had his head and shoulders deep in the stock car. The operator came back on the line. "No 800 number for QwikFoto."

"Any other number, not 800?"

"Not in New Orleans. Somewhere else you want me to try?"

"Ohio?"

"Where in Ohio?"

"Try Dayville."

A moment went by. "Nothing, sorry."

"How about Columbus?"

"Sorry, sir. No number there, either."

"Thanks." It had been a long shot, anyway. He hung up, stared at the girlie calendars on the wall without seeing them, waiting for the ten minutes to crawl by. At nine minutes, he called the precinct, asked for Petey.

"Got 'em," Petey said softly in answer to his voice. "Grab a pencil." He reeled off two numbers, their addresses, then said, "This office is mighty fucked up. We just lost that information for a couple hours. That do?"

"I owe you, Petey."

"Nah. Listen. Maggie used her charge card at the airport, bought a seat on an American flight to Chicago."

Sam swallowed the bile that suddenly rose in his throat. She really was running. Until now he hadn't been able to convince himself of it.

"Sam, you still there?" Petey's voice was insistent in his ear. "Chicago ring any bells?"

"Yeah, I'm here. No. Chicago? No."

"I don't know what's going on, Sam, but you watch yourself, y'hear?"

"Yeah. Will do. Thanks, Petey." He disconnected before Petey could ask questions he couldn't answer. He tapped out the first of the numbers Petey had given him, an address on Bullerton, close to the drugstore.

A young girl's voice said, "Hello?"

Sam could hear domestic noises in the background, the rattle of china, a dog barking, an evangelist on TV being moved by the spirit.

"I'm sorry to trouble you, but I'm trying to find out if some-one called you from the Poinciana Drug Store this morning be-tween the hours of nine and ten?"

"What?"

"Who's that on the phone, honey?" A faint female voice call-ing from another room.

"I don't know, Aunt Jewell. Someone wants to know about phone calls—"

Footsteps, a rustle, then, "What do you want?" A woman's voice, not friendly.

"Sorry to trouble you, ma'am. Can you tell me if my wife, Maggie Cady, called you this morning between ten and eleven?"

"What makes you think she called here?"

"She made a call from the Poinciana Drug Store, and I'm try-ing—"

She cut him off. "How did you get this number?"

Good question. "Well, it was on a slip of paper—"

The woman did not let him finish. "My niece here made a call about her grocery list. Sorry if your wife's cheatin' on you, but she didn't call us."

The phone banged in Sam's ear as T'bird came into the of-fice and hovered at his shoulder.

"Gotta check my driver for tonight, Sam. Important race, wanna be sure the sumbitch stays sober. You about through with the phone?"

"Yeah. Thanks, T." Sam pocketed the scrap of paper with the addresses. The other number had to be the one she'd called. "I need some wheels for a couple of days. You got anything I could use?"

"You can take that old Merc. Don't look like much, but she'll get you where you're going." T'bird rummaged in a drawer, threw Sam a set of keys. "Make a note of the mileage and we'll settle when you bring her back." He turned to the phone, spoke over his shoulder. "You want me to work on your rides, you bet-ter get them in here early tomorrow, Sam. Busy day, Monday."

"Okay, T. Thanks. Good luck tonight."

T was already banging out his driver's number. "Yeah, we gonna take 'em, sure. Sumbitch drives better with a skinful at that."

The Mercury was littered with debris, empty coffee contain-ers, overflowing ashtray, the back seat piled with oil-stained cov-eralls, but Sam knew it would be pristine where it counted, under the hood. He pulled out onto the highway, turned toward the New Orleans bridge and the second address Petey had given him. From his years in the NOPD, he recognized it as being on the edge of the Vieux Carré, outside the high-rent district.

Who did his gentle, innocent Maggie know in Sleazeville?

* * *

348 Chartres was a small white office building almost hidden behind palmetto and bougainvillea gone wild. Sam sat in the Mercury, studied the building. Two storeys, nothing special, stucco walls pierced by a row of windows on each floor.

He scanned the tree-lined street. It was Sunday-afternoon quiet, everyone sleeping off Saturday, getting rested for the start of another night's business. No dark green Cherokee, but he hadn't expected it.

On the corner across the street a liquor store was open, a sign outside indicating a public phone was available. Sam got out of the car, made his way across the empty street, pushed open the door. The overweight young kid behind the counter looked up without interest. "Hi. What you need?"

"Thanks, just using the phone."

The clerk went back to his magazine and Sam picked up the public phone hanging on the wall, called the number that matched the address Petey had given him. On the first ring, a male voice answered.

"I'm still waiting. Come on up."

Sam hung up without speaking.

The front door of the building was glass, unlocked no doubt for whoever it was the guy he'd spoken to was expecting. Sam crossed the black-and-white tiled floor of the small lobby, opened a glass door into an interior garden. Scraggly mimosa trees, tangles of lantana, a fountain in the middle half filled with scummy green water. Above, an open second-floor gallery edged with wrought iron scrollwork, doors to various offices. More iron scrollwork on the stairs at either end of the gallery. On the far side of the garden a passageway led through the building to a parking lot behind.

He found a discarded Marlboro Light packet, jammed it under the door so that a simple push would get him from the lobby to the courtyard, no fiddling with turning knobs, losing precious seconds if he needed an alternative exit. He crushed an abandoned liquorice candy box, shoved it under the front door, then turned to the directory on the wall by the stairs.

On the ground floor, the building housed a secretarial service, a computer technician, Madame Sylvie Couturier to the Elite, and something called The Naked Face—Electrolysis and Facials. The floor above housed an attorney, an insurance agency, and Mama Celestine, Charms, Curses, Love Potions. Ersatz stuff—no voodoo queen worth her chicken blood would be caught dead doing business out of an office building.

He worked the ground floor, found every door secure. The same with Napoleon Chambord, Attorney at Law in 210. No Mama Celestine in 208. Everything was Sunday silent. At 206, the corner suite—George Menton, Insurance, the gold lettering on the opaque glass looking a bit worn—the doorknob turned. Sam eased the door open.

A small reception office. Desk and computer, plaque that said No Smoking Zone on the desk, a nameplate beside it. Johanna Menton. Hatrack in the corner hung with half a dozen fancy *chapeaux,* feathers and flowers, in place of the usual dusty plastic plant.

The door to the inner room was open.

"Anyone working today?" he called.

"How did you get in here?" The same voice Sam had heard minutes ago, answering the number that Maggie had called. The man coming from an inner office was of medium height, solid, fortyish, in his shirtsleeves.

"Door's open downstairs. Careless thing to do on a Sunday. Or are you expecting someone?"

"Who the hell are you?"

"Name's Sam Cady." At the mention of his name, all expression left the other man's face. "My wife, Maggie Cady, called you this morning."

"I don't think so, Mr.... What did you say your name was?"

"Cady. Sam Cady. My wife is Maggie Cady. And, yes, I think she did. Where is she?"

"I don't know what you're talking about."

"Are you George Menton?"

"Yeah, that's my name. Now, we're closed here—"

"Listen, George," Sam said. "I've taken about all I intend to take today. My wife, Maggie Cady, called this number at this address at 9:23 this morning, and she hasn't been seen since. Now, you can tell me where she is, or I can beat the shit out of you first. Your choice. What's it going to be?"

"I tell you I don't know any Maggie Cady—"

In two steps Sam was across the room. He threw his right forearm across the man's throat, slammed him against the wall, was not surprised to feel the series of short hard jabs Menton delivered to his kidneys, the swift attempt to hook him behind the knee to throw him off balance. The guy was a player, no stranger to physical action.

Sam increased the pressure, took pleasure in burying his fist in the man's gut. He felt the sudden deadweight, held Menton up with the crushing forearm across the throat.

"Where is she?"

Menton took a couple of gasping breaths, his face pale, then choked out, "You're pushing your luck—"

Sam delivered another heavy blow to the same spot, stood back, let Menton sag to the floor. He took out the Sig, drew back the slide, shoved it against the man's teeth.

"Where is she? Where's my son?"

Speechless, Menton turned onto his side, his knees drawn up as he fought for breath. Keeping the weapon trained on the prone figure, Sam went to the door to the inner office, leaned in, swept his eyes around the room. Framed certificates on the walls, Southern Atlantic Assurance Company, Completion of Training, awards for salesmanship. George Menton, Johanna Menton. Bookshelves loaded with books on insurance. Couple of chairs, a partner's desk in front of the window. Innocent as hell.

"Okay, George Menton." Sam dragged the man to his feet, pulled his arm back and up, duck-walked him into the inner office, threw him into his seat behind the desk.

The man was shaking his head when his skull exploded. Bone, brains, blood, shards of glass sprayed the room. The body fell across the desk then toppled in slow motion to the floor.

Sweet God Almighty.

One shot from the street, through a closed window—Sam's thoughts were simultaneous with his dive into the safety of the corner, the protection of wall and bookshelves. He crouched against the wall.

Two minutes, three, passed in silence. Heart still hammering, Sam crawled across the bloody floor, grating on glass and bone, sliding over pieces of Menton's brain. He got to his feet in the reception office, crossed to the outer door, opened it. The gallery opposite was empty, the inner courtyard as peaceful as it had been when he arrived. He looked around the office, grabbed a hat from the fancy hatrack, threw it into the gallery in front of the office, followed it, the Sig at arm's length. Nothing.

Sam sprinted toward the staircase, took the steps three at a time, raced across the courtyard, through the passageway that led to the back parking lot. He peered out. The parking lot was empty. Nothing moved. Carefully he exited the passage, inched his way along the wall toward the alley that ran down the side of the building to the street and his car.

Warily, he put his head around the corner, took a quick look. Blank walls, a bunch of stray cats busy at an overturned trash can, and, halfway down, a rusted orange Dumpster with its lid propped open.

He stared around, evaluating his options. He could go back the way he came, across the courtyard, into the lobby, into the sights of the gunman maybe now hidden in the building. Or he could go on down the alley toward the Dumpster, into the sights of the gunman if he was still on the street. There was no way of knowing where he was. But Sam was sure of one thing: whoever he was, the gunman knew something about Maggie.

Sam took a breath, then raced down the alley, negotiating panicked cats, the overturned trash can, before hurling himself against the Dumpster. Noises reverberated from inside the metal skin and he leapt up, shoved the Sig over the top. Cats jumped in every direction, and he fell back against the wall, shaking.

He caught his breath, allowed his heart to slow its beat until it felt like it was going to stay in his chest, then warily made his way around the Dumpster. Staying close to the wall, he inched to the end of the alley. He waited, then cautiously poked his head around the corner. The door to the liquor store was shut tight, the Merc was twenty yards away. The exposed street lay dozing in the sun as it had been when he arrived, half an hour ago.

Then the wall by his head turned into a cloud of white pulverized stucco, the sound of a volley of shots following in a nanosecond. Sam hurled himself back along the alley, gained the safety of the Dumpster, hunkered down behind it. The shots had come from the direction of the liquor store. Either the marksman had lost his eye, or he was playing a game. Or it wasn't the same shooter. George Menton had been capped with one shot.

He waited for more shots, but could hear nothing but his own heaving lungs.

He stood, looked over the top of the Dumpster, saw a head peering around the end of the alley as cautiously as he had himself checked the street. Sam raised the Sig, yelled, "Son of a bitch, what the hell's going on?"

Another volley of gunfire answered him. The gunman appeared like an outline against the light at the end of the alley and Sam brought up the Sig. He fired. And missed. The gunman raised his weapon.

Then the gunman's head burst like a rotten pumpkin into a bloody, filmy cloud.

Mouth dry, heart threatening to explode his chest, Sam dropped behind the Dumpster, slid down the wall, back pressed against the stucco. One shot. One fucking shot. He waited—for another attack, for a voice making a demand, for police sirens. Minutes passed in the strange hush that always followed gunfire. Then sound picked up, hesitant at first, becoming louder. Birds in the parking lot trees, the rustle in the weeds clinging to life along the base of the building. Gingerly, a cat made its way back to the overturned trash can in the middle of the alley.

Sam got to his feet, ran toward the street. He glanced down at the gunman's body as he jumped over it.

The guy was black, dressed in Hawaiian print shirt, chinos, skinny bare feet in polished loafers. The stink of a sphincter loosened by death mingled with something Sam hadn't smelled since he left the police force.

A hand-rolled cigar the size of a fifty-dollar Cuban smoldered between the fingers of the guy's left hand.

Ganja.

NINE

Maggie scanned the crowd as she hurried toward the airport's exit. Kennedy was bustling, noisy with a cacophony of languages, so different from the soft tones of the South she had become used to. She attached herself to the edge of a party of Hasidim, hoping to lose herself in their midst, then realized the women with their closely covered hair, calf-length dresses, the bearded men in wide-brimmed hats and long black overcoats merely highlighted her own jeans-clad figure. Swiftly, she moved on, found a bunch of teenagers, bounced along in their wake until they swerved off.

Everywhere she saw men, twos, threes, groups, searching for her, ready to kill. She kept walking, purposefully, head down, face hidden by the peak of her baseball cap, past the innocent, unknowing strangers.

Outside it was dark. Rain spattered the sidewalk. Maggie shivered; the October air had the chill of a New York autumn, weather she was no longer used to. A good-humored dispatcher handled travelers waiting impatiently for cabs, calling the destination to the cabbies as he slammed doors on departing passengers. Maggie walked to the front of the line, slipped a ten-dollar bill into a receptive palm, murmured, "I don't want to wait. And I'll tell the driver where I'm going."

"Okay, lady. You got it." Ignoring loud complaints from the waiting crowd, the dispatcher opened the door of the cab standing at the curb, and banged on the top of the car as soon as she got in, sending it off.

How quickly it came back, Maggie thought, that New York edge she'd worked so hard to eradicate in her years in Louisiana. Sam had been the example she'd followed, his sweet easygoing charm... But she couldn't afford to think of him now. As soon as the cab drew away from the curb, Maggie leaned forward.

"Take the Van Wyck to Queens. I'll tell you where."

The cabby nodded without turning his head. Maggie stared out of the window, the lights of airport buildings, the darkness of the trees, the clapboard duplexes facing the racing traffic on the expressway. The passing scene dropped into its slot in her brain as if she'd never been away, familiar, still a part of her.

"Okay, so you're in Queens." The cabby broke into her thoughts. "Where do you want to go?"

"Somewhere I can make a phone call."

The cabby took the next exit, pulled into a gas station. Maggie climbed out. "Wait for me," she said.

"So what else am I going to do?" the cabby replied.

Rain-soaked pages from the telephone book littered the ground around the metal shell, the nearby wall smelled of urine, but mercifully the telephone was still attached and it worked. Maggie punched out the number that came back to her over the years, remembering the last time she had used it, when she was desperate to find him, to find James and her father, to warn them. She ran a dry tongue over drier lips. She didn't even know if he had returned there after Rome—

The ringing stopped, a soft pleasant voice said in her ear, "This is Father Patrelli."

Maggie tried to swallow, but without saliva her throat wouldn't work. She took a breath, then said, "Bobby." It was all she could manage.

For two heartbeats, there was silence. Then, "Who is this?" The voice was sharper.

"Bobby, this is Andrea."

"What? What? Who is this?"

"Bobby, it's Andrea. I need you to meet me at the place we saw each other last."

TEN

Sam pulled over like a good citizen to allow the NOPD vehicles roaring toward him, lights and sirens at full tilt, to pass unimpeded, then turned onto the first quiet side street he came to, and took stock of his appearance. His shirt, pants, his face, even his hair, were streaked with blood and bits of George Menton's brain. He reached behind him, pulled T's oil-stained coveralls over the back of the seat. None were designed for a body of his size, but he struggled into the largest, scrubbed his face and hair with the two that didn't fit, then checked in the rearview mirror. He was now oil-streaked, but that was a hell of a lot less sinister than being covered with George's blood and brain matter.

He turned on the ignition, rejoined the thickening traffic, crossed the New Orleans Bridge, drove to the Wal-Mart on Esplanade. To be safe, he kept his eye on the rearview mirror, but he guessed he wasn't being followed. For some reason the marksman, whoever the hell he was, no longer wanted him. If he did, Sam knew he would be dead by now.

In the store, he aroused little attention in spite of the filthy ill-fitting coveralls with Thunderbird Racing Team, New Orleans plastered across the back. He picked up chinos and a T-shirt, a windbreaker, sneakers, underwear and socks, stood in line to pay, got back to the Merc without incident.

North on Kerlerec, Sam turned into the Paradise Motel—"TV and phones in every room."

"You want a video or anything? It's extra." The receptionist kept her eyes on her own screen showing a Sunday afternoon gospel service, the mixed black-and-white choir rocking their way to heaven. She pushed a registration card toward him.

"No, thanks." Sam kept his head down, scribbled "Bob Jones, Louisville, Kentucky," added an imaginary license number, paid cash, took the key to No. 16, and breathed easier when the door closed behind him.

He showered, lathering his hair until he had used the last drop in the tiny bottle of cheap motel shampoo, and dressed in the fresh clothes. Then he picked up the phone, punched out a number, waited impatiently until Petey Le Pont barked into the receiver.

"Hey, Petey," Sam said softly. "Got anything? Anyone call?"

"No. There's been nothing. Wait a minute." Sam heard the sound of a door closing, then, "Where the hell are you?"

"At a motel. I had to get off the street."

"Yeah, hear a couple of guys got their heads blown off over on Chartres. An address that matches one of the numbers called from the Magnolia Shopping Plaza this morning. Nothing you'd know about, I guess."

"Turned out to be an insurance agency," Sam said. "What was she doing calling an insurance agency? The guy knew her name, but before he could tell me anything, he was blown away. Swear to God, Petey, one head shot, through a closed second-floor window. Guy's brains were everywhere."

"No shit!" Admiration was clear in Petey's voice. "Hell of a marksman."

"Yeah. I left in a hurry, and someone came after me waving a cannon."

"And of course you fired back, endangering innocent women and children—"

"What the hell was I supposed to do? Call 911? I thought it was the same guy coming after me. Turned out I was wrong. Guy was firing at me when he had his own head blown off. One shot. Same thing."

"No shit!" Petey said again.

"Black guy, probably Jamaican."

"How'd you figure that?"

"You know of anyone else dry out their brains with those Bob Marley *ganja* cigars? When I got out of there, the damn thing was still throwing up enough smoke to give half of New Orleans a high."

Sam heard Petey blow out a breath and knew his former partner was shaking his head with the same confusion he felt himself.

Petey said, "Weston's reported in that she can't find you. The guys over there checked all the johns in your house, so they know you ain't taking a leak somewhere. Washington's damn near having a coronary."

"The feds looking for me?"

"Not yet. Washington can't stand those tightassed bastards. The way he figures, you put in your twenty, so unless you mess up big time you're still NOPD's business and fuck the feds. He's cutting you some slack, Sam, because he knows you're going after Maggie, and we know where she's going. He's counting on our guys to pick you up before you get out of the city. You got any take at all on what this is about?"

"I've been racking my brains, but no, nothing." Sam felt the blood pound in his temples. He closed his eyes for a minute, then said, "They connecting me to it?"

"The Chartres thing? No, not yet. Won't be long, though,

cher. The Eighth District caught this one, but as soon as Washington connects the dots, he'll have to bring the feds in on it."

"Any more word on Maggie?"

"Chicago PD will pick her up when she arrives at O'Hare around 3:15 this afternoon."

"Oh, Christ, Petey."

"Yeah. Well. I gotta say this, Sam. If she were my lady, I'd be on the next plane to Chicago, FBI or no fucking FBI. Just don't fly American, our guys are watching."

"Yeah. Right. Thanks, Petey."

"*Rien, mon ami.* Watch your back, y'hear?"

He hung up.

ELEVEN

"You sure you want me to leave you here?" The cabby leaned across the seat to get a better view of the sign attached to the gate. "St. Savior's Cemetery," he read out loud. He turned, looked at Maggie. "Spooky sort of place, late like this."

"It's okay. I'm meeting someone." Maggie handed over the amount on the clock, added a tip.

"Sure as hell hope it ain't Dracula." The cabby hesitated, then said, "Listen, lady, this is New York. I'll wait if you want."

Touched, Maggie shook her head, gave the cabby what she hoped was a reassuring smile. "No, I'll be all right. Thanks."

"Okay, your call." The cabby gunned the engine, shot away from the curb, as if embarrassed by his own kindness.

The engine noise faded, the silence deepened. Streetlights just beginning to come on barely penetrated the heavy canopy of trees, and on the other side of high black railings that reached into the darkness in both directions, the night seemed a solid wall.

Then, slowly, the surrounding city reestablished its presence, the hum of traffic on Springfield Avenue, the wail of a distant police siren, the heavy beat of rap from a passing car. Maggie walked briskly to the guardhouse in the center of the closed gates.

A guard stepped out. "I'm sorry, ma'am. The cemetery's closed. You'll have to come back tomorrow." He gestured to the signboard. "We open at eight, close at six."

"But I've come directly from the airport. I'm leaving early to-morrow and I arranged to meet someone. Maybe there's a note?"

"Oh, wait a minute. I just came on shift, there's something here." He went back inside the gatehouse, picked up a note, poked his head back outside. "Are you the lady meeting a Father Patrelli?"

"Yes. Is he here?"

"No, he called. You can wait for him in the guardhouse if you like, drier in here."

"I'd rather go into the cemetery now, if that's all right."

"Okay by me. Most people are scared of this place, know what I mean? Me, I think it's the safest place in town with the streets full of punks. Shoulda kept old Rudi on. Great guy, cleaned the city up with all his law and order stuff, even before September 11..." He stopped. "You know where you're going?"

Maggie stared at him. Did she?

"Lady, do you know where you're going, your deceased's plot? Do you need a map?"

"No. Thanks. I know where I'm going."

The rain had turned into a fine mist and the lights from the guardhouse began to dissolve as she walked away, then disap-peared completely, screened by the night and the rows of moldering headstones that dated from the early years of the nineteenth century lining both sides of the gravel path.

Maggie shoved her hands into her pockets, and in spite of the autumn chill, forced herself to walk without hurrying. Bobby was coming from Manhattan, he'd be a while, and the guard was right, there was nothing to fear in this place of the dead. No one knew she was here.

At home, when they'd first met, Sam had often taken her to visit the old cemeteries: Metairie, Lafayette, St. Louis. Strange places for him to take a date, she'd thought at first, but that was before she understood what they meant to him. They still visited when they could, wandering among the ancient tombs, stopping here and there while Sam told her tales from the early days of his city. The Irish and Germans who labored to clear swamps, their lives cheaper than those of expensive slaves, the Quadroon Balls and the Civil War, yellow jack and voodoo, the past and present mingling for him as so often happens in New Orleans.

But that was in sunlight, walking hand in hand with Sam.

And this was New York. The danger zone, they'd called it when they had warned her never to return. But she'd broken that contract and no one would protect her now. She had only herself. No Sam to hold her hand.

The trees dripped moisture, and Maggie pulled up the collar of her jacket. A journey that had lasted only minutes the last time she had been here—following the flower-laden hearses along the broad tree-lined road to the crypt—seemed endless on foot at night with the avenues of stone closing in around her.

She walked quickly, sure of her way, keeping her mind resolutely on the many times she had been here in daylight as a way of containing the panic that urged her to race back to living human contact at the guardhouse. Then, there it was, the crypt under the protective screen of the giant willow planted at the turn of the nineteenth century to weep in perpetuity.

The silhouette of the ornate little building was not as she remembered. A large angel had been added at the side, wings spread, head drooping in sorrow. In the dark she couldn't see the names of the occupants recorded in marble on the front of the vault, but she didn't need to. They were imprinted in her memory. She moved close so that she could run her fingers over the two most recent: Salvatore Bellini, Giacomo Bellini, the dates of birth a generation apart, the date of death the same. She had no tears left. There was only rage now, a cold, hard source of strength.

She was lost to time, standing there, until the sound of footsteps crunching over gravel brought her back to the present. Quickly she moved across the path, melting into the group of granite figures kneeling by the neighboring vault, carved hands pressed together in supplication, stone eyes turned piously heavenward.

The man striding toward her was bareheaded. He wore a black trench coat, a flash of white at his neck. Slim, medium height. The Bobby she remembered, walking as he always did—going somewhere in a hurry. He stopped by the crypt, bent his head in prayer, a dark outline against the density of the angel towering over him.

"The angel is new." Maggie stepped from the shadows, crossed the few yards, the five years, the abyss that separated them. "Paul's idea, no doubt."

At the sound of her voice he turned, peered into the mist. "Andrea?"

Without speaking Maggie took off the baseball cap shadowing her face, allowing her hair to fall around her shoulders as he would remember it.

His eyes moved over her face. "I knew your voice the minute I heard it. I never believed you were dead."

"Why not? The day after this," she ran her fingers over the names of her father and brother, "you ran away to Rome. You knew what it was like then. Anything could have happened here in New York."

"I was ordered to Rome."

"You could have said no. You could have refused to take your final vows. I thought you would. You let me believe you would."

There had never been a time when he was not part of her life, Giacomo's best friend, six years older and her first love. She'd thought her only love until she met Sam.

He looked away, then back at her. "I'm sorry I wasn't here for you, Andrea. I would have been—"

"No, you wouldn't. You chose Rome."

"Andrea—"

"Andrea is dead. My name is Maggie Cady."

"I like Andrea better."

Maggie turned onto the path, started to walk. Patrelli fell into step beside her.

"What brought you back?" he asked. "It must be very dangerous for you here."

"They came for me, Bobby. Early this morning." As she said the words, they seemed unreal. Only this morning Jimmy slept in his own bed. "I wasn't there, I'd gone to an early mass. They took my son, instead. He's four."

Patrelli's step faltered. "A son. You have a son?" He turned his face to her. "Andrea. I'm sorry. So sorry."

"I want you to take a message for me."

He was silent.

"Bobby, you can do this for me. I don't know what they want. Whatever it is, tell them I am here. The minute I know my son is safe with his father in New Orleans, I will go wherever they want, do whatever it is they want. They'll listen to you."

"You expect me to deliver you to them? Is that what you think of me?"

"This is not about you, what I think of you, what I don't think of you. This is about my son. I'm asking you to deliver a message. That's all. Whatever comes after that won't concern you."

"I can't do that. Things are not as they were before—"

"I know they're not. While you were safely tucked away in the arms of mother church they really did try to kill me."

"I know. I heard about it. Andrea, I—" He stopped in the middle of the path. Maggie turned cold eyes onto him, daring him to continue. He looked away from her challenge, resumed walking.

"Who was it? Did the FBI find out?"

"No. So they said. But they knew. They kept a watch on me, followed me everywhere."

"I didn't hear about it until much later, you must believe me. Too late to do anything, even if I'd been able to." His voice trailed, then picked up. "In spite of what you think, I wasn't asked whether I wanted to go to Rome. I was injured, half drugged. The cardinal... I was just shipped off."

Maggie turned to him. "Bobby, I don't care anymore why you went. *They've got my son. I want him back.* His father wants him back." She fought the sobs closing her throat—she couldn't afford anguish. Whatever emotion she had from now on had to nourish her rage and her energy. "They lost people. We lost people, my father, my brother." She didn't add that she'd lost him, too, that day. And later, their unborn child. All of that heartbreak had faded into memory. Only the present was urgent. "Now they have my son."

"Do you know what they want?"

"Take the message, Bobby." She felt suddenly drained. "Then go square your conscience, as you always manage to do. You and the cardinal."

He ignored her jibe. "Where are you staying tonight?"

"I haven't thought about it. I'll go to a hotel."

"Come back to the rectory with me."

She shook her head. "That'll raise some eyebrows. But the cardinal will fix that, too, no doubt." He didn't answer, and she said in a softer voice, "Thanks, anyway, but that's the first place they'll look for me."

"No, I think you'll be safe there."

She thought about the night stretching ahead of her—finding a cab, a hotel. And tomorrow, sitting by the phone in a strange room, not knowing what was happening, waiting for him to call. And then there was the Beretta. She'd taken a chance on sending it to the rectory, the last address she'd had for Bobby, intending to ask him to deliver it to her, or if he no longer lived there, to find a way to intercept it. But if she stayed at the rectory, she could get the weapon, and no one would know she was armed.

She nodded. "All right. Thank you."

They walked through the dripping trees toward the gatehouse and the parking lot behind. A large black BMW stood under a light. Not the car one would associate with a priest in a run-down parish in Manhattan. But then, she thought, Father Roberto Patrelli was not your usual neighborhood priest.

He opened the passenger door, waited until she was settled then slid behind the wheel, turned onto Springfield, headed toward the Van Wyck Expressway. Maggie leaned back against the rich leather, her head turned away from him to watch the light and dark of traffic, the small clapboard houses and shops that came and went.

Patrelli broke the silence. "Do you ever think of me, Andrea?"

She answered without turning her head. "Not anymore. I have a husband, and I love him. He is everything you could never have been." She felt the pain emanating from him, and said, "I'm sorry, that was cruel." But her words were perfunctory, polite only.

He waited as if wanting her to say something more. When she didn't he said, "I really did love you—"

She cut him off. "Don't. The girl you knew no longer exists. If you harbor any illusion about that, you'd better talk to your confessor."

"I have. I do. All the time. Andrea—"

"My name is Maggie. Maggie Cady." She sat up. "Bobby, take me to a hotel. Somewhere quiet and out of the way." She was describing the places where they had spent so many stolen hours, never the same place twice. "That would be better."

"No. You need to rest tonight." He glanced at her briefly. "And at the rectory, I can guarantee your safety."

Maggie stared out of the window. She was right. He was still connected.

TWELVE

Sam left the Mercury on a side street off Airline Highway and walked the rest of the way. Inside the airport terminal, he checked the counters. No uniformed cops hanging about watching passengers, no plainclothes he could make at first glance. He went to Midwest Express, a small commuter line, used his credit card to buy a ticket on the next flight to Chicago, found he had an hour to kill before it left.

He kept his eyes sweeping the crowd as he made his way to the bank of phones by the men's room, carefully avoiding the American counter. He dropped fifty cents, called T'bird, left a message on the answering machine about the location of the Merc, and about the keys he'd hidden among the roots of a fig tree close by. T would know to get there in a hurry before the car was dismantled right there on the street. T had no love of the authorities—he'd deal with the bloody bundle of clothes in the trunk, then he'd wait for an explanation from Sam before bothering the cops.

That done, Sam went into the men's room, locked himself in a cubicle, sat on the toilet and leaned back to wait for the time to pass until he could get to his flight. He studied his ticket as if it could tell him what he needed to know—what had happened to his son, what his wife knew. Where she had gone...

He sat up. *Sure as hell not to Chicago.* He was following the path Maggie had laid down for the police. She was too damn smart to leave a paper trail unless she wanted it followed. She'd bought a ticket for her true destination with cash. She must have had a money source he didn't know about.

He left the toilet, went to the USAir counter. "Did you sell a ticket earlier today to a woman wearing a black leather jacket? Five-two, about thirty, dark hair, big dark eyes?"

The clerk grinned, showing large irregular teeth. "I don't remember passengers, they're all just bodies to me. Like I told the other cop who asked this morning, I just sell tickets. He was looking for a woman in a red suit, five two, dark hair. What's going on? You guys misplace a basketball team of little women?" The guy snickered.

Sam resisted the urge to pull him over the counter by his lapels. He nodded his thanks, didn't bother to correct the mistaken assumption that he was NOPD. Jerk should have asked for his ID.

He checked with Delta, Florida Air, Alaska. No one asked him to identify himself, and no one had seen her.

He glanced at his watch. If he was to make his flight, he had to get to the boarding gate within the next few minutes. But he had a feeling that Midwest was going to Chicago without him.

The United Airlines counter was crowded. He went to the side, beckoned to the ground attendant.

She flapped a hand at him. "Sir, you'll have to come and take your turn like everyone else."

"NOPD doesn't wait in line, lady."

"Excuse me a moment," she said to the woman in front of her.

She approached Sam. "If you're asking about that missing woman, I can't answer a lot of questions, I'm very busy. I've already told the police I didn't see her."

"A woman in a black leather jacket?"

"Black leather?" She thought a moment. "Black jeans, baseball cap? Yes, I think that was a Gucci jacket. I noticed her. They asked about a red suit—"

"Where did she go, do you remember?"

"Yes, as a matter of fact I called the gate to tell them she was on her way. She had to run."

"So where did she go?"

A moment's hesitation as she appraised him. "New York."

"Kennedy? La Guardia?"

"Kennedy, arriving 6:00 p.m. Eastern Standard Time."

"Thanks. Get me on the next flight to Kennedy."

"My. What did she do?"

"Just write the ticket please." He handed her his credit card, a signpost for the feds, but there was no way around it.

"Hope you're on expenses. Gate 10, boarding in ten minutes."

Sam turned away from the counter and came belly to belly with Frankie Lans. Sam looked over Frankie's thick shoulder, relieved to see he was alone.

"Hey, Sam. Long time no see." Frankie had put in his twenty-five and had left the force a couple years after Sam. Now he made real money for the first time in his life, running airport security. He put a heavy arm over Sam's shoulder, eased him out of the crowd. "What are you doing here? I thought you had enough problems at home to keep you busy awhile."

"Deke Washington call you?"

"What do you think? Tells me your wife's done a run. Looks like she took your boy, huh? Too bad."

"That what Deke said?"

"No, I was listening to the backbeat. I been through my share of marital grief. I know what happens, these women get a bee up their ass."

Sam felt the breath come back into his lungs. Frankie hadn't got word yet about the Chartres Street killings.

"Yeah, well, I've got to go, Frankie. When you speak to Deke again, tell him I'm following Maggie to Chicago."

Discreetly, Lans patted Sam's back as they walked. "You're carrying, Sam. How were you planning to get through security?"

"The usual way."

"Not in my airport, buddy. Not with the restrictions we got now. You're a civilian, you don't get to use service corridors."

"Okay. Well, I've got a plane to catch, Frankie. You want this, you better take it. Here." Sam reached toward the small of his back, gambling that Lans wouldn't want a weapon waving around in a crowded airport, everyone was jumpy enough.

Lans looked around at the crowd. "Keep your piece where it is, Sam. You want to frighten the old ladies?"

"In New Orleans? You gotta be joking."

The burly ex-cop laughed. "Yeah, well, just the same." He herded Sam toward the airport security office.

"I haven't got much time, Frankie. I've got a plane to Chicago in five minutes."

"Let's just get that weapon, and the backup I'd lay a bet you got on your ankle. Then I call Deke, get the go-ahead. You're on the next plane, no hard feelings."

He opened a door, politely stood back to allow Sam to go through, then half turned to close the door behind them. Sam slammed his clenched fist hard below Frankie's right ear, caught the heavy body as the security chief fell, eased him to the floor, checked his pulse. Out, but breathing easy. Sam crossed to the other side of the office, opened the door that led into the quiet interior hallway. The phone was ringing as he closed the door behind him.

He sprinted along the service corridor, guessing that no internal security checks had been put in place. He was right. The corridor was empty. He slipped unnoticed through the door marked Gate 10, mingled with the last of the boarding passengers. He kept his head down as if examining his ticket, but no one from NOPD was checking United to New York.

Sam settled into his aisle seat, leaned forward to pick up the magazine from the seat pocket in front of him and flipped the pages, seeing nothing. The flight attendant stood by the open door checking a list on a clipboard. The phone behind her buzzed, and she picked it up, listened. Sam turned his head, giving her a profile in case she was being given his description and tried to make himself smaller in the seat. He peered across his seat mates, an old man grumbling at his wife as he fussed with her seat belt, and looked through the window. Small airport vehicles buzzing around, loaders in orange coveralls, triple baggage trailer heading for another plane. Nothing out of the ordinary. No police action on the tarmac, no Guard.

Sam turned back to the magazine. The door should have closed five minutes ago, the plane already rolling. He ran a forefinger over his top lip—sweat was a dead giveaway. He'd always check a suspect's sweat level first when he was a cop. The attendant hung up the receiver, picked up the microphone.

"Will passenger Tim Salazar please make himself known. Mr. Tim Salazar."

A buzz of panic ran through the passenger compartment. Several people started to struggle from their seats.

The flight attendant spoke into the microphone. "Please keep your seats. This is not an aircraft emergency. There is nothing wrong on this airplane."

A tall skinny black man made his way down the aisle, spoke to the attendant. His face anxious, he went back for his hand luggage, murmuring a few words to each line of passengers as he passed.

"My pa's had a heart attack, I gotta go home. It's okay."

He left the plane and the attendant pulled the door closed. The plane moved. Sam's heartbeat steadied. He was out of reach of the cops.

Three hours to New York. Sam put a hand into his inside pocket, pulled out the photograph he'd found in Maggie's dressing table. Two guys he didn't know. Not much to go on, but it was the only connection he had now to his wife and son.

THIRTEEN

Maggie knelt at the small prie-dieu in the corner of the room, and looked up at the statue of the Virgin. Nothing came, no prayer, no peace. Her heart felt as if it was bleeding into her chest cavity, draining away everything she had been, or wanted. All that was left was Jimmy....

She must have slept a few hours. She'd come awake to the anguish of Jimmy's disappearance flooding back with renewed ferocity, as if it were a living, breathing entity that had fed on her blood and gathered strength during the night.

By rote she started the rosary, tried to concentrate without success. The words she was murmuring sounded in her ears like a foreign tongue, making no sense. Only Jimmy's return would bring peace. She gave up, got to her feet, dropped the rosary onto the bedside table and picked up her backpack. Then she opened the door of her room, looked both ways along the corridor.

The air inside the rectory was cold—to mortify the flesh no doubt—and smelled of furniture wax with an undertone of in-

cense and dead flowers. The hum of a vacuum cleaner somewhere in the house seemed only to deepen the immediate silence. Maggie pulled the door closed quietly behind her, made
her way toward the stairs, down to the entry hall.

"You want something?"

The housekeeper, something more than middle-aged and
stout, her broad flat face surrounded by wisps of gray-blond hair
straggling from a babushka, stood in the doorway of a small
room off the foyer. She turned off the vacuum.

Maggie nodded. "Good morning. Has FedEx made a delivery? I am expecting two packages."

"*Nyet.* You stay here? Father Robert told me you an old friend
of his." She swept Maggie with her eyes. "You don't look so
old."

"We grew up together."

"Coffee in the kitchen," the woman said. "And food. Muffins,
oatmeal."

"Well," Maggie looked at the door. "Could you let me know
when the packages—"

"You don't look so good. Go. Drink some coffee, eat something. You feel better. I get your packages." The housekeeper
turned back into the small book-lined room, noticed Maggie's
hesitation, jabbed a finger in the direction of a door at the end
of the dark wood-paneled passage running alongside the stairs
toward the back of the house. "Kitchen. Go. You see."

"You'll have to pay the FedEx man." Maggie fumbled in her
bag, handed the woman a hundred-dollar bill, then turned and
followed the pointing finger, glad to be away from the statue of
Christ the Redeemer that faced the front door, the luridly exposed bleeding heart a mirror image of her own.

The kitchen was huge and comfortless, a large expanse of
white tile. Church funds apparently did not run toward modern
appliances—stove, refrigerator, sinks, all looked as if they'd
been in place for fifty years. The coffee was a surprise, a rich

Italian brew that teased her memory. Then she remembered. Bobby's mother. She'd always had beans sent from Sicily. According to Mrs. Patrelli, no one could roast coffee beans like they did in Sicily.

She hadn't thought of Mrs. Patrelli for years—she'd had to build a wall to keep out the past until her new life had encompassed her as securely as a turtle's shell. Maggie held the cup with two hands, breathed in the aroma of her childhood.

A man entered the kitchen, not yet old but nudging the years. He had a full head of white hair, and was dressed in beat-up gray pants, a rusty black shirt, dog collar. His face had settled into a perpetual sag of defeat. He stopped at the sight of her.

"You must be Father Patrelli's guest. He left me a note."

Maggie put down her coffee cup and wondered how soon she could get back to her room without appearing rude. Small talk was beyond her.

The priest poured coffee, lifted the lid of a pot on the stove. "Oatmeal. Our Mrs. Grotka seems to think all priests must have Irish oatmeal for breakfast. Strange, isn't it? She's Ukrainian, I'm Polish and Bob's Italian. But you know that." He glanced at her. "Can I get you a bowl?"

Maggie crumbled a piece of the muffin on her plate. "No, thank you. This is more than enough."

"Well, now. I'm Father Lachinski." He sat, hacked a knob of butter off the rock-hard slab on a plate on the table, rubbed it over the oatmeal then sprinkled sugar. He looked up expectantly when she didn't respond. "And you are?"

"Sorry. Maggie Cady. How do you do, Father?"

"Well. Welcome to our little rectory. Not often we have social visitors, and a charming lady at that." He spooned his oatmeal, touched his lips delicately with a paper towel. "So what brings you to New York, Maggie?"

Lachinski did not sound as welcoming as his words. Maggie hesitated, then said, "I have some family business to attend to here."

"Ah. Well." He slid her a glance. "You and Father Patrelli are old friends, I understand."

"Yes, that's right. We grew up together." Clearly he wanted more. Maggie gathered her dishes together, preparing to rise. If he thought her rude, so be it. "I will be leaving today, so I'll take this opportunity to thank you for your hospitality—"

"Andrea! This is far too early for you to be out and about. You should have slept in. Good morning, Wen. I see you two have met already." A cassocked Bobby Patrelli strode over to the coffeepot, trailing a whiff of incense as he passed. "Quite a good house this morning, Wen. Ten old ladies, and Manuel Lopez." He brought his coffee mug to the table, returned to the stove, speaking over his shoulder as he filled a bowl with oatmeal. "Lopez has been beating his wife again so he's trying to head off the wrath of God with daily mass, as usual. We have to get them both in for counseling again before he kills her or the children. I think it's time to insist she take the kids and go to Grace House. It's a home for battered women," he said to Maggie. He pulled out a chair and sat. "So, did you manage to get some sleep?" He saw the puzzled expression on Lachinski's face and said, "Andrea and I have known each other since childhood, Wen. Our families were close."

"Yes, so you said, but there seems to be some confusion over the name. Your childhood friend here seems to think her name is Maggie."

Maggie got to her feet. "Andrea's my middle name. I prefer not to use it." She took her mug and plate to the sink, rinsed them, looked for a dishwasher, and realized there wasn't one. She found a dish towel, dried the two dishes, opened cupboard doors looking for a place to stow them.

"I have something I must do this afternoon, Wen," Father Patrelli said. "I was wondering—"

Maggie turned. "No, you can't wait that long. You have to go now, this morning."

"What? What does she mean?" Lachinski looked from one to the other. "Is someone in trouble?"

"Bobby, please," Maggie said. "You have to go this morning."

Patrelli silenced her with a look. "Andrea, the appointment has already been made." He turned to Lachinski. "Something personal has come up I have to take care of, that's all. So, can you take the teens at risk group meeting for me at four?" He pushed the bowl of oatmeal away, reached for a muffin. "I'll take the six o'clock mass tomorrow morning for you, and you can sleep in."

Lachinski's eyes darted from face to face. "I never sleep in, Robert. You know that. What's the matter—"

"Personal stuff, nothing to concern you," Patrelli said. "So if you do the teens, I'll owe you. Just name it and I'll do it."

"That means I have to rearrange my schedule—"

Patrelli jumped in. "Good. Thanks, always know I can count on you in a pinch."

How did he reconcile the two sides of his life? Maggie wondered. Mob negotiator. Parish priest. She caught Patrelli's eye as she crossed the kitchen to the door, and knew he read her mind. He always had. She closed the door behind her.

The FedEx packages and a stack of change from the hundred were on her bedside table, beside the bible and a small breviary, neither of which she had opened. Maggie ripped off the brown paper, unwrapped the silk scarves, and stared down at the gray plastic and metal weapon. She ran a thumb over the stylized *AB* on the barrel, then held it at arm's length, one hand curled beneath the other as her brother James had taught her, refamiliarizing herself with the balance. Satisfied, she loaded it, placed it in her backpack. Immediately she felt better. Armed, she was her father's daughter.

How could she ever have imagined she could be anything else?

FOURTEEN

"Petey, for Christ's sake, man. There's been a mistake. He was an insurance agent, not a fed." Suddenly needing air, Sam crossed the room to the window, the phone locked to his ear. Seventeen storeys below, people looked like ants scurrying from a disturbed nest. He searched for a way to crack the window open, but it was fixed in place. "The name was on the door. George Menton Insurance. He even said that's who he was. George Menton. And he knew Maggie, no question about it."

"Yeah, well, his wife identified the body, Sam. Johanna Menton. There's no mistake," Petey Le Pont said. "It seems he moonlighted selling insurance but he was a U.S. Marshall, all right."

Sam took a breath, trying to process what Petey was saying.

"Sam, you see how this is shaping up?" Petey let the silence stretch, then said, "Maggie disappears. She calls a U.S. Marshall on a private line no one knows about. He gets shot dead couple hours later. You gotta know, at least suspect that—"

"Now, wait a minute." Sam interrupted before Petey could

give substance to the unthinkable. "That's a hell of a stretch." He ran a hand roughly over his face, struggling with what Petey was implying, trying not to believe it. But he knew that Petey was right. The U.S. Marshall's Service administered the Federal Witness Protection Program.

In an instant everything had suddenly changed. Now the question seemed to be not only where Maggie was, but *who* she was.

"Sam, it's the only thing that makes any sense of all this," Petey said. "Maggie's in the WPP. George Menton was her case officer."

"Christ Almighty, Petey, that's Maggie you're talking about. Maggie. Jesus." Sam felt suddenly overwhelmed. He had to put all this aside, consider it later when he was off the phone. Right now he had to deal with the rest of the tonnage Petey had just dropped on him. At least, that he could understand. A federal warrant had been issued for his arrest for murder. Armed and dangerous. "I didn't kill him, Petey."

"Shit, I know that, Sam," Petey said. "But I got to tell you, it's not looking too good. We found the green Cherokee. It had been reported stolen Saturday over in Abbeville..."

Sam tried to listen while his mind threatened to spin out of control. He knew Maggie, lived with her, loved her. Had a child with her... He forced himself to concentrate on what Petey was saying.

"...it's being torn apart but they doubt they'll find much. It's been cleaned up by someone who knew what he was doing."

"And that fits me, too, right?"

"Deke still doesn't see you as a killer, but it's out of his hands now and the feds are sure wondering why the body count keeps going up."

"What do you mean, going up? The insurance guy and the Jamaican—"

"And the liquor store clerk. Couple of our people discovered the body when they went to question him about the shootings across the street. Poor bastard was behind the counter. Head shot, like the other two."

"Oh, Christ, Petey." Sam thought of the young face of the clerk, untouched by life, the overweight body—soft, dumb kid in the wrong place at the wrong time. "What about the Jamaican? How do they explain him? Why am I supposed to have killed him?"

"They figure that will fall into place when you're picked up. Of course they're thinking drugs, you being a 'copter jockey and all."

"Sure," Sam said bitterly. "Makes as much sense as anything else. Why not?" He wrestled with the window again, without luck. He was trapped in this goddamn box, high above goddamn Manhattan. "So the guy, the shooter, must have popped the clerk first, then used the liquor store as a blind until he could get the other two."

"That's what it looks like." Petey Le Pont sounded grim, no longer filled with admiration for the marksman's skill. "A pretty cool killer, bro. He waits to get George Menton while his other vic's lying dead behind the counter. Only luck no one came in for the Sunday paper, or I'd bet my ass there'd be another body."

"So he takes care of Menton, sends his buddy the Jamaican after me and caps him before he can do it. That doesn't make any sense, Petey. Did he leave any sign in the store, anything that can be used to get me off the hook?"

"They're still working the scene. We don't know much yet."

"So why didn't he come after me himself?" Sam said. "I was a sitting duck for a guy like that."

"I don't know, *cher.* So far, nothing adds up worth shit."

Sam said, "I should have heard the shot that killed George Menton, and I didn't hear a damn thing. You thinking what I'm thinking?"

"A silencer."

"Yeah. A professional hit." The world Sam knew had tilted

out of focus. A sea of blood swirled around his wife and son. "Explains the Jamaican. A contract killer brought in from the island. But he probably won't be in any database, Petey, if he was brought in just for this job. It's the marksman who's the main man."

"The informed assholes in the FBI say that's you, Sam. They ain't telling us doodoo, as usual, but if Maggie was in the Federal Witness Protection Program..."

Sam heard the words, tried to match them with the woman he knew, his Maggie. His wife, his lover...

Petey's voice hummed in his ear, "...and Menton was her case officer, there's the key right there. You just won't be able to turn it, bro."

"You got anything I can work with, Petey?"

"Nothing. It's heavy shit, whatever's going on. The big dog from New York's still here. The local bureau men are pretty stiff-legged around him, and he's pissing Deke off every time he blinks. These guys are going to be on your tail sooner rather than later."

"Yeah." For a moment neither spoke. Then Sam said, "Petey, listen." He could hardly get the words he wanted to use past his lips. "Can you lift Maggie's prints from the house and run them, see if you can get a match somewhere? Get a set of DMV prints, too. Maybe it'll give me a lead. Something."

Petey said, "Sam, if she is in the protection program, you know there's no penetrating that. There'll be a fire wall, no prints, no records, nothing connecting her to her other life. Everything will have been obliterated."

"I've got to start somewhere."

A beat of silence, then, "Sure, buddy," Petey said. "Yeah, sure, Sam. Consider it done."

"Thanks. If you get a word on Jimmy, or anything else, you can reach me at—"

"Sam," Petey interrupted. "I don't want to know where you

are. We heard from Cook Country PD so we know that neither of you turned up in Chicago, and that's all I want to know. If we get anything on Jimmy, I'll leave word with Elle, so you call my home whenever you want, and she'll know what I know. Just don't use your cell phone, we don't know who's listening. Anything else, you tell Elle what time you'll call back. I'll try to be there."

So they hadn't picked up his credit card trail yet, didn't know he was in New York. "Yeah, okay. I owe you, Petey, big time."

"*Rien.* Sam, I got a bad feeling about this one, it looks like some strange goddamn territory, so watch your back, y'hear?" He hung up.

Sam stared down at the street below, hating it. People that looked like ants, buses the size of beetles. He'd checked into Loews at 51st and Lex, the hotel he'd used when he'd attended a seminar for police helicopter pilots several years ago, just before he'd gone down during the Colombian bust. Before he'd met Maggie.

Or whoever she was.

Fuck it, he thought. Maybe he should just go home, leave her to it. That's what she'd said, anyway. *Don't follow.* He got the note she'd left him out of his wallet, the familiar handwriting mocking him.

Sam, I love you.

Who the hell was she, the woman who wrote that? Not the woman who had murmured those words to him in a voice thick with desire, and softly sated with love. His heart seemed squeezed in a vice as he remembered—the passion between them as urgent now as it had ever been, and even sweeter, the intimacy afterward, the hours spent talking, sharing...telling her everything, his life, his thoughts, his feelings. His soul mate... he'd known how lucky he was to find her.

And all of it, a lie.

He crushed the note in his fist, lobbed it at the wastepaper basket and missed by a couple of feet. He thought of Jimmy shooting into the kid-size basketball hoop he'd put up in the backyard. He'd missed every shot at first but he kept on, every day. The look on his son's face the first time the ball dropped sweetly into the basket was something he would always treasure.

Sam retrieved the note, smoothed it out, replaced it carefully in his wallet. Then he picked up the photograph from the bedside table, the priest and his buddy, important to his wife, whoever they were. Whoever she was.

He turned it over, reread the small lettering at the bottom. QwikFoto 322. He remembered the little blue-and-yellow booths, drive-in, drive-out film development. Once every supermarket parking lot seemed to have one, but no longer. Without much hope, he picked up the phone, dialed information and was surprised when he got a corporate office number in New York.

"I'd like the location of store number 322," he said to the woman who answered. "Can you tell me where that is?"

"Transferring you," the voice sang in his ear. "Hold on, please."

The spiel lauding the superiority of QwikFoto products and services was mercifully interrupted by another female voice. He repeated his question.

"322? That series of numbers is not active now, hasn't been for years."

"Well, where would that location have been when it was active?"

"Somewhere in New York City."

"Where, exactly?"

"I don't have that information. Sorry."

Sam studied the photograph in his hand, then said, "This is the Atlanta Police Department. Sgt. Leo Smith. That information is vital to an ongoing investigation. Can you get it for me, please?"

"Oh. Well. It'll take time. I have to search—"

"Don't you have it in your computer?"

"Well, yes."

"Okay. I'll hold on."

"Sgt. Smith, you'll have to leave your number. I'll call you—"

"Ma'am, just make the search now, please. I'll hold on."

"I'm sorry, as I say, it will take time. I'll have to call you back. Please give me your telephone number, and I'll get back to you." The voice had become stubborn and chilly.

He couldn't wait for her to find out there was no Sgt. Leo Smith in Atlanta. Leo had been a twenty-five-year veteran of NOPD. The guys had given him a great send-off last year after he'd drunk himself to death. Sam said, "Thanks. I'm out in the field. I'll call you."

He picked up his windbreaker, slipped it on. It looked as if he'd slept in it, but it did the job, hid the Sig in his belt. With luck he'd be okay as long as he didn't get picked up for some dumb-ass thing like jaywalking. He was in a labyrinth, couldn't see the beginning, couldn't see the end. One thing was sure, though, this was no time for him to be walking around naked in New York City.

FIFTEEN

Maggie sat on the edge of the hard single bed, stared out of the window at the lowering sky. Kept her thoughts away from Sam. Waited. The day stretched ahead, hours in which she could not allow herself to think of Jimmy.

A knock at the door startled her—she must have dozed. Maggie straightened, her hand automatically seeking the backpack.

"Missus, you want to eat?" The knock was harder. "Missus, you want lunch?"

"No, thank you."

The door opened. "Yes, I think so." Mrs. Grotka stood squarely in the doorway. "I make potato soup, good meat in it. You come down."

"Thank you, but—"

Mrs. Grotka stood her ground stolidly. "Yes, you come. You eat in kitchen. Come."

Maggie stared at her. Mrs. Grotka was not going to give up. Then, suddenly Maggie felt herself soften. The housekeeper was concerned for her—she could allow that much in without losing the edge she needed for what lay ahead.

"Father Lachinski gone," Mrs. Grotka said. "Father Bobby gone. You be alone, peaceful."

Maggie forced a smile and nodded. "All right. Thank you." She hadn't eaten for so long, and for Jimmy's sake, she had to keep her strength. She picked up her backpack.

A place was set at the kitchen table. Mrs. Grotka ladled soup into a bowl, placed it in front of her, pushed a basket of warm crusty bread closer. "Eat. After, apple pie. Coffee fresh in pot." She left the room.

Maggie ate without tasting, reached for a newspaper from a pile teetering on a chair, ready for recycling. News of New York, weeks old, of no interest to her. Nothing much seemed to have changed since she left. The same crime, the same corruption, the same political wheeling and dealing. Sickened her years ago, sickened her now. She dropped the paper back on the pile, picked up another, flipped the pages, skimming the newsprint. Her eyes slid over a picture. Then went back.

The mayor at the annual Sons of Sicily League dinner. On one side was Cardinal Matterini. On the other was her father. But it couldn't be.

Maggie picked up the page, looked closer, realized it was her brother, Paul. Paolo. Older and thicker, more like their father than ever, his hair springing back from his forehead as their father's had done, although Paul's was still dark where her father's had turned silver—in his thirties her mother said. The caption identified him as Paul Bellamy. Behind the group was the partly obscured figure of Father Robert Patrelli.

Maggie felt very still, her lungs barely moving with each breath, if she was breathing at all.

Why hadn't they gone after Paul? Or his daughter? Why come after her? Why Jimmy?

She couldn't write to Paul, or call him, she didn't even know how to find him—certainly not in the telephone book. He wouldn't take her call, anyway. Her brother didn't know Maggie Cady, and Andrea Bellini was officially dead.

Requiescat in pace, she thought bitterly. As if that had ever been possible. The longing for Sam, the sound of his voice, his arms around her, the only peace she'd had in the last six years, caught her under the heart, a physical pain surrounding the core of agony that was Jimmy. She went to the old-fashioned black phone on the counter and dialed. On the third ring, a sweet, drawling voice answered.

"Elle," Maggie said quickly. "It's me. Don't ask me anything. How is Sam?"

"Oh, honey," Elle said, "I don't know. He's not here."

"Did he follow me to Chicago?"

"Cook County police said neither of you arrived, sugar. No one knows where he is."

Maggie caught the careful note in Elle's voice. Panicked, she said, "Has someone called about Jimmy?"

"No, no. We've heard nothing. But, honey, the FBI is saying that Sam killed three people."

Maggie groped for the counter. Icy sweat bathed her skin and she swallowed, fighting nausea. "Elle... No... Not Sam. Not my Sam. He couldn't do that—"

SIXTEEN

Sam dodged through the traffic on Lexington Avenue, turned west on 50th toward Fifth Avenue, passing the bank on the corner. He lengthened his stride, glad to stretch his legs. Noise assaulted his ears: too much traffic, construction hammers, boom boxes, the voices of street vendors selling an assortment of unlikely products out of suitcases on the sidewalk, one eye cocked for the police, ready to pack and run. Twenty-five-dollar gold Rolexes, Chanel handbags, genuine antique carvings straight from ancient kingdoms in the heart of Africa, made in the Bronx last week. A gas if he and Maggie were here together, celebrating a brave, wounded city that had struggled hard to get its life back to normal, spending money, shopping for Jimmy.... He dragged his thoughts back.

He entered the next bank he came to, kept his head turned away from the surveillance camera. He caught the eye of a guard watching him, and held his hands visible, casually clasped behind his back as he joined the line filtering customers to the tellers' windows.

A turbanned bank teller beckoned and Sam stepped up to the window. "I want to draw $5,000 from my account in New Orleans." Enough to make him solvent, and leave the rest available for— His mind stumbled over her name, not wanting to use the name by which he knew her, loved her—then made himself complete the thought. For Maggie. He slid over a check, his bank checking card, his ATM card, his driver's license.

"This account is not in our bank, so it will take a few minutes, Mr. Cady. Please wait." The teller, Mr. Rasid Singh, according to the sign in front of him, gathered up the documents, retreated to the back of the bank. Sam could see him conferring with a supervisor, and he smiled pleasantly as the woman looked at him. The security guard hovered close by, his right hand looped in his belt, close to his weapon. An ex-cop, Sam guessed. Second nature for him to check body posture, facial expression. The guy could smell trouble at a hundred paces.

It took forever. Sam tried not to sweat. He knew he was taking a chance. The feds would watch for him to lay down paper so they could pinpoint his movements, but better to take a chance with this one stop and get enough cash than leave a daily credit card trail.

Mr. Singh came back to the window. "Please, I need a sample of your signature so that we can fax it to your bank."

Sam complied. He waited, suddenly certain he'd overplayed his hand. *They'd put a marker on the account, wired into the New York Police Department, the FBI field office.* He felt the hairs rising on the back of his neck, the sweat beading his upper lip, and had to force himself not to swivel his head, to search for a SWAT team clad in Kevlar body armor.

Mr. Singh returned, smiled.

"How would you like this, Mr. Cady?"

"Forty-five hundred in one-hundred-dollar bills in an envelope, please. Four hundred in fifties, a hundred in twenties." Sam reached for the cash, relieved to see that his hand was steady.

He nodded at the security guard as he left.

In spite of the crowds going up and down, the immense stone lions couchant flanking the steps of the New York Public Library on 42nd Street were silent—word was they roared each time a virgin passed between them. He'd laughed when he'd heard that the last time he'd been in New York. Now he gave it a passing thought, a joke told to someone else.

Sam went to the information booth, told the librarian what he needed and was directed to Room 100, ground floor. Everything was on microfilm, and he started with Manhattan, worked back through the years, struck pay dirt in 1995. QwikFoto booth 322 had been attached to the A & P supermarket on Pike Street. He checked the street map he'd picked up at the hotel, and saw that Pike Street was on the Lower East Side. If the roll of film had belonged to the priest, if his church was close by, if he used QwikFoto 322. Too many ifs, but at least it was somewhere to start.

He took a cab downtown. The neighborhood was in the shadow of the on-ramps to the Manhattan Bridge, the streets narrow and treeless, littered with garbage, the gutters pooled with stagnant water. The A & P was now a Chinese supermarket.

Sam took a moment to study the area, to get a sense of it. The scene matched the one in his mind, the Lower East Side of New York familiar from film and photograph. Only the teeming cast of characters had changed.

A hundred years after the influx of Europeans, a new kind of immigrant scrabbled for a foothold—Asians and Hispanics, some recent refugees from communist East Europe. A sprinkling of white-bearded Orthodox Jews with prayer shawls and yarmulkes still clung stubbornly to their roots. Across the street from the Hong Kong Supermarket, a large stone building that had once been a substantial synagogue—the Star of David was still visible in the round leaded windows—sported a sign across the front proclaiming it to be The Song Tak Buddhist Association. Everywhere, signs above the small stores were in Spanish, Chinese, Korean, Cyrillic.

Sam turned up Broadway, away from the enormous blocks of the public housing projects facing the East River, turned onto the first street he came to, entered the open door to a tiny general goods store. Merchandise hung from the ceiling, plastic buckets, cheap children's toys, remnant bolts of fabric leaned against the wall. The woman behind the counter looked old before her time, though it was hard to tell if she had black hair streaked with blond, or blond hair streaked with black. Either way, it looked as if rats had been chewing at it.

Sam smiled, got nothing in return. He took the photograph out of his pocket, showed it to the woman.

"Do you recognize this man?" He put a finger on the priest. The woman stared at him without answering. Sam repeated the question, tapped his finger on the photograph for emphasis. She shook her head without speaking. Sam said, "Look at it. This is a church. Is it around here somewhere?"

"*Nyet.*"

Sam glanced at her, saw that she was frightened. His old police antenna told him she was scamming but, considering the surroundings, it was probably small time. He nodded his thanks. It was going to be a long day.

Sam quartered the neighborhood: Canal, Hester, Grand, Delancey, under the ramps of the Williamsburg Bridge, working the small shops below crumbling tenements on Broome, Ridge, Pitt, Stanton. He thrust the photograph under the noses of passersby getting the same response in half a dozen languages, sometimes embellished with fractured explanations.

Midafternoon he had a couple of bites of a doubtful cheese sandwich in a small luncheonette, stale bread, coffee that had only a passing relationship with a coffee bean—a far cry from an oyster po'boy, or a mug of Aunt Pellie's famous blend of chicory and black Arabica.

At 7:30 he realized he'd have to call it a day, get back to the hotel, phone New Orleans for an update. He was in a part of the city that would not go easy on strangers strolling after dark, asking questions. Garbage littered recessed doorways, shops were shuttered with metal grilles, the neighborhood was closing down, law-abiding citizens getting off the street.

On Forsyth he stopped by a small park to take note of where he was. Across the street a once Norman Rockwell-innocent neighborhood grocery had turned on bright fluorescents. The store was empty, no kids buying ice cream or boosting the latest horror comics, no mothers hurrying in for a bag of sugar. A group of young toughs lounged against the wall, cell phones in hand, tattooed arms bulked with muscle bare to the damp October night. Courtesy of the jailhouse weightlifting equipment, Sam thought grimly, your tax dollars at work. But if these guys were members of *Los Latinos Reyes,* they'd know every inch of their home turf.

He turned away to remove the Sig from the small of his back. He shoved it into his belt in front, covered it loosely with the windbreaker, then crossed the street, conscious of half a dozen pairs of dark eyes watching his every move.

Sam took out the photograph, held it up. "Any of you guys know this priest?"

They slid their eyes at each other. No one looked at the proferred photograph. Someone said, "Hey, man, we look like we hang with a bunch of fags in skirts?"

"Just take a look."

A short, stocky homeboy with a teardrop tattooed under his left eye, the sides of his head shaved to the skull, a smooth swath of long black hair swept back from his forehead, hung his thumbs in his belt, deliberately exposing the grip of a .357 Magnum shoved behind the buckle.

Sam refused to play. He kept his eyes instead on the tattooed spiderweb emerging from the homeboy's T-shirt, reaching around his neck, the black widow spider spread across his throat, the red spot on the spider centered on his Adam's apple. The *pistolero* swallowed a couple of times, causing the spider to jump. Leaning back, knee raised, one sneakered foot flat against the wall, he made a show of looking Sam over, dark eyes starting at Sam's feet, moving upward, top lip raised in a sneer that said he wasn't impressed with what he saw.

"Don' you hear so good, old man?" he asked. "We don' know no fuckin' priest." His crew sniggered.

Sam held the picture up at eye level, moved it around the group of hostile faces. "What about the church? Is it around here?"

Spider Web said, "You hear wha' we sayin', man? We don' hang at no fuckin' church—" A buzz on a pager interrupted him. He leaned forward, thrust his face at Sam. "You wanna keep your *huevos,* man? You take your fuckin' questions and stick them up your fuckin' ass. Get outa here."

Sam said, "You know, you might want to rethink that tattoo."

"Wha' the fuck you sayin', man?"

"The male black widow spider gets eaten by the female immediately after he's done the business, know what I mean? She's got it all over him." Sam let his windbreaker fall open, showing the Sig. "Thanks anyway, guys. It's been great."

He started back across the street, his whole being concentrated on the point of impact in the middle of his back. Then a late-model Jag drew into the curb in front of the store, the young white driver blocking Sam from the homeboy's view. Sam turned toward a still busy Houston Street, and breathed easier.

He turned up the collar of his windbreaker against the chill and damp, and caught the eyes of a kid, ten, maybe less, hovering in a doorway. The lookout.

"Hey," Sam said. "Looks like it's going to rain any minute, you better get on home."

"What's it to you, man?"

"Nothing, I guess." Sam took out the photograph, showed it to the boy. "I'm looking for these people. Do you know them?"

"I don' talk to no cops."

"I'm not a cop. I'm a private eye. This church around here?"

The kid glanced at it. "Yeah. *Mi madre* go there. She pray all the time. It's over on Rivington."

Sam raised a hand to rub the moisture from his face, and the boy flinched as if avoiding a blow. A wave of sadness flooding him, Sam rummaged in his pocket, careful not to let the child see the Sig—not that it would frighten him, he was probably packing himself—and retrieved a twenty-dollar bill. "Go on home to your mama, kid. It's safer."

The kid put the bill in his pocket, grinned at him. "Make more money on the street," he said.

SEVENTEEN

Maggie lay on the bed, stared at the ceiling, listened to the beat of her heart that seemed to repeat the two words: *Jimmy, Sam.* The minutes ticked by, the hours dragged on until the light outside the windows had faded. She didn't turn on the bedside lamp, the forty-watt bulb threw a depressing light, only barely enough by which to pray. And she couldn't quiet her mind long enough for that to bring comfort, even by rote.

Then at last a tap on the door and Bobby's voice. "Andrea. Are you awake?"

Maggie swung her legs to the floor, crossed the room, opened the door. "What did they say?"

"We can't talk here." He indicated the hallway.

"Come in." Maggie turned back into the room leaving the door open.

Patrelli took a step backward. "No. I'd rather not do that. We'll talk in my study." He waited until she joined him in the hall, led the way downstairs without speaking, held the door open for her to precede him into the study Maggie had glimpsed earlier.

The room held the scent of woodsmoke, and the bowl of yellow chrysanthemums on the green leather-tooled desk were fragrantly autumnal. As different from the rest of the house as if in another world, the room reflected wealth and good taste. The modern crucifix over the fireplace was the work of an artist; richly bound books lined custom bookcases, the art on the walls could be religious or secular, teasing the consciousness of the beholder. Logs crackled in the fireplace.

Clearly Bobby's family saw to it that he lived well while he put in his time wearing the hair shirt of the humble priest serving an impoverished parish.

Patrelli pointed to a leather armchair, went over to a discreet bar in the corner of the room. "Do you want a drink, Andrea? Is it still Manhattans?"

She wanted to scream at him, but with an effort she kept her voice steady. "No. Bobby, please." She remained standing just inside the door. "What did O'Malley say?"

He turned slowly, whiskey bottle in hand, as if reluctant to speak, to inflict more pain upon her. "The Irish don't have him, Andrea. O'Malley says he knows nothing about a missing child."

EIGHTEEN

Sam walked down Rivington, passing a tiny sweatshop, Ho Wong Tailoring, still open at 8:00 p.m., a couple of men bent over sewing machines under a yellowing light, steam rising from the presses in the back room, past Rosengarten's Apparel, its windows thick with grime. A used furniture store was already shuttered and dark, but a dab of color came from the red-and-blue neon flickering over Bernie's Luncheonette. Lights were coming on in the tenements above the shops, illuminating struggling plants in pots on the rusty fire escapes that festooned the dirty brick buildings, shining down on the old cars lining the curbs.

And, on the other side of the road, toward the end of the block, steps led up to a stone church.

Sam crossed the street, stopped in front of the weather-beaten board announcing the name of the church. Gothic letters that long ago might have been gold, arced across the top: Christ the Redeemer. Below the name, the services: Masses 6:00 a.m.,

8:00 a.m. daily. Sundays High Mass at 10:00 a.m. Confessions 7:00 p.m. Wednesday and Saturday. Monsignor Wenceslaus Lachinski, OMI. Monsignor Robert Patrelli, OMI.

Obligates of Mary Immaculate. The thought floated up from his parochial school education. Sam's eyes went back to the name of the church. Christ the Redeemer. He took the photograph from his pocket. The same steps. The same door. The same Gothic style letters. MER. The end of the word matched the fragment in the photograph.

He ran up the steps, tried the doors, not surprised to find them locked. He returned to the sidewalk, started toward the next building, built of the same stone, guessing it was the rectory.

"Can you spare a dollar?" A ragged arm waved at him from the basement steps of the church.

Sam looked down at a face streaked with dirt, topped by a dark woolen watch cap. Behind him several prone bodies were stacked on the steps leading down. Like street people everywhere, they were dressed in layers of ragged garments, whatever color they had once been now melded into one depressing shade of mud. The man smiled, keeping his lips closed over his teeth. Not so far gone that he wasn't embarrassed by their rot, Sam thought.

"Five would be better, pilgrim. Plenty of us here to share it."

"A John Wayne fan, huh?" Sam said pleasantly.

"In a former life, pilgrim."

Sam pulled out some bills, dropped a five into the open palm, heard a blessing following him, and waved an acknowledgment without turning.

He went up the steps to the rectory, pressed a finger to the bell. Minutes passed. He peered through the frosted glass, saw a shadow approaching. The door jerked open. A woman stared at him. Broad flat face, blond hair beneath a pink babushka, blue eyes that went blank as she looked at him. She waited for him to speak.

"I was wondering if you could tell me whether this is Msgr. Lachinski?" Sam stepped forward, photograph in hand. The woman seemed to retreat without moving her feet.

"No."

"Then it must be Father Patrelli?"

She did not answer. Sam met the blue eyes. Not hostile, not confrontive. Just carefully blank. The eyes of a woman who'd experienced firsthand the crash through the front door before dawn, the disappearance of friends and family, the all-powerful authority of a police state. She was scared to death of him.

He smiled at her. "I'm looking for some old friends of my brother who died recently." He offered the photograph again. "This is the only picture I have—"

The woman shook her head, started to close the door.

Sam shoved his foot against the jamb. "Perhaps I can speak to one of the priests?"

"You come tomorrow in the day." The door pressed hard against his foot, and reluctantly he removed it. The door closed firmly, the light inside went off. Sam stared for a moment at the door, thought about leaning on the bell, decided against it. She was alone and too scared to say so. God help parishioners in trouble, they'd have to find succor elsewhere. He recrossed the street, walked to Bernie's Luncheonette.

The air inside smelled of frying grease and old cigarette smoke, something else that was probably the rotting corpses of generations of cockroaches. He took a seat on a stool at the counter, ordered a cup of coffee, decided to take a chance on a couple of the donuts under the protection of a glass dome on the counter. When the counterman served the food, Sam slid the photograph toward him.

"Is this one of the priests from the church across the street?"

The man glanced at the picture. He took a swipe at the counter with a damp cloth stained with use. "Who wants to know?"

"I do."

"Yeah? So who are you?"

Sam gave him the story he'd told the housekeeper, without much hope. As he spoke, the counterman, his eyes on the photograph, swung his head doubtfully from side to side.

"Nah. You better ask over there, you want to know anything. Me, I don't see nothing on the street. Work in here all day, know what I mean? Don't take much notice of what happens outside. They got a Russian housekeeper living there. Go ask her."

"I already did. Not very forthcoming."

"Russian, know what I mean? You're lucky she even answered the door after dark. They got robbed coupla times over there. Now you gotta make an appointment. They don't trust nobody, Russians."

"Yeah. An attitude that seems to be catching." Sam held the counterman's eye until the man shrugged. "Yeah," Sam said again.

He picked up his coffee and donuts, took them to a table by the window where he could see the rectory. Sooner or later a priest was going to go in or come out, and he could be through the door and across the road in seconds.

"Say, buddy, we close now. You want something more to eat, you gotta go to the Plaza." The counterman grinned, pleased with his witticism, wiped his hands on an apron that in another life had been white. "That's uptown on 59th, y'know it?"

"Sure. An old hangout of mine." Sam looked at his watch and found it was 10:30. He dropped a five on the table for a tip—he'd been taking up space for two hours drinking one cup of coffee and a refill—and nodded a good-night. The lights went out as the counterman closed the door behind him.

The rectory was dark. Most of the streetlights were out, the few remaining threw dismal pools that made the darkness around them even more sinister. Sam walked a block east, then turned. He waited until Bernie's neon light went off, then retraced his steps. He'd noticed that the luncheonette was without a metal grille, and he settled in the recessed doorway. He couldn't remember the last time he'd been on a stakeout, but it was like riding a bike. Once learned, never forgotten.

NINETEEN

Except for the red votive lights in front of the statue in the hall, the house was dark at 1:30 in the morning, and freezing. Maggie kept her eyes on the flickering candles as she descended the stairs and crossed the hall. The door to Bobby's study was ajar, and she pushed it open. The room was warm, the melange of scents now deepened with a touch of good whiskey, and the logs in the fireplace still glowed. Maggie perched on the edge of the leather chair behind the desk, switched on the green desk light, reached for the phone. She tapped out the number, listened to it ring. A voice thick with sleep but fully alert answered.

"What? What's happened?"

What else would her mother expect in the middle of the night but disaster? "Mom. It's Andrea."

"Honey." The voice sharpened as if the speaker had suddenly sat up. "What's wrong?"

"Is the phone tapped?"

"I don't know. Maybe. What's the matter? Where are you?"

"I just wanted to hear your voice."

"Is everything all right, honey?" A rising panic was clearly discernible. "Is Jimmy all right?"

"I just wanted to hear your voice, Mom," Maggie said. "I'm okay, but I'd better hang up now that I've heard it. Don't worry, I'm okay. I love you, Mom."

Her mother was still speaking as Maggie put the phone back in the cradle. She rose to her feet, went back into the hall, made her way down the corridor. The kitchen was icy, smelled damp, with the slight gassy odor that lingered in old kitchens. The high strip of windows above the sink gave enough light from outside to allow her to negotiate past the table and chairs without noise. She unlocked the back door, slipped out into the darkness, closed the door behind her.

The rectory basement smelled of garbage, some nocturnal creature had knocked the lid from one of the cans. Maggie put the lid back on—she didn't want to be swarmed by rats when she returned. She climbed the basement steps, stopped as soon as she could peer into the street.

A patrol car, filling the narrow street made even narrower by cars lining the curb, slowly cruised past, then came to a stop half a block away. A couple of cops climbed out and the beam of a flashlight swept the basement steps of the church.

"Come on, buddy," she heard a voice say. "You can't sleep here."

"Too many rats down at the rectory," a peeved voice answered. "They need new garbage cans. We always sleep here."

"You mean you always start out sleeping here. And I always roust you because I don't like people like you on my beat. Now come on, asshole, get out of there."

"Son of a bitch fascist commie bastard, ain't you got nothing better to do, terrorists taking over the city—" The voices continued arguing. The second cop was on the other side of the street running his nightstick along the metal grilles of shopfronts, making enough noise to wake the dead.

Maggie went up the steps of the rectory basement, peeked into the street. Both cops were busy. Across the street, a man who had been sleeping in the doorway of the luncheonette, left without argument, a dark figure slinking away close to the wall while the cop watched, nightstick slapping his palm, to make sure he didn't slip back.

Keeping close to the wall herself where the shadow was deepest, she ran toward Houston Street, waiting for someone to shout after her, but no one did. On Houston she flagged a passing cab, told the cabby her destination, surprised him by agreeing to his price without an argument.

They crossed the Queensboro Bridge and, once clear of the city, the traffic was light. At two in the morning the journey to Port Washington took less than an hour. They turned off the Long Island Expressway, and fifteen minutes later they were in countryside that could have been anywhere in New England. Maggie leaned forward. It had been more than five years since she'd seen these narrow tree-lined lanes, the stone pillars flanking driveways leading to unseen houses.

"Here. You can let me off here."

The cab slowed. "There ain't nothing here—" The cabbie looked out at the stone wall only barely visible on the other side of the line of trees. "There ain't even a sidewalk."

"I know. Let me off."

The cabbie stepped on the brake right where he was, stopping in the middle of the deserted lane.

Maggie got out, breathed in the damp, green-smelling air leavened by the sharp tang of the Long Island Sound. She paid what they'd agreed, added a generous tip. She waited until the taillights, winking flashes of red, disappeared into the night, leaving her in darkness, then walked along the wall until she reached a pair of tall iron gates. They were closed as she knew they would be, and unguarded, which was something new. She retraced her steps for about ten feet, then ran her hands over the front of the wall, found what she was looking for. She grabbed a jutting stone, heaved herself up, feeling with feet and hands, her body remembering every projection she and Bobby and her brother, James, had used as kids, coming and going as they wished when the house was under surveillance by the FBI. The boys used to fall about laughing after they'd sauntered anonymously past the cars parked outside the gates. Later she found out the FBI always knew who they were. They were just not interested in children.

She grabbed for the tree, inched along the limb, dropped to the ground inside the wall. Within minutes she was running under the canopy of maples that lined the driveway. The graveled forecourt was floodlit. She stopped at the edge of the trees, scanned the house, almost surprised to see nothing here had changed when everything else in life had. The pale limestone walls were still softened by Virginia creeper, the wall sconces her father had brought back from some old wreck of a house in Sicily threw artistic patterns against the pair of wooden front doors exactly as her father had planned. The paint was fresh, the shutters gleamed, the vines around the windows were carefully manicured. Obviously there was no shortage of money. The whole place looked as if the *patrone* were still in residence.

She left the forecourt, circled the house to the back. A light glowed in a window on the second floor. Her parents' bedroom. Her mother had not gone back to sleep after her phone call. Sleep never came easily to Bianca Bellini. Once awakened—disaster so often seemed to happen in the night in her husband's business—she would read until morning. For a minute or two Maggie stared at the window, remembering. Racing her brothers to her parents' room early on Sunday mornings. Proudly holding her father's hand as they led the way into church for mass, Paul and James flanking their mother behind them.

The sound of dogs barking in the distance surprised her. They'd never had dogs, her father's prized landscaping didn't allow for dogs in his garden. She realized they were coming closer—and they did not sound like pets. Male voices shouted back and forth, and the crash of bodies racing through the underbrush was becoming louder with every second.

Maggie ran back around the house to the front door, jammed her finger on the bell.

"Mom, it's Andrea. Let me in." She hammered on the door with both fists, shouting her name, her heart pounding. The dogs were very close. The door opened, she fell into the house.

"Mother of God!" A heavy hand steadied her. The other held a sawed-off shotgun. "Andrea! Christ! You're dead. You're supposed to be dead!"

"Donnie! Call off the dogs!"

Donnie Provanto was ashen with shock. "Yeah, yeah." He yelled into a radio transmitter, "It's okay at the house. Hold them back." He racked the shotgun with several other weapons on a wall rack just inside the front door. "Jeez! Andrea, we thought you was dead."

"I know, but I'm not, Donnie." She looked at the weapons. "What's all this? You expecting a siege?"

Provanto looked as if he was conversing with a ghost. "Nah, nah. Someone's always here with your mother at night is all. You know, with your old man gone and Paolo..." He looked down. "You know how it is, Andrea. We ain't got no one who's strong these days. For your old man's sake, we look out for your mother."

"Honey? Andrea? Oh, my God. What's happened?"

Maggie looked up at her mother, coming down the stairs. Dark hair still without a trace of gray, large, dark eyes. Where she'd once been slim, she was now thin. Thinner than the last time they'd been together at the monastery in Ohio where they spent three precious days twice a year, once in spring and then again before Thanksgiving. Thin and strong.

Maggie ran to her, felt her mother's arms enclose her. But now that she could let herself go, the tears wouldn't come.

"Oh, sweetheart. Sweetheart, it's okay, I'm here." Bianca Bellini motioned Provanto away, kept an arm around Maggie as she led her into the kitchen. The red gingham-covered armchairs were still on either side of the huge brick fireplace, logs still smouldered. Bianca pushed Maggie into the chair she pulled away from an ancient refectory table that had once served a congregation of French monks.

"Something's happened. It's Jimmy, isn't it?" Bianca said. It was more a statement than a question.

Maggie's head went from side to side, trying to shake the swirling pain, in her head, her heart. "He was taken, Mom. They came on Sunday morning. They shot up the house, and they took Jimmy. He was asleep, and they took him."

Bianca Bellini let out a soft moan. She felt behind her, grabbed on to the edge of the granite counter to steady herself.

"Who? Who did this?"

"I don't know. I thought it was O'Malley, I thought the Irish came for me. But now I don't know. Maybe I'm wrong. Maybe it was someone else." Now that Maggie had started talking, the dam broke, words tumbled over each other. "I'd gone to an early mass. They attacked the house, and they took Jimmy from his bed."

"Oh, my God. They called here."

Maggie found herself on her feet. "Who?" Without realizing she had moved, she was at her mother's side. "Mom, who called here?"

"I don't know—"

"Was it the Irish? Was it O'Malley?"

"Honey, I don't know. I've been frantic, trying to reach you, I tried to tell you on the phone earlier—"

"Did you call my house?" Maggie asked in alarm.

"No, you know I wouldn't do that, not ever. I called the emergency number you gave me, your case officer. George Menton. He wasn't there and the man who answered the phone kept asking who I was, what I wanted. I knew he was trying to keep me talking so I hung up, I didn't want the call traced back here. I was frightened they'd find out you were still connected to me." Bianca was shaking.

Maggie heard Bianca's voice through the roaring in her head.

"Mom, please." She knew she could not afford to give way to the hysteria flooding her, or they would both start shrieking. She grabbed at a remnant of calm, drew a shaky breath into her lungs, forced herself to speak slowly. "Mom, when did they call?"

"Sunday morning, about ten." Bianca's face was gray under its normal olive tone.

"What did they say?"

"It was a man's voice. He said, 'We hear you've got a grandson. You'd better watch out for him, see he doesn't get into trouble, young kid like that.' Something like that. Then he said, 'Give our best to your daughter, Maggie.' I didn't answer. I just hung up." Bianca looked suddenly ten years older.

"But they already had him by then— Oh, God—"

"It was a threat. Everything's a threat, every word... I should have known..."

"Mom, don't." Maggie couldn't find the words to reassure her. "It was O'Malley, it has to be, there's no one else. But why didn't he go after Paul? And his daughter? That's what I came to find out, I didn't want to talk on the phone. I saw Paul's picture in the paper. Why me? Why my Jimmy? And why now, so many years later?"

Bianca shook her head. "I don't know."

"Has Paul said anything to you?"

"I haven't seen Paolo—"

"But you speak to him, don't you?"

Bianca shook her head. "I don't see Paolo, I don't talk to him."

"Oh, for God's sake, Mom." Maggie wanted to scream. Who cared who anyone slept with when there was so much else that was important?

"I see his wife when she brings Jolie to see me. She hasn't said anything."

"Then Jolie hasn't been threatened. So why us? They had to search for me, for my Jimmy. How could they find us?"

The two women stared at each other. "They must have heard something," Maggie said. "Someone's been talking."

TWENTY

Sam flagged a cab on Delancey, climbed gratefully into its muggy warmth. "Loew's, Lexington and 51st."

The car pulled into still heavy traffic—New York living up to its twenty-four-hour-a-day reputation. The cabby glanced at Sam in his rearview. "Had a wet night, huh?"

Sam rolled his shoulders under the soaking windbreaker. "Yeah."

A hellish night. He'd avoided being rousted by taking off before the cop got to him. After that, somehow he'd managed stay one step ahead of the cruiser, although the damn thing drifted by every couple of hours. So far, New York's finest were still unaware that the bum in the doorway of Bernie's Luncheonette was Sam Cady, wanted for the murder of three men in New Orleans, and considered armed and dangerous. Cops on the street would interpret that as shoot first, ask questions later.

Sam knew how that worked.

He'd kept telling himself to call it a night, get some sleep—

no one was going to leave that rectory now, not in the early hours of the morning. But the church was his only link with his son, with Maggie, and he hadn't been able to force himself to leave Bernie's doorway. Then around four he'd had a thought that had snapped his head back. He'd made a world-class error checking in at Loew's. The feds were bound to discover that he'd stayed there last time he was in New York, and the minute they did, they'd check to see if he'd returned. That meant he had to get out of there, now, tonight. He'd decided to risk heading back for a quick shower, change into the dry clothes he'd bought earlier and get back to the rectory before the 6:00 a.m. mass. Hammer this priest in his own pulpit if he had to.

"How you liking New York City?" the cabby asked. "Pretty great, huh?"

"Yeah. You guys have made a great recovery." Sam leaned his head back, closed his eyes to discourage conversation, listened to the whoosh of tires on the wet street, the nonstop voice of the driver celebrating the accomplishments of New Yorkers in general and Rudi in particular, as if he was still the mayor. He'd had the luck to get into the cab of the only chatty, native-born driver in the city.

"So, here it is, buddy. Loew's."

Sam jolted upright. He paid off the cab, crossed the wet pavement, head down against the rain. He pushed at one of the glass doors flanking the revolving door, swept a glance around the lobby, picked up the two dark-suited figures leaning against the bar to the right, watching the door. No drinks in front of them.

He let the door fall back in place, turned, ran across the street, dodging traffic. Seconds later, the two men burst out of the hotel, weaving through honking, braking cars, ignoring the shouts of angry drivers.

"Cady!" a voice shouted. "Sam Cady. FBI. Stop."

Sam hit the sidewalk at a dead run, sprinted through the forecourt of the bank building on the corner of 50th, knowing they wouldn't draw weapons—a bunch of conventioneers, unsteady on their feet, were spread out all over the place, laughing and shouting, making for the hotel. They'd never risk firearms. He doglegged along Park, got onto 52nd, found the road half blocked by a trailer in front of a construction job, wooden steps stretched across the sidewalk. He hit the steps, leapt for the plywood fence around the site. The fence rocked ominously beneath his weight, and he scrambled over, dropped on the other side.

And found himself on the edge of a crater. One day it would be a multi-storey underground parking garage. Now it just looked like a giant grave.

He struggled to catch his breath, head down, a hand on each knee. His breathing slowed and he listened for sounds of pursuit, but heard only the hum of distant traffic. No shouts, no pounding feet.

"Stop right there!"

Sam felt as if a lead weight had dropped from throat to crotch. He turned to run, but blinding floodlights brought the pit into sharp focus, and he could see there was nowhere to hide. He waited for the feds to announce their presence. They didn't and he put up a hand to shield his eyes against the light and the pouring rain. He peered at the approaching figure.

He looked for the other fed, then realized there was only one man, covered in a black slicker. By his side was a dog.

Sam felt the weight in his belly dissipate.

A security guard and his dog, a Rottweiler that could have been Max's twin, except that his face was wrinkled in a snarl, exposing canine teeth an inch long.

"I'm sorry, I know I'm trespassing." Sam allowed his south Louisiana childhood to sweeten his tone, a visitor from out of town, a rube out of his depth. "Can you turn the floods off? I can't hardly see you." He waited, his hope of escape revived, knowing he had to talk fast. Sure as shit the FBI hadn't given up. Any time now, they'd be banging at the front gates to the site, flashing their credentials. "I was mugged, and had to run like hell, two guys chasing me. I'm from out of town—"

The watchman interrupted. "And you just managed to get over the fence by accident. Spare me the bullshit, I've heard it before."

"Listen, I don't want trouble here, I truly don't," Sam said. He held out his hands, showing them to the watchman. "I'm going to reach into my inside pocket here, get out my wallet. We can negotiate this." Rain was dripping off his chin, finding the space between his neck and collar. In his oilskins, the security man had the advantage. "I just want to get back to my hotel across the street—I'm at Loew's—take a shower, drive out to Kennedy, get my plane back home. That okay?"

"Buddy, you know what's good for you, don't fucking move a muscle." The watchman put his radio transmitter to his mouth.

"Fifty bucks," Sam said. "Listen, I know this looks bad but it's a mistake. I'm telling you the truth, here. I can show you the card key for my hotel room, if you let me. And the fifty."

He knew he had it when the man lowered the transmitter.

"What the hell you doing wandering around New York City at night?" Shaking his head, the security man waved the hand with the transmitter. "Ah, shit, don't tell me. I don't want to know." He put the transmitter to his mouth again. "It's okay, Lennie, cut the lights. I got this." He yanked on the dog's leash, murmured a command. The dog sat, its unwinking eyes never leaving Sam's face. The overhead lights went out, leaving only the perimeters shimmering through the driving rain. "So what you're saying is you ain't casing the job to steal this shit." He waved at the construction equipment. "I got that right?" The man studied him. "Okay, I believe you, fifty bucks worth. For another fifty, my partner Lennie over there believes you, too. The dog comes free."

Sam relaxed. He held up his hands. "In the inside pocket, okay?" The man nodded. Sam half turned to keep the bulging envelope containing the rest of the money from the bank out of the man's sight—he might be dealing with an honest crook, but it was wiser not to tempt fate—and reached into his pocket for the wallet. He extracted two fifties and held them out.

The security man reached for them. "I'll take you through the fence. Even if they're looking, your *muggers,*" he emphasized the word, "won't find you, the guys rigged it so they could get out for a smoke without management busting their balls. But do yourself a favor, buddy, don't come back here. Not all our guys are as understanding as I am."

Sam trod warily around the edge of the pit, followed the security man to the fence where it abutted the next building. The guard shifted a couple of boards, Sam squeezed through, the boards slapped back into place and he was alone on 53rd Street. A cab was passing, a miracle on a rainy night. He climbed in, told the cabby to take him to the nearest YMCA.

Three hours later, Sam walked past Ho Wong's Tailoring and Rosengarten's Apparel, making for Bernie's. As soon as the luncheonette opened up, he'd use their phone to call Petey. In the gray of a moisture-filled morning, the gutters on Rivington were even more choked with sodden filth, but at least the night of rain had cleaned off the sidewalk a bit. It had been after five when the cab dropped him off at the Y on 45th Street. He'd checked in, had a shower, brushed his teeth with soap on the corner of a washcloth, and lay on top of the bed to rest for a few minutes. Next he knew it was past seven, and he'd missed the early mass at Christ the Redeemer. He'd had another quick shower, put on yesterday's underwear and the socks that had seen some heavy duty in the last twenty-four hours. At least he felt he could deal with the day ahead. He'd never needed much sleep.

"Top of the morning to you, pilgrim." A voice penetrated his thoughts. "What the hell were you doing in Bernie's doorway last night?"

A black-shrouded figure had swung into step beside him.

Sam looked under the large plastic garbage bag, saw that it covered the beggar on whom he'd dropped the five.

"Hey, how are you doing?" Sam said.

"Felt any better, I'd check in at Bellevue." The beggar looked up at Sam. "If you're thinking of growing a beard, pilgrim, don't. Looks like shit."

"Thanks," Sam said. "Appreciate the input."

The old man stroked his own grubby white whiskers. "So what's up? Lady wife throw you out?" A throaty chuckle accompanied the words.

"Something like that," Sam said. "Where'd you go last night?"

"Got me a spot over on Seward. Lot of people scared of the projects, but not me. The cop there's got a brother on the street. Lets me stay sometimes, long as it's not a regular gig. Saw you slip away before you got rousted." He gave Sam a look that was suprisingly sharp. "What you doing down here, anyway? I know you got dough, you gave me a fin. Should have asked for a tenspot. Where'd you go?"

"Dodged around cars, mostly, in the lot at the end of the street. Waited until the cops left. Then I went back to Bernie's."

"You got the look of the law about you, know that? Must be a hell of a handicap." The throaty chuckle morphed into a fit of coughing.

Sam took another look at the bloated face he'd last seen in the crowd staggering away from the church in the early hours of the morning. This guy had some education, quite a bit of it by the sound of him. Certainly he wasn't the usual street crazy.

"What do they call you?"

"Why do you want to know?"

"Being polite, like my mama told me." Sam kept his voice casual, he didn't want to spook the old guy. Just ask a few questions.

"You can call me Asshole."

"Jesus. I'm sure not going to do that."

"Then how about Yankee, Southern boy."

Sam laughed. "You spend a lot of time at the church?"

"Some. Say, you want some grub? The housekeeper there is good for a touch. I eat there most mornings. Not inside, of course, she's frightened of my lice." The old man laughed. "She lets me sit on the basement steps. Bet she'd find enough for two."

"No, not for me. Come on, I'll buy you a hot meal at Bernie's."

Yankee slid him a look. "I'd sooner have a drink. You pop for that and I'll eat at the church. Don't want the Russki to think I don't appreciate her cooking."

"I'll buy you a hot meal, and give you enough for a drink. How's that?"

"Yeah?" The man punched Sam's arm. "Your good deed for the day, boy scout. I'll tell the Russki I went to the Black Sea on vacation."

They waited in the recessed doorway in which Sam had spent a goodly part of the night until the same counterman opened the door. He looked at Yankee.

"Get outa here. I told you before, go over to the church you want a handout."

"Fuck you. I got a patron." His bag of empty cans clattering, Yankee pushed his way into the warm interior of the luncheonette. "Fire up the stove, my man, I'm starving."

The counterman turned to Sam. "You can't bring that bum in here."

"What's the matter? Think my fleas are going to beat up on your cockroaches?" Yankee dropped his cans and the plastic bags he was carrying underneath his homemade poncho, raised his fists, swung his shoulder in a parody of a boxer's weaving grace, danced a couple of little steps on the balls of his feet. "Dance like a butterfly, sting like a flea."

"Just give us breakfast." Sam seated himself at the same table he'd had the night before, the one with the clear view of the church. "And we'll be out of here."

Yankee picked up his bags, carefully stowed them on the chair across from Sam, took the chair next to them.

Muttering, the counterman went to the coffeepot, came back, smacked down a couple of stained mugs that were cracked and chipped, coffee slurping over the edge. Yankee pushed his away.

"I'd like a glass of milk with a couple of raw eggs whipped up in it. For starters." He looked at Sam. "Gut rotted with booze. That'll settle it."

"Ever thought of quitting?"

Yankee reached for his bags. "You start holy rollering me, Southern boy, I'm outa here."

"No, no." Sam looked at the counterman. "Get him his milk and eggs. In a decent glass." He pushed at the cracked mugs. "And you can take these back, bring a couple of clean coffee cups. Then eggs over easy, pancakes, sausage, bacon, toast." He looked at Yankee. "Anything else?"

"I'll let you know."

Sam gave a fleeting thought to Aunt Pellie's beignets, her coffee and chicory, and ordered a short stack for himself. He kept his eye on the church. He waited until Yankee had drunk half his milk and eggs, then slid the photograph across the table. "You know this priest?"

Yankee looked at it, then up at Sam. "Knew you were a cop." He drank the rest of his milk, touched a paper napkin delicately to his lips.

"I'm not. I used to be, but I'm not now." What the hell, Sam thought. "My wife left me and I'm looking for her. I found this photograph in her drawer. The housekeeper over there says she never saw these guys before."

Yankee leaned back to allow the counterman to place a plate loaded with food in front of him. Sam shoved the picture closer. "Look at them. Is that one of the priests, Patrelli or Lachinski?"

Carefully Yankee forked up an egg, carried it whole to his

mouth. He chewed, swallowed before answering. "A bottle would be better than one drink."

Sam tapped his finger on the picture. "Have you seen them before?"

"Some real good stuff. Chivas used to be my drink of choice in a previous life. Royal Salute, the twenty-year-old stuff. Be nice to have another taste."

"Yankee, whatever you want. Do you know them?"

"We're talking the quart bottle, right?"

"Yeah, sure, the big bottle. Whatever you want."

"Guy in skirts is Father Patrelli. Don't know the other one. Probably before my time around here. I haven't always been in this neighborhood." Yankee swept a piece of bread around the last of the egg yolk on his plate. "For two bottles, I'll ask around."

Sam nodded. He wasn't in the business of saving souls. That was the priest's job. "You got a deal. I'll get you a copy of this."

TWENTY-ONE

The Trinity Church clock at the top of Wall Street was sending out the musical chime familiar to everyone from the investment program on public television. Maggie ran up the steps of the subway station with the rest of the crowd hurrying to jobs in the financial offices—to anyone watching, a worker among workers. Not that she thought she could be under surveillance now—no one had been following when Donnie Provanto drove her to the subway station before six that morning. Donnie hadn't been her father's bodyguard all those years without developing a sixth sense about watching eyes, but she'd changed trains several times, anyway, squeezing out of cars as doors closed, into others as they were about to. Everywhere she looked people seemed familiar, seen an hour ago, ten minutes ago, leering like faces in a fun house mirror.

Heavy rain had eased into a fine mist, enough to slick the pavement, bead in the hair, dampen skin. At the edge of the curb, Maggie waited for the light to change. The instant it did so, she stepped off the pavement. A hand grabbed her, jerked her stumbling backward. She fought for balance, whirled, the Beretta in her hand, as a helmeted courier in black Lycra sped by against the light, his racing bicycle brushing her body.

Her rescuer, a girl with an umbrella protecting a large hairdo, an imitation leather bag over one shoulder, dropped her eyes to the gun. Her face paled with shock, and she clutched her hands together across her chest as if the stem of the umbrella could ward off a bullet.

Muttering an apology, Maggie shoved the Beretta back into her pocket, crossed the street at a lope, losing herself in the jam of people and for once thanking God for her lack of height. She glanced once over her shoulder, saw the frightened girl stop a passing security guard. And the guard, probably getting off the night shift, his disinterest apparent even at a distance, shrugging, his hands raised, indicating the crowd—"what the hell do you want from me?" in every gesture.

Maggie joined the mass of bodies converging on Number Sixty Wall Street, swept through glass doors into the marble lobby. Just inside, she stopped short, causing hurrying workers to swirl around her as she fought a sudden surge of the panic that was never far from the surface.

She'd never get even close to Paul's office. Access to the rest of the building was blocked off by a barrier of turnstiles like those in the subway. The lines in front of them moved quickly as people swiped cards, pushed through, hurried toward the banks of elevators.

She needed a card key.

On her left, three security men sat watching a row of monitors. Standing behind them another guard kept his eyes scanning the lobby while dealing with a deliveryman.

Maggie studied the crowd, an idea forming. It could work. A few minutes passed until she found what she was looking for. Head down, a dark-suited woman walked rapidly as she juggled her briefcase open to retrieve a file. Without slowing, the woman locked the case, started flipping through the file, reading as she crossed the lobby toward the turnstiles, seemingly oblivious to everything around her. A woman with a purpose, and in a hurry.

Maggie watched to see which turnstile she was aiming for, then hurried to get there ahead of her. Ignoring a murmur of protests, Maggie jostled her way into line directly in front of her mark, whose attention was still on her file. The line moved quickly, people swiped card keys, pushed through, ran to catch the elevators. Then Maggie was inside the metal embrace of the turnstile, the steel bar pressing against her stomach. She fumbled in her bag as if searching for her card. She heard an exasperated sound from the woman behind her, and glanced around with an apologetic murmur. People grumbled and peered over heads to see what was causing the holdup. One of the security men in front of a monitor leaned back, spoke to the guard talking to the deliveryman, nodding toward the restive line.

"Hurry up, please." Pressing against Maggie's back, the woman spoke impatiently. "I have a meeting to get to."

"I can't seem to..." Maggie said.

The woman clicked her teeth against her tongue. "Oh, for God's sake." She leaned over, swiped her own card, pushed Maggie through the turnstile, swiped again for herself, rushed by to get to the elevator. Maggie, hard on her heels, forced her way in just as the door closed.

The small space was a battleground of aftershave and perfume, coffee, the surprising odor of garlic wafting from a brown box held by a deliveryman, sickening at nine o'clock in the morning.

Still reading her file, Maggie's unwitting benefactor exited on the 34th floor. Maggie stepped out on the 46th, took a deep breath, pushed open the carved front door of Bellamy Associates, Stockbrokers.

"Good morning. Can I help you?" The receptionist, raven

hair twisted into a chignon low on her neck, took in Maggie's Gucci jacket, swept dark eyes over black jeans that had lost any semblance of freshness, came back to regard Maggie without smiling.

"I'd like to see Paul Bellamy, please." She hadn't seen Paul since the joint funerals of their father and brother. He'd never even sent her a message after someone had tried to kill her, and there'd certainly been time for that before she'd had to disappear. But even as children, they had never been close.

"Do you have an appointment?"

"No. I don't need an appointment—"

"Everyone needs an appointment to see Mr. Bellamy."

"I don't. I'm his sister. Tell him I'm here, please."

"I'm sorry, Mr. Bellamy does not—"

Maggie placed both hands on the curved antique desk, leaned toward the receptionist. "I don't think you heard me. I am Paul Bellamy's sister, Andrea Bellamy. Tell him that I am here. Do you understand?"

The receptionist nodded. She picked up the telephone, pressed a number, her eyes never leaving Maggie's as she waited for an answer. Then she said, "I have a Ms. Bellamy here. She claims she is Mr. Bellamy's sister." She listened, then said, "Well, I think you'd better come and talk to her yourself." She hung up, said to Maggie, "Mr. Bellamy's personal assistant will be here. Please sit down." She indicated a pair of handsome sofas, several upholstered easy chairs, a low coffee table.

Maggie looked at the grandfather clock in the waiting area, watched the pendulum swing back and forth. She'd give this assistant one minute, and then she'd go looking.

"Can I help you, Ms....er, Bellamy, is it?"

Maggie turned toward the voice. A young man, improbable blond hair slicked back, impeccably tailored black suit cut to show off a slender body, crisp white shirt, brilliant tie in parrot colors, hyacinth, scarlet, green.

"I want to see Paul Bellamy and I don't have time to argue. Please take me—"

"Well, Ms. er, Bellamy, you say?" the voice held an amused question. "I wasn't aware that Mr. Bellamy had a sister."

"And now you are."

"Well, not quite."

"So you'll have to take my word for it. Now, where is my brother?"

A number of people passed back and forth across the hallway, papers and folders in their hands, their eyes on the three people confronting each other in the quietly elegant front lobby. The receptionist retreated behind the desk, disassociating herself from the unpleasantness.

"Maybe I can help you?" the young man said. "If you'd like to tell me your business—"

Maggie pushed past him, walked rapidly along the hall toward the wall of glass framing a view of the East River at the end.

The young man ran along beside her, protesting. "Ms., er, Mr. Bellamy isn't here. You cannot just—"

"Where's his office?"

"He isn't here, I tell you."

They passed a windowless bull pen of shirtsleeved brokers imprisoned in small cubicles, phones locked to their ears, eyes glued to the computer screens in front of them, oblivious of passersby.

"I'm going to have to call security if you don't leave right now." The young man's distress was increasing. "I don't know who you are. I tell you Mr. Bellamy isn't here. He hasn't been in the office for a week."

Maggie stopped and stared at him. "Why? Is he on vacation?"

Clearly rattled, the young man answered. "No. I don't know—"

"Have you checked with Julie?"

"You know Mrs. Bellamy?"

"Of course I know Mrs. Bellamy. She's my sister-in-law, for God's sake." Maggie softened her tone. The threat of security men had caught her attention. "I also know his daughter, Jolie." Everyone had tried to head off that little eccentricity. Julie was dim and good-natured, but she had a hell of a stubborn streak and had refused to listen. She'd thought the two names cute together. Paul hadn't given a damn what the child was named. "Does Mrs. Bellamy know where he is?"

The young man was like a balloon losing air. "No. She just said he wasn't at home, that's all. She didn't seem to know where he was, but she wasn't...she didn't seem to be concerned."

Not surprising. Paul came and went as he pleased, always had. His wife knew better than to ask where he was going, or when he'd return. He'd been forced into marriage and had proved his manhood by fathering a child. Too bad it was a girl but his duty, as far as he was concerned, was done. He made it clear the family could expect no more children from him. "Does he often stay out of the office?"

"Well, no, not without telling me."

Maggie resumed her stride along the hall—Paul's office had to be somewhere close to that view. The young man, seemingly torn between his desire to stop her, and relief at having someone who shared his anxiety, danced along at her side.

"Have you called the police?" Maggie asked.

He looked suddenly frightened. "No. No, we haven't, of course not. Mr. Bellamy often takes a few days off—"

"This long?" Maggie insisted. "Without telling you he'd be gone?"

"Well, no."

An anteroom opened up off the hallway, like a luxurious sitting room in a country house, the discreet desk and computer showing it to be the personal assistant's line of defense against unwanted intruders. Maggie crossed the anteroom, opened the inner door onto breathtaking views of the river on one side, the city on the other. The enormous space was filled with art, on walls, on pedestals, all discreetly spotlighted.

"This is Paul's office?"

"Really, Ms. er, er, Bellamy, please. You can't go in there—"

Maggie pushed him out, slammed the door in his face, pressed the lock. A fist banged against the wood, and then Maggie heard the voice retreating, calling for security.

The desk was about the size of a playing field, and bare except for a piece of modern sculpture—of what, it was hard to say. No photograph of wife and child. No laptop, no papers. She tried the row of narrow drawers in the cabinet behind the desk, found sheets of Paul's personal letterhead. Slick brochures about investments, here and abroad. Nothing else.

Whatever she had hoped to find, a clue to Jimmy's whereabouts, anything, she wasn't going to find it here. If Paul had a laptop where he kept private data, he'd taken it with him when he left.

Maggie picked up the telephone, pressed buttons until she heard a dial tone. She tapped out a number, muttering impatient encouragement as the ringing tone seemed to go on and on.

Finally a voice answered. "Yeah."

She'd expected her mother, but Donnie was better. She said quickly, "Donnie, I'm at Paul's office in Manhattan—"

He interrupted, sounding shocked. "Andrea, jeez, Andrea, what you doing there? You're not supposed to be—"

"Donnie, stop. My mother gave me this address, she knows I'm here. This is important. I have to find Paul. He hasn't been seen for days, not at his home, nor his office. Have you seen him recently?"

"I don't go to Paulie's office, Andrea, know what I mean?" He sounded hesitant, as if not sure what she knew. "No one goes there, we gotta keep things quiet. Low-key, you know what I'm saying here?"

"Donnie, I know you know how to reach him, you let that slip this morning driving in. Now, where can I find him?" The line hummed with silence. Then Maggie said, "Donnie, this concerns my father." Donnie was a killer, but his loyalty to her father was never in question.

A heartbeat, another, then Donnie said, "Well, he's got a fuck pad, know what I mean?" He stopped as if embarrassed. "Andrea, you know, a place he takes his boys."

Maggie wanted to scream. "Donnie, for God's sake. Where?" She could hear voices now in the anteroom. Someone calling her name. A fist pounded at the door. "Come on, they're at the door."

"Who? Who's at the door? What's going on—"

"Donnie, just give me the address."

Donnie rattled off an address in the East Fifties. "You don't want to go there, Andrea. You shouldn't—" He was still protesting when the door burst open. Uniformed security men rushed in.

Maggie dropped the phone back onto the cradle, raised both hands. "I'm leaving."

"You got that right, girlie." The beefier of the two security men, his face red with importance, crossed the room. "You're under arrest."

"Don't be ridiculous, I am Paul Bellamy's sister. If you don't believe me, call his wife, ask her if she knows me."

Paul's assistant hovered behind them. "Just let her go. She might be his sister." He looked at Maggie, uncertainty writ large. "In fact, I think she is. Just make her leave." He seemed on the point of tears.

The red-faced spokesman said soothingly, "Okay, Mr. Angeli, you're the boss. We'll just escort her out of the building, okay? See she don't slip back. Come on, girlie, don't give us no trouble here." The man started to grab Maggie's arm, faltered when he looked into her eyes. He hitched at his belt instead, tucking his shirt more firmly into his pants. "Get your feet moving, you hear me?"

In the elevator, the other passengers stared curiously, somehow managing to move around casually without appearing to do so, isolating Maggie and her escort in the miniscule space. No one spoke.

They crossed the lobby in silence, the men staying with her until they reached the sidewalk. The smaller of the two spoke for the first time, establishing his own authority. "We'll be watching for you, honey. Don't come back."

On East 54th, close to the river, expensive apartment buildings faced the tree-lined street, awnings protected the residents from the intrusion of the weather. Maggie nodded in response to the smile of the doorman outside Paul's building, went through the glass door webbed in gold metal he held open. The lobby was an understated demonstration of wealth—etched glass, marble, inlaid woods, touches of satin finish brass, exquisite vases of fresh flowers.

"Ma'am?" A concierge came from behind a small table, advanced toward her. "Can I help you?"

"I'm visiting Mr. Paul Bellamy. Just tell me his apartment number, and I'll go up. I want to surprise him, so it's not necessary to call him." She knew he wouldn't go for it, but if he'd been doing this job for long, he'd see it for what it was—the opening of a negotiation.

The elevator door opened before he could answer. Two men, their ages spanning a generation at least, emerged, their glance taking in Maggie and the concierge by the desk. The older man murmured something to his companion, and both laughed as they crossed the lobby. They might have been alone for all the attention they paid to the two people watching them, the older man's arm resting possessively around the younger man's waist.

With a flourish, the doorman opened the gold-webbed door, rushed to hold the door of the Rolls-Royce that purred to a stop at the curb when they appeared, raised his fingers to his cap as the Rolls pulled away.

The concierge touched the small gold ring in his left ear,

raised his eyebrows, moved his head impishly to one side, a smile in his eyes as he looked back at Maggie. "I don't think Mr. Bellamy can be expecting you, do you?"

Maggie rummaged in her backpack, moving the Beretta to one side, and found her wallet. She opened it, extracted a hundred-dollar bill.

"Is Mr. Bellamy in, do you know?"

The concierge took the bill from between her fingers. "I haven't seen him today, didn't see him come in or go out."

"I'm his sister. He hasn't been seen at his office for a while. I just want to go in, see if he's okay."

The man looked pointedly at her wallet. Maggie took out another hundred, waited. The concierge looked toward the street as if he hadn't noticed the bill in her hand. Maggie counted out three more.

"Okay, that's five hundred. For this I want the key. If he's there, he'll call you and let you know that I am his sister. If he's not there, I want fifteen minutes. Deal?"

The man took the bills, went to a small room behind his desk. He reached into a numbered cubbyhole, brought out a key.

"702, 7th floor. I'm going to call up to let him know you're on the way. If there's any trouble, my friend out there," he indicated the doorman, opening the door now to a middle-aged man with a German Shepherd on a leash, "will back me up that I did not give you the key, you must have grabbed it when I was busy elsewhere."

He left the desk, crossed to pat the dog's head. "Dennis is looking good today, Mr. Feidler."

"Yes, he's on top of his game, Johnny. Always is, though, eh?" Mr. Feidler's voice was unnaturally deep, as if he had to work to pitch it from the bottom of his diaphragm. He gave Maggie a curious glance then strode with a long heavy tread to the elevator.

Johnny watched until the doors closed and the discreet brass indicator arrow above the elevator started to move, then turned back to Maggie. "Very butch, our Mr. Feidler. Thinks nobody guesses. God knows why he lives here." He grinned, gave a particularly girlish twitch of his shoulders. "As if anyone cares, anyway." He held out the key to 702. "Take it or leave it."

Maggie took the key, went to the elevator, waited impatiently until it returned. True to his word, Johnny was on the house phone as the doors closed.

The corridor was softly lit, deep apricot carpet absorbing all sound. Maggie pressed her ear to the door of No. 702. Silence hummed back at her. She inserted the key, turned it. Her heart thundered in her ears. Paul had to know something about Jimmy's disappearance, she was sure of it. He'd be able to explain why they hadn't come for him or for his daughter. Why they came instead for her and Jimmy. Then he'd help her get Jimmy back. *La famiglia e per famiglia,* was one of their father's favorite sayings. Even Paul would respect it.

She pushed open the door, called out, "Paul, it's Andrea." She didn't want to surprise him *en flagrante delicto.*

The foyer opened into a sitting room, cold and dreary in the gray light of the overcast day. The art here was explicit: male nudes in every kind of sexual configuration, singly, in groups, closely observed genitalia in the course of erection, the moment of erupting orgasm. Lamps in the shape of young men were alight, the voice of Edith Piaf warbled from a stereo, deepening a silence that was suddenly ominous.

The doors to the terrace were open, as if someone had checked outside, and hadn't bothered to close them properly when returning. Sheer drapes hung limply in the damp cold air. A sickening odor permeated the place.

"Paul?" She forced her voice louder. "Are you in? It's Andrea." The sound echoed in the emptiness.

The wall of gauzy white curtains moved eerily, and the back of Maggie's neck prickled. She walked outside to make sure no one was on the terrace, then pulled the doors shut behind her. She stood with her back to the doors and the view of the East River, took a moment to survey the space in front of her.

A light film of dust coated glass tables, vases containing bronze spider chrysanthemums, their leaves dried out, the stems standing in a couple of inches of stagnant water. On the other side of the room, a door stood partly open.

Reluctant now, and frightened, Maggie crossed the room. She hesitated, then pushed the door.

The bed was a sodden chaos of tangled sheets, burst pillows, blood. Two bodies in the room—she took in that much before stumbling away.

She managed to get to the kitchen, holding on to the counter while her stomach emptied into the sink. She wiped her mouth on a paper towel, then took down a glass, filled it with ice and water from the door of the refrigerator. She rinsed her mouth and spat into the sink. Body shaking, she sagged against the counter for what seemed an eternity before she had strength enough to turn on the water, clean the sink, wipe her face with a dish towel she found in a kitchen drawer. She took a moment to gather herself, then returned to the doorway of the dreadful room.

Paul was stretched across the bed. He had not died easily. Knife wounds crisscrossed his body, and he had been burned with a steam iron that was lying by the side of the bed. His mouth was stretched by his last scream. His own manhood filled the cavity.

Like the photographs they had shown her...

Another body was posed over a blood-spattered television set that was still on, legs splayed as if part of the entertainment, framing filmed bodies grunting, jerking in endless pornographic motion.

Pools of blood had congealed beneath both men. Dead men don't bleed, so they had been alive when emasculated. It looked as if the pile of hand towels on the floor had been used as gags to muffle the sounds.

Maggie restrained an impulse to turn off the awful movie. The police would need to see this room exactly as she saw it now.

She had to force herself not to run from the apartment, away from the stink of death that was everywhere. Instead, she turned back to the living room, searched quickly, found only domestic things, linens and china, silver tableware. She shook the art books on the glass coffee table, kept her mind closed against the bedroom door gaping like the mouth of some hellish cavern. The light flashed on the telephone, one message, and she pressed the button.

"Mr. Bellamy." A light male voice. "This is Chip at Flower Fling. Your order is on its way and I must say, the chrysanthemums really are quite divine. So, enjoy."

She opened the hall closet, pulled aside ski equipment, fancy dress costumes—a horned devil, a leather cowboy outfit with no crotch or rear. She replaced everything the way she found it, then went into the guest toilet whose walls were decorated with a series of pornographic drawings by famous artists: Picasso, Grosz, Hockney, Maplethorpe.

She found nothing. No laptop, no jottings from telephone conversations. Not even an address book to link Paul to anything or anybody outside this apartment.

For a moment she stood in the middle of the room, gathering her spirit, wrapping it protectively around her. Only Jimmy mattered, nothing else.

She crossed the room.

In the bedroom, she kept her eyes from the pitiful remains of what had once been two human beings, riffled quickly through the bedside cabinets, finding only sex toys, exotic jellies. Poppers of amyl nitrate.

The iron stink of blood seemed lodged in her throat, and she heard her breath catching noisily. She entered the walk-in closet, using one of Paul's monogrammed handkerchiefs to wipe her fingerprints as she went. Clothes, expensive cashmeres, hand-made shoes, silk pajamas, drawers filled with scanty underwear. Glass shelves in the bathroom were laden with scents and oils from Provence, soaps, shaving things. Quaaludes, other junk in the drawers.

Nothing of use to her.

She left the door as she found it, returned to the kitchen. She washed the glass she had used, dried it, replaced it in the cupboard in the kitchen, wiped the cabinets, everything else she thought she had touched, folded the dish towel across the bar inside a cabinet, then crossed to the front door. She took a last look around, used the handkerchief she had brought from the bedroom to pull the door closed behind her.

In the elevator she leaned against the smoked glass, too played out to raise her eyes. She caught sight of her feet, the bloody feathers from the burst pillow stuck to her boots. Moans of horror escaped her. She slid to the floor, rubbed at the soles of her boots with the monogrammed Irish linen. The elevator purred downward, passing every floor without stopping. When the door opened to the lobby, she was upright, composed. She stopped at Johnny's desk, handed him the key.

"Call the police. Paul Bellamy is dead."

"What? Dead? What do you mean?"

She didn't answer, didn't turn to respond to his panicked questions. She walked through the gold-webbed doors into fresh air, turned toward Madison Avenue, remembering Paul as he had been, at home in Port Washington, years ago. Paolo, Giacomo, Andrea Bellini.

Pampered children of the don.

TWENTY-TWO

Sam ran up the steps to the rectory and leaned on the bell. He could hear it ringing in the house, then the clatter of shoes on the tile floor as someone hurried to open the door.

"*Da, da.* I come."

Sam kept his finger on the bell until the door was flung open. "What you do, this noise so early." The woman stared at him. "What you want? Come later."

Sam pushed his toe against the jamb, held the photograph up in front of her nose. "I think you do know this man. His name is Father Robert Patrelli. He lives here, and I want to see him. Now."

"Not here." The housekeeper tried to close the door.

"Listen, lady. I don't know what your problem is, but I'm not going away. This guy is here, and I want to see him."

"No. Not here—"

"Where is he then? At the church?"

"What is it, Mrs. Grotka?"

A man peered over the housekeeper's shoulder. "Can I help you?"

Older, white hair, stocky build. Dog collar. "You must be Father Lachinski."

"Yes. What can I do for you?"

"I'd like to see Father Patrelli, please. For some reason your housekeeper seems to think I mean him some harm."

"Mrs. Grotka has not yet recovered from her fear of the police. I'm sorry, Detective—" He waited for Sam to fill in the blank.

"I'm not the police, Father. My name's Sam Cady. I'm from New Orleans, and Father Patrelli is a friend of my wife, Maggie. I just want to visit with him."

Lachinski raised his eyebrows. "Really now. Well, I'm afraid Mrs. Grotka is right. He's not here. He's left already for the hospital. We have several parishioners sick, and we attend them daily."

"I didn't see him leave."

"Well, I guess you need more than one pair of eyes, then. He left from the back of the house. By car."

Sam cursed himself. "Which hospital?"

"Oh, Bellevue, mostly."

Sam turned to run down the steps. The priest's voice stopped him.

"Of course, if it's your wife you're looking for, maybe Mrs. Grotka would be kind enough to awaken her." Lachinski spoke to the housekeeper. "I suppose she is still in her room?"

Sam turned back and made for the door, found Lachinski barring the way. Everything seemed to slow down, a tableau of three stone figures facing each other for eternity. Then Mrs. Grotka's words brought the moment back into real time.

"Nyet," she said. "No one sleep in bed last night."

Maggie got into a cab on Madison and 54th, slumped in the back, her strength gone. Even her bones felt as if they had no substance. Traffic was heavy, but she saw everything outside the cab as if it were in a movie, without any sense of reality. She stared out of the window, seeing Paul's body superimposed on the crowds on the sidewalk, flashing on the dreadful photographs she had shut from her memory.

What connected such brutal killings to Jimmy?

The stink of blood still filled her nostrils, forced bile into her throat, and she swallowed. Her heart felt crushed, and she longed for the quiet of the dismal little guest room at the rectory, the comfort of the prie-dieu in the corner, time to think of what to do next. Call her mother to tell her what she'd found. Or maybe not yet. Talk to Bobby again, get him to take another message to O'Malley. Try not to think of what she had seen...

Think of Sam. She ached for him. Needed him to hold her, to tell her that it was all right, that they'd get their boy back...their lives back...that these terrible deaths could not reach their son....

The cab stopped, and Maggie looked up.

"These bums park anywhere," the cabby fumed. "Look at that, think they live in this city by themselves." They were already on Rivington, the narrow street blocked by a delivery truck double-parked in front of a small used furniture store. The cab of the van was empty, the driver nowhere to be seen. The cabby stuck his head out of the window. "Hey," he shouted. "Other people gotta move in this city, too, y'know."

"This is good enough," Maggie said. "It's not far, I can walk the rest of the way."

She handed a few bills to the driver and got out. Still fuming, the cabby slammed into reverse, backed up into a cross street, shot forward and disappeared.

Alert now and walking fast, Maggie kept one hand in her pocket, fingers curled around the grip of the Beretta. If anyone was watching the rectory, broad daylight was no friend. Across the road, an old man sat with his feet in the gutter, surrounded by plastic bags, busy with a pile of empty soft drink cans. A few people were about, an Asian going into a garment shop, a cou-

ple of women browsing used furniture displayed on the sidewalk
on the other side of the delivery truck. No one threatening.

Maggie continued toward Christ the Redeemer. Then she
heard a car coming from behind her. Powerful engine. Slowing
as it came closer.

An ambush—and she had walked straight into it.

Sam leaned against the wall in Bernie's Luncheonette, phone
to his ear, and listened to the ringing, four, five, six, seven. He
had decided to wait and watch the rectory, alternating back and
front. He could search Bellevue for hours and still miss the
priest. But sooner or later Patrelli would return to the rectory,
and Sam intended to be there when he did. He was about to hang
up when a soft voice answered.

He straightened. "Elle," he said. "Hi. It's Sam. Heard anything?"

"Hey, Sam. No, nothing. I'm sorry." The distance from New
Orleans did nothing to mask the distress in Elle's voice.

Sam gripped the receiver of Bernie's public phone tighter,
pressed his forehead onto the greasy, moisture-stained wall for
an instant. *Nothing on Jimmy. Christ, what do they want? Who
are they? Who was Maggie?*

He raised his head. "But Petey's still on it, right?"

"Well, it's an FBI case, Sam. He's doing what he can, but you
know how that is."

"Has he heard of a lead? Anything?" Sam already knew what
Elle would say. If there had been anything, she would have told
him immediately.

"I guess not, *cher.* What about you, Sam? You got anything?"

"Not yet." Sam had his eyes on a small blurred figure he'd
been watching through the steamy windows. A kid from the
neighborhood, jeans, black leather jacket. Long stride for a short
kid. Familiar long stride. "Wait a minute, Elle." Still holding the

phone, he went to the front door, rubbed a hole in the steam-clouded window.

That was no neighborhood kid.

Sam let the phone drop from his hand, frightened that if he took his eyes away even for an instant to hang it up, she'd be lost to him again. Then a black Lincoln Town Car passed her, crossed Sam's line of vision, blocking her from his view. The car slowed, but kept rolling at a walking pace. Then it stopped.

Maggie moved closer to the buildings on her left and picked up her pace. The black car kept abreast of her for a few yards, then pulled ahead and stopped. The back door opened, a man emerged, hands raised to show he was unarmed. On the other side another man got out and leaned over the top of the car, grinning. Through the smoked glass of the windows, she could just about see the pale face of someone in the passenger seat, and beyond him the driver. Both no doubt holding weapons on her.

The delivery van had not moved.

Maggie pressed her back against the wall, arms extended, one hand cupping the other, the Beretta gripped between them. She thought with gratitude about her murdered brother, James, for the hours he had forced her to spend practicing in the sound-proofed firing range in the basement of the house in Port Washington.

"Hey, Andrea. Babe, hey, what's this? You don't need no piece." The taller of the two men walked toward her, a large smile that didn't reach his eyes spread across his face. "Hey, come on. This ain't called for. We just want to talk. O'Malley says to say hello."

"Keep away from me." She heard the delivery truck start up, saw it start to roll slowly. She'd walked into a trap.

"Andrea. He wants to talk, babe. That's all. Just talk."

"Tell him to call Bobby Patrelli when and where. Get away from me."

"Hey, do we need a go-between? Come on, what is this?" He

came closer, hands held waist high, away from his body. "Just talk, honey."

He looked enormous, beer belly over his belt, a layer of hard fat over a heavily muscled body. More than double her weight.

"Get back." From the smile on his face, she knew he figured she didn't have what it took to use the weapon in her hand. The second man, smaller, red hair combed into a pompadour, freckled skin blotched with sun damage, was circling to her right. Out of the corner of her eye, she saw the window in the car lower. The man in the passenger seat grinned as he let her see the muzzle of the weapon resting on the sill.

Sam slammed open the door of the luncheonette, the Sig already in his hand, his mind a tangle of confusion. The woman wasn't Maggie, not his wife. This woman knew all the moves. He'd caught a glimpse of her, back to the wall, knees easy, arms extended, weapon supported by both hands to take the recoil.

His Maggie hated guns.

He ran across the street, skirted a slowly moving delivery truck blocking his way. The truck stopped. Suddenly, Sam found himself flat on his belly, the van driver holding him down, slamming at his kidneys with heavy fists. The Sig skittered across the pavement, hit the curb. Sam twisted, brought both knees up, jammed them into the deliveryman's chest.

He couldn't see what was happening, Maggie was on the other side of the van. He managed to shout her name. But the guy pummeling him was a tank, kept on coming....

Maggie had a sense of another man running, then a shout. She heard her brother's voice, "Keep focused. Aim to kill," and kept her attention on the man in front of her, smiling, inching closer. "Come on, babe. Don't do this the hard way—"

Maggie lowered the weapon, aimed for his crotch, saw the smile replaced by panic. She fired, heard him scream as he collapsed. But it was sheer terror. She'd twitched her aim at the last minute—James would have been furious.

The redhead came from behind the car. He raised his gun.

A voice shouted, "Don't whack her, you fucking moron. Grab her, for Christ's sake." The heavy man was on his hands and knees, eyes bulging, his face purple. "Grab her."

Maggie listened to her brother's words resounding in her head, "Andy, don't think. Aim to kill. You won't get another shot." She fired at the redhead, saw him drop to the pavement. The man she'd missed moved faster than she thought possible with so much belly. He was on his feet, arms around her, dragging her. The car was already moving when he threw her in the back. A knee was in her chest, feet trampled her body as the man she'd shot was dragged by his coat into the moving car. Maggie kicked out, felt both boots connect.

"Fucking bitch." A fist slammed into her head, the world dimmed. She grabbed an arm, sank her teeth into a bare wrist. Another blow took her behind the ear, and then nothing.

Somewhere a horn blared and the deliveryman broke contact. He got to his feet, staggered toward the truck. Sam threw himself at his back, and the guy turned, slammed him against the side of the van. Sam dropped to the ground, the wind knocked from his lungs—the truck panels were solid, had to be reinforced metal. Then the van was backing up, and Sam rolled just in time, feeling the wheels brush his body as the van mounted the curb in front of the rectory, clearing out of the road.

Sam scrabbled for the Sig, got to his feet, raced to the middle of the street facing the Lincoln. It was picking up speed, coming fast. New Jersey license plate. He aimed at the driver. Fired. The windshield held.

Bullet proof.

Sam stood his ground, expecting a bullet in the back from the delivery van, fired again. Then the Lincoln was on him, forcing him to leap for the sidewalk.

Fearful of hitting Maggie...the woman...whoever she was, Sam got off a couple of shots at the tires, his view impeded by parked junkers, missed as the driver slalomed back and forth across the street, metal screaming on metal as he sideswiped parked cars.

The delivery van roared into life, aiming for him on the sidewalk. Sam hurled himself up the steps of the church. The van passed, found a small space between two cars, bumped back onto the street, picked up speed, covering the Lincoln's back as it took a left on two wheels.

Sam leapt down the church steps to the street, raced after them. He got to Delancey in time to see them turn again, the roar of supercharged engines fading into the general pulse of traffic coming off the Williamsburg Bridge.

The whole thing had taken only minutes.

Stunned, Sam stood in the middle of the street, the Sig dangling uselessly from his hand. Four men in the Lincoln, another in the van.

Adrenaline was draining out of his body. He took a minute to catch his breath—his kidneys ached, he felt as if he'd gone fifteen rounds with Tyson. The street was empty, stores shut tight, tenement windows closed.

He ran back toward the rectory, took the steps three at a time, pounded on the door, wanted to go on pounding on the priest who threw it open.

"I heard gunfire—"

"Where is Patrelli?"

"I told you—"

Sam grabbed the front of his cassock. "Where in Bellevue?"

Lachinski's eyes were on the Sig in Sam's right hand. He pulled at the hand twisting his cassock into a knot on his chest. "Mrs. Grotka, call 911."

Sam released his hold. "No police." He looked at the priest's face and modified his tone. "Father, listen. You know Maggie. I just saw her pulled into a car. She didn't want to go. I tried to stop it, that's what you heard. If the police get involved, it will get worse. Please believe me. Give me a couple of hours. Just tell me where I can find Father Patrelli."

Lachinski stared at him silently, his face tight and hostile. Sam felt he was losing it, fought to keep his hands off the man in front of him. "Goddammit. *Where is Patrelli?*"

Mrs. Grotka spoke from behind the priest. "By now, he goes from Bellevue. Go to St. Vincent's. Ask for Napoli. Maybe fifth floor."

St. Vincent's and this son of a bitching priest would have sent him to Bellevue. "Thanks."

Halfway down the steps he looked back at Father Lachinski. "Believe me, there's a reason for all this, and I'll explain it to you. Please don't call the police. Don't call anyone. You'll just put her in more danger." Fuck it, he was pleading and didn't care.

Sam held the priest's eyes until he answered. "I'm not the only one with a phone, you know. Someone else will call it in if I don't."

Not in this neighborhood, Sam thought, but he nodded his thanks. No one was on the street except the old man, Yankee, muttering to himself as he gathered up his plastic bags from where he'd dropped them when he took cover in a doorway. Passing him at a run, Sam caught a glimpse of a brilliant patch of color clutched to the mud-brown chest. Even when bullets started to fly, the old man hadn't parted with his down payment for services yet to be rendered—the big bottle of Chivas Royal Salute in its fancy purple velvet bag.

The cab dropped Sam in front of St. Vincent's Catholic Hospital on Seventh Avenue. He barged through the revolving door, went to the receptionist's desk beneath large stained glass panels of St. Vincent and a couple of other saints he didn't recognize.

He leaned over the desk. "I'm looking for—"

"You'll have to wait your turn." The receptionist threw him a brief glance, then went back to the patriarch of the large family in front of her, frowning, trying to understand what he was saying in the few words of English that peppered a torrent of an unfamiliar language.

Sam went to the elevator. He got out on five, found the nurses' station, spoke to the lone nurse on duty.

"Mr. Napoli. Is he on this floor?"

"Never heard of him."

"Well, who would have heard of him?"

The nurse caught Sam's intent blue eyes, took in the size and shape of him. She put a hand to the tendrils of blond hair arranged around her neck and smiled.

"Try the information desk," she said.

"I did. They were very busy, and I didn't wait."

Still smiling, she shrugged.

"I'm actually looking for Father Patrelli," Sam said. "I was told he'd be with Mr. Napoli."

"Oh, Father Patrelli. I saw him a while ago."

"When?"

"An hour, give or take."

"Do you know where he went from here? Napoli maybe?"

"I don't know any—"

"Okay, thanks." Sam turned to walk back to the elevators, and the receptionist downstairs.

"If you like, I could call around."

Sam returned to the station. "Yes, thank you, I'd appreciate that."

"No problem." The nurse smiled, giving him the full treatment. "You from the South?"

"New Orleans. What I need to know is whether Father Patrelli is with Mr. Napoli, or if he isn't, where Father Patrelli is heading now. Can you find that out?"

"Oh, sure." She punched out a number, said, "This is Patsy

on fifth. Patsy Van, honey. On fifth? Yeah. You got a Napoli up there? Yes, honey, I know you're not supposed to. Just make an exception this time, okay? I got a delivery guy cluttering up my station with a load of flowers." She raised her eyebrows at Sam, smiling. "Got his room number, hon?"

Sam leaned across the desk, watched her scribble 633 on a scrap of paper, push it toward him.

"Thanks, Trace," she said. "Is Father Patrelli with him? You know, the cute priest from Christ the Redeemer?" She listened. "He is. Okay, honey, thanks."

She looked up to find Sam halfway down the hall, waving without looking back. "Thank you, appreciate it."

"Sure," she called. "Anytime, sugah."

TWENTY-THREE

Maggie kept her shoulders squared, fought not to give in to an almost overwhelming desire to sag in her chair. Her head pounded, her body felt as if she had spent the entire journey rotating in the drum of a concrete mixer. She kept her eyes on the man sitting on the other side of the desk. He had pale skin and black hair, gray eyes—a typical Celt. Black brows arched below a smooth forehead, and at first glance he was handsome, until she looked into the eyes. It was like looking at a flat stone surface.

She thought of Paul's body, and that of his lover deliberately, obscenely posed, draped over the television, and felt her stomach quiver.

Behind her, she could smell another man and hear the thick sound of his breath in and out, but she did not turn. She kept her eyes on O'Malley.

O'Malley stared back, then nodded as if he'd come to an important conclusion. "You look like your old man, you know?"

He smiled, showing small even white teeth. "Good-looking guy, Salvatore."

"Why am I here?"

He assumed a look of surprise. "I thought you knew. Friend of yours came to see me. Father Patrelli. Said you wanted to talk." He shrugged, his hands spread. "I'm a good guy, right, Andrea? So I figure I'll save you the trouble of finding me." He leaned back in his chair, settling in for a long chat. "Jesus, Andrea, you're one tough lady. Old Kev may never recover. Poor bastard thought his balls were gone for sure." O'Malley gave a throaty laugh, the flat surface of his eyes remaining unchanged.

The unseen henchman behind Maggie's chair sniggered, the sound cut off at a glance from the man behind the desk.

Maggie said, "I want my son."

O'Malley regarded her over steepled fingers. "And you haven't even asked how old Tim's doing. You shot that poor son of a bitch, it's only polite to ask."

"Where is my son?"

"Ah, I knew you'd be concerned." O'Malley looked at the man behind Maggie's chair. "How's old Tim doing, Danny?"

"Lost a lot of blood—" the man started to answer, but O'Malley cut him off.

"Yeah, that's right. The doctor's still with him. See?" O'Malley said to Maggie, his voice reassuring. "You don't have to worry, he's going to be okay. Guy's a piece of shit, anyway. Right, Danny?" He laughed. "Matter of fact, you got better aim, you'd have done me a big favor. Fuck." He made a show of half rising to his feet. "I might just go right now, shoot the dumb son of a bitch myself." Then he frowned, shook his head as if having second thoughts and sank back into his chair. "Nah. The doctor works for us? Big-time dope fiend. Yeah. Probably fill old Tim full of the wrong shit anyway, save me a bullet." He laughed again.

Maggie curled her fingers around the arms of her chair, forced herself to keep the whimper rising in her throat from escaping. If these men had Jimmy— The thought curdled in her brain.

"Where is my son?"

"Yeah, I can understand your concern. You got yourself a hell of a problem there. I'd be the same if I'd lost a kid somewheres. Easy to replace though, kids." O'Malley leered at her. "A bit of the old," he made jabbing motions with a clenched fist, "a few months, a few pushes. And there you are. A replacement. Nothing to it. Am I right?"

With an effort Maggie kept her face still. "What do you want of me? Why am I here?"

"I told you already. You sent word to us—"

"Stop this. You have my son. You called my mother. Where is he? What do you want? Please..." Her voice suddenly broke and the breath she drew caught in sobs in her throat.

O'Malley's reaction was immediate. His face creased with rage, he slammed his fist on the desk. "Don't start that shit with me. I can't fucking stand it, sniveling women make me fucking puke."

Maggie swallowed the sobs, clenched her teeth to bring her erratic breath under control. "What do you want?" she asked again. Her voice was too loud in the quiet room.

O'Malley leaned back, his face smooth, all trace of anger gone as if it had never been. A smile hovered around his well-shaped mouth. He leaned back in his chair. "I tell you what. Why don't we help you find him?" He looked up at the man behind Maggie. "Danny, take our little Italian mama here and let her search the house." To Maggie he said expansively, "Go where you like, sweetheart, the place is open to you. Who knows, you could get lucky and find your kid." The smile dropped from his face. "Then come back with a changed fucking attitude and we'll talk."

"What do you want?" Maggie's voice rose. "O'Malley—"

The man behind her put a heavy hand on Maggie's shoulder. She pulled away.

"Why are you doing this?"

"What?" O'Malley sounded incredulous. "You lose your kid, which is pretty fucking careless if you ask me, and here I am trying to help you find him, and this is the thanks I get?" He shook his head sadly. "Andrea, Andrea. Where's your fucking gratitude?" He leaned forward again. "Now, you know what's good for you, you'll shut up and get the fuck out of my face. Understand?"

"O'Malley, please. Whatever you want, just tell me. Please—"

O'Malley looked at his henchman. "Get her out of here, for Christ's sake." He picked up the telephone, spun his chair until only the back of his head was visible, tapped out a number. "Hey, Mitchie," he said in a loud voice. "That stuff we was talking about? Well, my man, you are in luck." He was finished with her.

Danny put huge hands beneath Maggie's arms, lifted her to her feet as if she weighed nothing. The man was enormous, smelled of beer and cabbage, mingled with the rank animal sweat of a man who ate too much flesh and used too little soap and water. An arm around her, he hustled her out of the door, her struggles useless, her feet barely brushing the floor.

In the hallway, he dropped her to her feet, grinning into her face as his hands found her breasts and squeezed hard, daring her to complain. Silently, Maggie struggled with him, managing to feel for the weapon she knew he must be carrying. Found the holster under his arm.

Her mind darted back and forth, seeking an escape, an idea, something, anything. A plan began to form, the only avenue she could see that was open to her. She looked at the gross man feeling her body, and made little protesting sounds in her throat.

"Please, don't." She pushed weakly at his wrists.

"You Eyetalian babes. All that," he pitched his voice into a soprano, "'don't, don't, you're hurting me,' bullshit. You're hot for it, all you Eyetalians. Known fact."

"Tell me where my son is. Please."

He tweaked the nipple of her left breast, grinning when she winced. "Come on, you heard what the Mick said. Maybe we find him, maybe we won't. You wanna try, though, right?"

He pushed her ahead of him down the hall. The house seemed to be a pair of duplexes that had been remodeled into one, the rooms used mainly for storage. Paint was chipped, stained wallpaper was peeling from the walls, gray duct tape covered tears in a filthy carpet that once maybe had been pink. The house was silent, the only sound came from the street outside, rising and falling in waves, an indeterminate hum of sound. Somewhere there was a basement, Maggie thought. These houses always had basements. *Please God, let him show me the basement.*

Her captor opened a door. Heavy pieces of Victorian furniture were piled haphazardly, chairs on top of tables, sideboards, headboards without the beds.

"We got a container full of this shit." He laughed. "Mick got the word it was military hardware. Opened it up, thought he was gonna have a heart attack, he was so pissed. Got rid of most of it, though. Faggy antique dealers. They love it." He grinned, exposing nicotine-stained teeth. "Hey, you got a fag brother, right? Maybe you should talk to him, see if he wants what's left here." He pursed thick lips, shook his head. "Jeez, that's right, I forgot. Heard he don't got much use for beds and shit now."

Maggie closed her mind to the images his words evoked. She said, "What do you want to let me go? Money?" He stared at her, grinning, let his eyes travel the length of her body, back to her breasts. Maggie said, "You want to do it to me? Then let me go, tell O'Malley I got away—"

He ran his tongue moistly over his lips. "You ain't going nowhere, honey. Not until the Mick's good and ready, and that ain't yet. So shut up with that shit."

He pushed her across a narrow hallway, threw open a door into what was once a dining room. Light leaked from around the edges of torn drapes, and Maggie could see cardboard cartons stacked on a scarred wood floor. Elaborately Danny opened one of the cartons, peered inside, looked up as if surprised.

"No lost kid. You wanna see?"

Maggie stayed where she was against the door and stared at him without speaking. The man grabbed her, dragged her into the room, forced her head into the box he had opened. It was filled with machine parts, and the smell of oil made her gag. The thought of grabbing for the weapon in the holster under his arm passed through her mind, but she couldn't take the chance. Not yet. She closed her eyes, struggled against the hand on the back of her neck, wriggling her body until she knew he would feel the movement of her buttocks against his thighs.

Grunting like a rutting animal, he ground into her.

Maggie jerked sideways, frightened she'd gone over the line, that she wouldn't be able to stop him. "Let me up. Come on, please." The strength of sheer terror coursed through her, and somehow she managed to break his hold. "Listen, please, let me speak."

He released her, his breath ragged, his forehead beaded with sweat.

"Danny, listen. Listen to me. You let me go, and we can work something out. What do you think?" She touched the backs of her fingers to his chest, let them drift toward his belt and tried again not to gag. She was taking a risk; he could rape her here and now without giving her the chance she needed. Holy Mother, she prayed, protect me, protect my son.

He was breathing hard. "Sounds good to me, babe." He nodded. "Yeah, great idea. Let's just figure out what I tell the Mick. We had a fuck and then she got away? Yeah, sure, Danny, he'd say. Happens all the time. Then he'd hang me up by my balls and fucking shoot me." He grabbed her arm. "Come on, you gotta see the rest of the house, or he'll be pissing blood."

He hustled her into another room, twitched more torn drapes. "Okay, nothing here. So you gotta see the kitchen. Make Mick mad, you don't get to see the kitchen, good Eyetalian girl like you."

He threw open a door and she followed him into the filthy room. Unwashed dishes piled in the sink, pizza boxes, Chinese food containers overflowing on the table, nude centerfolds pinned to the walls, a poster advertising a porno flick.

Maggie stood in the middle of the kitchen, breathing through her mouth. She pointed to a door, guessing where it led, praying she was right. "Where does that go?"

"The cellar. You wanna see?"

"No." Her heart was pounding, fight or flight. Her mind was steady with the answer. Fight.

"Sure you do, honey. Never know what you might find in cellars." He threw open the door, releasing a drift of cold, dank-smelling air. "In the old country our people, they stored potatoes in the cellar. Course, here, we don't grow potatoes we got groceries, so we use cellars for other things, know what I mean? Yeah, course you do. You know all about that being Eyetalian. You think your kid could be down there?"

Maggie shook her head.

"Why not? Come on, let's have a look. Mick don't want you should miss the cellar. Could be the best part."

"Then put on the light."

"Nah, we don't need a light." He leered at her.

"I do." Maggie pointed to the switch on the dingy white-washed brick wall just inside the door. "Put it on."

"Ah, shit, Andrea, you spoil all the fun." He flipped the switch.

Maggie looked quickly at the small landing lit by a forty-watt bulb, the rickety wooden stairs, the concrete floor at the bottom. "You first."

He made a little puffing sound. "You ain't afraid of the dark, are you?"

"No. I just don't know the stairs, and the light's not good. If I trip, I can hold on to you." She let him see the tip of her tongue.

A spark came into the man's muddy green eyes. He opened his mouth, his breath coming fast.

"Sure, babe. Yeah." He started down the stairs. "Sorry I said that about your kid being down here. Just kidding around, joking, know what I mean?"

Maggie glanced at the door. No key in the lock. God help me, she thought. She stepped onto the landing, held on to the rail, lifted her knee to her chest, drove her booted foot into the middle of the man's back. He grunted, stumbled down the steps, grabbed at the handrail as he tried to turn toward her, his body off balance.

"Hey, what the fuck—"

Maggie ran down, raised her foot again, connected hard. He crashed backward. Maggie caught a glimpse of him lying motionless at the bottom of the stairs before she ran back up the stairs, closed the door, and flipped the light switch. The cellar plunged into darkness.

She couldn't see him, but neither could he see her.

In the pitch-black, she felt her way down the stairs, listening for movement from him, hardly breathing herself. She counted a dozen steps, thirteen, fourteen, the next step was soft. She'd stepped on him. He groaned.

She should have left the light on, she thought. This was madness. She bent, felt his body. He groaned again, stirred.

Somehow she managed to straddle him. She ran her hands over his body, looking for the weapon and began to panic. He'd twisted as he fell and was half on his belly, his coat caught beneath him. She grabbed what felt like a shoulder, struggled to push him onto his back. Murmuring unintelligibly, he moved, helping her to turn him over. Her hands found the holster. She pulled the gun free, started to crawl toward the stairs. A hand grabbed her ankle, the grip weak. Maggie kicked and the hand slipped away, unable to keep a purchase on her leather boot.

She raised the gun, then changed her mind. If she shot him, O'Malley would hear the noise.

The cellar was more than dark, it was an airless space, with a blackness that seemed almost solid. She heard him grunt, felt him moving behind her. She retreated up the stairs, stopped, waited for him to follow.

"Hey, you fucking bitch—"

The voice was thready; she'd hurt him. She wrapped her hand around the metal weapon, giving her hand weight.

"You want me, come get me." Deliberately she goaded him, willing him to speak again, to give her a target. "Come on, lover, I'm waiting."

"Fucking bitch."

He was close, a step below. She was sick with fear, with the stink of his sweat and breath and blood. With all the force of her anguish and terror behind it, Maggie swung her weighted hand at the voice. She felt the crunch of metal against bone, swung again, heard the heavy body fall backward. Then silence.

She raced back up the stairs, opened the door, found the switch, flipped it. Weak light revealed the unconscious man sprawled against the bottom step, his mouth open, the side of his face bloody and concave. She turned off the light, shut the door, raced through the kitchen, along the hall, slammed into O'Malley's office.

He was leaning back in his chair, fiddling with a small tape recorder. He looked up, his pale blank eyes widening at the sight of the gun in her hand. His glance flickered behind her, looking for her captor. He recovered quickly, grinned at her, rocked his chair back and forth.

"Keep both hands on the desk where I can see them," Maggie said.

"Sure. Okay." He pointed two forefingers at the weapon in her hand. "That's got to be Danny's, right?" He threw up his hands in disgust. "Shit! You see what I got here? Fucking idiots. What do you think, would Salvatore's men come and work for me? Speak to them for me, Andrea, okay? Tell them I pay them good money, better than Salvatore—"

"Put your hands on the desk where I can see them."

Obediently he leaned forward, put the recorder on the desk, clasped his hands together in front of it, and looked at her, a bright attentive expression on his face.

"Where is my son?"

He opened his eyes wide. "You didn't find him?" he asked in mock surprise. "You search the house?"

Maggie advanced into the room, the gun trained on his chest. "You called my mother and threatened my son. I know you have him. So what do you want, O'Malley?"

The smile left his face. "Let me tell you something. You need a fucking lesson on how to behave. I send men to pick you up. Friendly, no harm. But no. You're like your old man. You got a fucking attitude, and you don't trust no one. You start shooting. Fucking Italians, you got no class, so I gotta teach you some manners. Right? Now what have you done with the stupid fuck I sent with you?"

Maggie advanced into the room. "What do you want, O'Malley?"

"Me? Forget that. You should be thinking about what you want. Heard someone paid your fag brother and his boyfriend a little visit. You know about that? Yeah, I see you do." His eyes glued to hers, O'Malley pressed a button on the recorder in front of him. A child crying, a muffled little voice. "Where's my mommy? I want my mommy. Mommy, Mommy—"

O'Malley snapped another button and the small voice stopped. He grinned. "You want to hear more, honey?"

The room started to close in and Maggie pressed her thighs against the desk in an effort to keep the heavy weapon in her hand steady. "Where is he?"

O'Malley shrugged. "I'm a businessman. I don't give nothing for nothing. But I got a proposition. You interested?"

TWENTY-FOUR

Sam took the stairs two at a time, opened the door to the sixth floor. A bright-eyed old man in the bed closest to the door looked up as Sam entered Room 633. His expectant smile faded quickly and he turned back to the television suspended over his bed. Sam took in the other bed—a still form attached to drips and machinery, either sleeping or unconscious.

Sam addressed the old man. "Mr. Napoli?"

The old man didn't answer. Sam approached the bed, spoke over the cheerful voice of a newsreader reporting the sinking of a crowded river ferry in India, hundreds presumed drowned.

"Mr. Napoli?"

"What?" The old man fiddled with his hearing aid. "Keep the damn thing off, nothing I want to hear. What did you say?"

"Are you Napoli?"

"Who are you?"

"My name's Sam Cady. I'm looking for Father Patrelli, he's supposed to be visiting a Mr. Napoli."

The old man laughed. "Well, it ain't me."

Sam looked at the man sleeping in the next bed.

"Ain't him neither," the old man said.

"Has Napoli been discharged?"

"Maybe, by now." The old man laughed again.

Sam turned back to the door and the nearest nurses' station.

"Room 680," the thin voice behind him said. "That's where they got him. They always give out the wrong room number for these guys. But it's 680. Cesare Napoli. I went down there one time to have a look. Got hustled out before I could see anything, though."

"I'm really looking for Father Patrelli."

The old man had his fingers twiddling at his hearing aid, his eyes on the screen above his bed. "I don't know nothing about him. But Napoli's in 680 if he ain't already gone. Full of the cancer."

"Thanks."

Sam walked quickly along the corridor counting off the rooms. 660, 662, 664. He passed a nurses' station without being noticed, turned the corner. No doors, no numbers. No room 680. Only the distant sound of bleating machinery broke the silence of a corridor that ended in double doors bearing large white letters: No Admittance. Sam pushed through.

He swept his eyes around the waiting room. A bank of windows spanned the end wall. Overstuffed couch, armchairs, a couple of tables lined the wall on the right. Two doors on the left, one unnumbered, the other bearing the number 680. Both doors were closed. A group of men, expensively tailored in dark suits, clustered in front of the windows and the farthest door, 680, talking in hushed tones. Before he could move toward them, Sam found his way blocked.

"Who the fuck are you?" The voice was New York, the speaker young, olive-skinned, thick dark hair. His right hand was ostentatiously out of sight in his bulging coat pocket.

"I'm looking for room 680," Sam said. "Should be along here somewhere." The room was filled with huge ornate flower arrangements, the air heavy with a mix of their funereal scent, high-priced colognes, cigar smoke clinging to the men. And another smell. Sam recognized it from his days with NOPD. He could smell death in the room.

"What is it, Gino?" A large figure detached himself from the group of men and started across the room toward them.

"Guy says he's looking for room 680, Joey," the younger man said.

"What do you want?" Dark eyes embedded in pockmarked doughy fat swept over Sam as if measuring him for a suit. A concrete suit. "What is it with you guys? Can't you read?"

"Read?" Sam said. "Read what?"

The man nodded at the door. "The sign says No Admittance. He's dying, for Christ's sake. Would it hurt you to let him go in peace?"

"I'm looking for Patrelli—"

Joey cut him off. "So get a warrant. Now get out of here, leave us alone."

Before Sam could respond, a woman's voice rose in muffled grief. The door to room 680 opened allowing the sound of anguish to fill the room. A black cassocked figure appeared in the doorway.

Every face turned toward the priest. Voices died away, and the rise and fall of the woman's keening seemed louder in the sudden quiet. The priest looked over the assembled men, then said, "Where is Joey Butters?"

"I'm here, Bobby," Sam's interrogator called. He started toward the priest, then looked back at Sam. "Now I asked you to leave politely, so why don't you just do that, okay? We're not looking for trouble here." He glanced at Gino, gestured with his head toward the door, then hurried toward the priest, a trace of musky cologne trailing in the air behind him.

Sam stared after him. They might have put their years in, moved up from the street, provided the next generation with the smooth edges of fancy educations, but New Orleans, New York, wiseguys looked the same, smelled the same. He heard pieces of the puzzle surrounding Maggie start to crash into place, the questions he didn't want to voice become louder.

"You heard what the man said." Gino laid a hand on Sam's arm, smirking as Sam jerked away. Gino brought his other hand, and a Smith & Wesson 9 mm, out of his pocket. "You got no warrant, you got no business here."

"You got a permit for that thing?"

"Sure." Gino lowered his eyes to look at the weapon. Sam slammed the edge of his hand against Gino's wrist. The gun jumped out of his grasp, and Sam grabbed the wrist, twisting the arm back and up behind him. The young man turned, slowly forced to his knees to prevent his shoulder from popping out of its socket.

Sam bent, grabbed up the gun. He straightened, called out, "Patrelli."

The priest turned, the shock on his face deepening as he took in the scene, the young man on his knees, the nine in Sam's hand.

Joey Butters started to reach under his jacket, and Sam raised the weapon and covered the room. Swiftly, men held their hands away from their bodies, palms forward, fingers spread showing they were empty. Shaking his head briefly, the priest touched Joey Butters's arm to restrain him. He walked toward Sam, Joey Butters with him. Six feet short of where Sam held Gino in a lock, Joey held an arm across Patrelli's chest, forcing him to stop.

"What is all this?" Patrelli asked. He looked over Sam's shoulder as if expecting more men to enter, then back at Sam. He gestured to the open door behind him, bringing attention to the sound of the grieving woman. "Cesare Napoli is dying. The police can have no further business with him."

"My name's Sam Cady." Sam said. "I'm Maggie Cady's husband." He watched Patrelli's face for a glint of recognition when he said her name, but saw nothing. Not the movement of a muscle, the tremble of an eyelid.

He was good, this priest.

Patrelli said, "If you're not on official business, you have no place here." He nodded toward Gino without removing his eyes from Sam. "Release this man, then leave."

"Patrelli." Sam eased the lock on Gino's arm, allowing him gradually to get to his feet, and beckoned the priest closer with the Smith & Wesson. Joey Butters tried to stop him, but Patrelli patted his hand in reassurance. When he was within arm's reach, Sam shoved Gino hard at Joey Butters, and held the gun on the priest. "I've just seen Maggie snatched off the street outside your rectory," he said softly.

For a second, Patrelli was still. Then he said, "I have no knowledge of a Maggie Cady. I'm deeply sorry, but I don't understand what this has to do with me. If you are not the police as you say, then I suggest you contact them."

"For God's sake, man, don't you understand what I said? Maggie was shoved into a car by a gang of thugs with guns."

"I'm sorry. You'll have to excuse me."

Patrelli turned away. For a split second, Sam stared after him, the only connection he had with his son, with Maggie, moving away, crossing the room, disappearing... *He couldn't afford to lose him, not now.* He leapt forward, threw an arm around Patrelli's throat, jerked the priest back against his chest, shoved the nine under Patrelli's chin. There was a wave of movement as men reached hands beneath their coats.

"Don't do it," Sam called. "This is private business but I'll kill anyone who moves. We're just going to have a little talk, that's all." He tightened his hold around Patrelli's throat. "Tell them."

"Do as he says, it's okay," Patrelli said.

"Let's see the hands," Sam said to the room at large. "Slowly." Hands reappeared, empty of weapons.

Sam took a step backward toward the doors, dragging Patrelli with him, sure the men would allow them to leave as long as he had the priest close against his chest.

He'd taken only a few steps when the woman emerged from the dying man's room, a young man close behind her. Weeping, wrapped in her own crumbling world, unaware of anything except her pain, she pushed through the group of men. Tear-drenched dark eyes bounced from man to man, came to rest on Joey Butters. She ran toward him.

"Joey. Joey, he's asking for you. What are you doing? He's asking for you, Joey."

"Sure, honey, I'm coming. Just give me a minute."

The distraught woman looked at Patrelli, her eyes moving on to Sam, to Joey Butters and back to Sam, as if for the first time taking in the weapon, the tension. She stepped closer, and Sam could feel the fetid heat of her grief, the dry stink of a long death watch with too little food, not enough liquids, mingling with stale perfume.

She held Sam's eyes. "Leave him alone, he's dying. Aren't you satisfied, you hounded him, and you hounded him." Her voice was rising into hysteria. "You killed him, why can't you leave him alone?" Suddenly she reached across Patrelli, slashing with long pale nails at Sam's face.

Instinctively he jerked his head back, instantly felt himself go off balance, and knew that he'd lost it.

Patrelli grabbed his arm, dragging the gun from his throat in the same instant that Joey Butters lunged forward and bore them both backward into the wall. Sam grabbed at the priest's cassock in an effort to hold him, but Patrelli slipped from his grasp. Blindly Sam swung the flat of the weapon at Joey Butters, felt it connect and Butters go down, his hands clutching Sam's windbreaker to break his fall. Sam stumbled, kicked himself free, held the gun on the room. Patrelli was nowhere to be seen. Surprisingly, no one had moved.

In the sudden silence, the woman's sobs rose. As if drained of strength, she leaned against the young man who'd followed her from the inner room. His arm held her protectively. Sam caught his eye and knew he had connected with the man in charge. The young man nodded once, an almost imperceptible dip of his chin. Sam backed through the doors into the empty hallway, turned and raced along the hall, past the nurses' station. Without slowing, he shouted at the surprised faces turning toward him.

"The priest, did he come this way?"

Too stunned to answer, no one moved. Feet pounded the hallway behind him, voices yelling for security, and he knew he'd been allowed to leave the room only to spare the woman more grief. Now they were going by the book, calling for the law, gunfire and assassinations in hospital corridors not fitting the new image. Sam yanked open the door to the stairs, leapt down three at a time. The stairwell echoed with the sound of his feet. No one was ahead of him. No one followed.

In the lobby, he waited a few minutes, caught his breath, tried to make himself inconspicuous while watching every descending elevator. Doors opened, passengers emerged, the priest not among them. He knew it was useless. Patrelli was gone.

He walked past the reception desk, through the glass doors into the street. A couple of NYPD cruisers were slamming to a stop outside the hospital, and uniformed cops raced by him.

Somewhere, Maggie fit into all this. Not the Maggie he loved, but a Maggie he would find. Now, at least, he knew where to start.

He flagged down a passing cab.

TWENTY-FIVE

"Hey, you don't look so good." O'Malley's voice was full of concern. "Why don't you sit down." He started to rise from his chair.

Maggie wrapped her finger round the trigger of the weapon, trained it on the middle of his chest. With an effort, she kept her eyes away from the connection with her son—the small tape recorder in the center of the desk. "Where is he? I want to talk to him."

"Nah, you know you can't do that. It's a recording, look, a tape. There's no kid here." He spoke as if to a two-year-old, toying with her. He picked up the little recorder, opened up the back and showed her the tape. "See? No little Jimmy." He smiled at her, snapped the back of the recorder in place, put it on the table. "Come on, you worry too much. You want your kid back? You can have him. You give me something I want. A fair trade. What do you say?"

Maggie knew she was close to killing, but to find Jimmy, she needed this monster. She took a breath, then another. When she could trust herself to speak, her voice was steady. "What do you want?"

"Salvatore Bellini. I want your old man, honey. Your son for your father." O'Malley laughed.

She'd half expected the demand, but still Maggie heard him through a hollow chamber in her head.

"You know where to find my father. In the Bellini family crypt at St. Savior's Cemetery in Queens."

"Cut the bullshit, or you're going to make me mad and you don't want to do that, babe, believe me. Now, I'm going to find your old man with or without your help. What you have to do right now is decide whether you want your kid back." He grinned, showing his fine white teeth. "Of course, the question really is if you want him in one piece, or a little bit at a time."

Maggie fought to keep herself from shrieking in terror.

"You're a father yourself, O'Malley. You're not that evil—"

O'Malley cut in. "Yeah, well, we can get off on a discussion of good and evil, but why don't you save it for the boy-friend—" He stopped. "Hey, that's a thought. The kid's his. Right? The priest?"

She stared at O'Malley without speaking, her mind spinning frantically—where to go with this, how to get to Jimmy, how to stop herself from pulling the trigger, pulverizing the grinning face before Jimmy was safe.

"You in or out?" O'Malley asked impatiently.

"I get my son back first," Maggie said. "Then we talk about my father."

O'Malley threw himself back in his chair, slammed his hands together. "That old bastard. I fucking knew it."

Maggie felt as if a river of ice had replaced the blood moving through her veins. She kept her face still, a lesson learned at her father's knee: Never let an opponent see when they've scored. She had just signed her father's death warrant.

She said, "I didn't say that he was alive, O'Malley. I said I get my son first."

"Keep talking, Andrea. One phone call, one fucking word from me, honey, and little Jimmy gets a visit from the friendly neighborhood chain saw guy. If you want him in one piece, start dealing."

Sweat beaded her upper lip and Maggie felt herself start to retch. She swallowed convulsively, willing herself not to vomit. O'Malley met her eyes, the knowing grin intact on his handsome face. Maggie said shakily, "If you want Salvatore Bellini, you give my son back to me. Today. Now."

"Yeah, well, that's not how this is going down. You don't hold one fucking card here."

Maggie raised the gun in her hand.

O'Malley looked at it. "Don't make me laugh, I'll get a hernia. You shoot me, the kid's finished. So, come on, babe. Speak to me."

"I don't know where my father is."

"Bullshit."

"The truth. I don't know where he is. And if I did, I don't for one minute believe he'd give himself up to you."

"Sure he would. I'm the guy got the trump card here, you might say. Giacomo died in the fucking firestorm at Bear Mountain. Paolo—well, just let's say poor old Paolo's out of his misery, and he wasn't doing too good, anyway, with his boyfriends and all. So who's left? What's her name? Jolie, right? But the old man would never come out for her, a girl, a dim bulb from what I hear. I got the only male left in the Bellini family line. That Sicilian *patrone?* He'll come." O'Malley was still smiling. "Gotta say, when it came right down to it, your brother Paolo was stand-up. That's what I heard, anyway. Didn't give up a word about the old man. Too bad he was a fag."

"My father doesn't even know of Jimmy's existence."

"Yeah? Well, I think he does. Your mama knows then old Sal knows."

"She doesn't know. I don't see my mother—"

O'Malley leaned forward. "You see your mama twice a year, babe."

Maggie kept the shock from reaching her face. *No one knew that. Only herself and her mother.*

O'Malley was still talking. "So, old Sal knows he's got a grandson. Now, you go tell him this. He comes out. You get your kid back. Win win, like they say. Except for Sal, of course. He loses. Otherwise..." O'Malley shrugged.

"First I see Jimmy."

"Oh, for Christ's sake. What do you think you're bargaining with here? A gun?" O'Malley threw up his hands. "So fucking shoot me. Then what happens? Someone offs your kid, someone else does you. No one knows nothing, and old Salvatore keeps on going at the Happy Home for Retired fucking Mobsters."

Maggie twitched the gun in her hand, aimed at the floor at the edge of his desk, pulled the trigger. The explosion was deafening, magnified in the enclosed space of the room. Maggie retreated until she felt the wall against her back and had a clear view of the door and the rest of the room.

"I see my son first."

O'Malley stared at the hole in the floorboards at his feet, then back at her. He reached across the desk, punched a finger at the recorder. Jimmy's voice came into the room. "Where's my mommy? I want my mommy..." O'Malley snapped a finger at the button. The voice stopped. Maggie felt her knees begin to sag, and she pressed her back against the wall. *Never let them see when they've scored...*

"You're really pissing me off here," O'Malley said. "Giving your old man up should be like falling off a fucking log for you. It's not as if you haven't done it before. Shit, you gave the fucking FBI where to get him. Get all of us."

Maggie's breath caught. The last time she saw her father, he refused to even look at her. Never sent a message when the Irish, or their own people, or whoever it was had tried to kill her. She'd been the child of his heart, but he was a product of an ancient tradition, and she'd violated those traditions, she'd broken his trust, and to him, Andrea Bellini was dead.

O'Malley was right. She had no leverage.

"Let me use your phone."

TWENTY-SIX

Sam approached the desk at the 42nd Street library. The woman on duty was the same one who'd helped him when he was looking for the QwikFoto address. Tight jeans, figure-hugging sweater, no one's idea of a librarian except for the spectacles on a ribbon hanging around her neck, bumping against her chest every time she moved.

Sam got her attention. "Where can I find your old newspapers?"

"All our newspapers are on microfilm. Room 100, ground floor." She pointed the way, and Sam nodded his thanks.

Room 100 was crowded, every microfilm reader in use. Sam prowled the room, came to rest behind a young man in a yarmulka shoving a pile of books into a backpack.

"You finished here?" Sam asked.

"Yeah, give me a minute and I'll get out of your way."

"Hold this spot, will you? I need to get some files."

"I'm leaving, buddy, so you better hurry it up."

Sam went to the files, retrieved film of the *New York Times* and *New York Daily News* for the two years before he and Maggie first met in New Orleans, returned to the cubicle, nodded his thanks to the young man. He started with the *News,* scanning back from that magical July when all he'd been able to think of was Maggie Jameson, the woman who'd captured him from the moment he'd seen her.

Screaming headlines in eight point type skimmed by—June, May, April, March, February, January. Disasters, scandals, New York Yankees. The year ended. He took out the film, loaded the file of the year before he and Maggie had met. December, November, October, September. The months passed. Then, a small headline caught his eye. Bellini Daughter Dead. The name rang a bell. Sam went back, zeroed in on the one-column report.

It was a follow-up to another story, one already covered. The daughter of dead Mafia Don Salvatore Bellini had been killed in a boating accident while on vacation in Honduras. No body had been recovered. A brief reprise of the events surrounding the death of Andrea Bellini's father followed, but Sam did not read it. His eyes were riveted on the small photograph that he'd scrolled up.

Maggie. Sam sat back. His Maggie Jameson was Andrea Bellini, the supposedly dead daughter of Mafia Don Salvatore Bellini. His son, Jimmy, was the grandson of the man who had been the head of one of the five Families of New York.

"This is a busy place, mister," a voice behind him said. "If you're finished here, you should go nap someplace else."

Sam glanced around at the woman who spoke and shook his head. "I'm nowhere near finished."

The woman gave a small, annoyed grunt and moved on. Sam looked at the date of the story: April, one year and three months before he and Maggie met. He printed out the article, then continued the search for the main story, passing the follow-up reports without reading them. He stopped at a headline shrieking

Bellini Bloodbath above a full-page color closeup of bodies, men dead from gunshot wounds, sprawled and bloody.

It was the start of the news story. And it was the genesis of the life he shared with Andrea Bellini.

Sam scanned the text, taking in the high points. A mob meeting at Bear Mountain, upstate New York. FBI raid. Gun battle. Seven men dead, among them Giacomo Bellini, the son and presumed heir of Salvatore Bellini, alleged don of the notorious Bellini Family. Also dead were Kevin O'Malley, Brian O'Malley, younger twin brothers of Michael O'Malley, alleged boss of the Butcherboys, offshoot of the Westies, the Irish gang that had controlled the meat packing district since the 1890s; plus Louis "The Nose" Nobiani, Sean Hargrave, Kit O'Connor, and Padraig O'Donnell, an Irish national. Salvatore Bellini, believed wounded, was spirited away by a priest thought to be a mob mediator, also maybe wounded. Lawyers for the Bellini family produce motions signed by Federal Judge Peter Fairbanks refusing FBI entry to the Bellini estate in Port Washington, Long Island, citing insufficient cause for search.

The following day, the headline was Bellini Dead, subhead Mobster Dies Of Wounds. The story contained little of substance, no direct quotes, a lot of lush descriptions of the Port Washington estate where Bellini was reported to be lying dead of his wounds—Sam guessed the reporter had never been inside the gates—and a recap of Bellini's career, his numerous appearances in front of congressional committees. It came as no surprise to read that he had never been indicted for any crime.

Sharing the front page was a picture of a smiling Michael O'Malley showing off a newborn. According to the proud father, he'd been pacing the corridors of New York Catholic Hospital at the time of the raid while his wife was giving birth to their fifth child. He had no knowledge of the deaths of his twin brothers, hadn't seen them in years. Direct quote beneath the picture of father and new daughter: "Who the f--- are the Butcherboys?"

The following day Cardinal Defends Pal headed an official statement from the office of the Archdiocese of New York denying mob connection, describing Bellini as a generous friend of the church, his son Giacomo as a good Catholic. A sidebar to the story stated that death certificates for both men had been produced. Then, three days later, front page, column left Cardinal To Officiate announced that Cardinal Matterini planned to conduct the funeral mass for Salvatore Bellini and his son Giacomo.

The only follow-up was a dramatic picture on the day of the funerals. The caption read Federal Agents Attend Funeral Mass.

That was it. Nothing more about the FBI, continuing investigations, search warrants, state police involvement. The story was dead.

Obviously, the Bellinis had powerful friends in powerful places.

Sam went back to the funeral picture, searching for Maggie among the black-clad, heavily veiled women, accompanied by a priest, emerging from St. Patrick's Cathedral. At the bottom of the church steps was a group of men in dark suits, short haircuts. Hard, grim faces were raised toward the women, who at a casual glance looked, in that microsecond caught by the camera, as if they were cowering in fear.

Sam studied the picture. One of them could have been Maggie, but he couldn't be sure. What he could see was that the paper had chosen to print a frame showing an incomplete movement as the women turned toward the priest. Clearly they were not cowed, they were surrounding him protectively. He was not surprised to see that the priest was Robert Patrelli, his face drawn in pain, leaning heavily on crutches. A figure among the feds looked familiar. Sam leaned closer, unable to believe his own eyes. The fed was turned toward the camera, his hand raised as if to prevent the picture.

Sam felt as if the breath had suddenly been knocked from his body.

He was looking at FBI Special Agent Stephen Adashek.

* * *

Awkwardly Sam juggled the file of articles and the telephone and waited for someone to pick up, praying that Petey was off duty and at home. The buzz of the 42nd Street library receded into the background as a familiar voice yelled into his ear.

"Le Pont."

"Petey, it's me," Sam said. Early in their partnership, Petey had heard him announce himself by saying, "It is I," and he'd damn near fell off his chair laughing.

"Sam. Hey, buddy," Petey said. "How's it going?"

Sam's heart felt as if it had landed hard in the pit of his stomach. If Petey had anything, he would have told him right away. He asked anyway. "Heard anything, Pete?"

Petey's voice softened. "*Rien, ami.* I am sorry."

"Nothing at all?"

"No. No ransom demand, no phone calls. Nothing."

His strength suddenly draining from him, Sam slid his back down the wall until he sat on the grimy floor of the library. He put the manilla folder he'd bought to carry the articles he'd printed out in front of him and took a minute before he opened it. He could hear Petey breathing, waiting for him to continue.

"Well, I got something, Pete. I've been looking in the newspapers. The Bellini Mob bust, remember that?"

He guessed Petey would pick up the name of the city he was in, but Sam was past caring. Petey had been known to bend a rule or two when it suited him. Now he was going to have to decide on his priorities.

"Yeah. I remember it," Petey said. "Six, seven years ago. Some godawful mess up north. New York. Fucking fiasco. Lot of scumbags dead. No one went down for it."

"That's it. The feds blew apart a fancy country inn, then couldn't make a single charge stick. Mob lawyers claimed they attacked innocent businessmen without warning. Everyone had permits to carry."

"Figures. So what about it, *cher?*"

"Maggie's name is Andrea Bellini. She's Sal Bellini's only daughter." The line hummed. For once it seemed Petey was lost for words. "Pete, you hear what I said?"

"Yeah, man. Jesus. Are you sure?"

"Yeah. I got her picture from the newspaper here in front of me. It's attached to a report of her death about three months after the shoot-out. Boating accident some place in Honduras."

"Honduras? Cute. Piranhas ate the body, right?"

"If they have piranhas there, sure."

"She went into the FWPP." A second or two passed, then, "She should have told you, Sam."

Sam surprised himself by saying quickly, "How could she? I was law enforcement." He ran through the salient points of the story. He got to Adashek and heard Petey grunt.

"Shit. Are you sure?"

"Got that picture in front of me, too. It's Adashek all right."

"He's gone back to New York, Sam. It's a federal case now, NOPD is no longer involved."

"What about the clerk in the liquor store. And George Menton?"

"Federal," Petey said.

It made sense. "Okay, Pierre, listen. Are you up for looking into something for me?"

"What you need?"

"I got a New Jersey plate I'd like you to run." He gave Petey the number he'd taken from the Lincoln that snatched Maggie.

"Where can I reach you, Sam?"

"I'd better call you—"

"Hey, that shit doesn't matter," Petey said quickly. "It's okay, I got a rough idea where you are. It goes no further than my ear. You can count on that."

"I know I can. It's not that, Pete. I don't have a place." Sam told him about the FBI waiting at the hotel—it seemed like weeks ago, hard to realize it was only the night before. "I'll call you. Leave a message with Elle if you get anything."

"Okay, buddy. Watch your back."

"Sure thing." Sam hung up. It took him a hell of a lot longer than it should to gather the folder together and get to his feet. He needed sleep, but he'd have to make do with Bernie's coffee.

TWENTY-SEVEN

Maggie looked at her mother. The kitchen was warm and smelled of garlic and spices and rich Italian coffee. The brass on the coffee machine reflected the dancing flames of the fire, the refectory table that had been used for a couple of hundred years in a French monastery gleamed, but Maggie's soul felt as cold and gray as ashes.

"I think he died quickly, Mama," she said. Later, her mother would have to know the awful truth of Paul's death. Right now, Maggie's only thought was to keep Bianca focused on Jimmy.

O'Malley had wanted to drive her back to the rectory, but she'd insisted on being taken to the subway. She'd boarded the train to Grand Central, and from there to Port Washington, no longer caring whether or not she was followed. O'Malley knew she would not disappear, and with Paul murdered, the FBI would be here soon enough to talk to Bianca. What mattered now was finding a way to keep ahead of them.

"How do you know he died quickly?" Bianca asked.

"I saw his...I saw him. I went to that apartment he had. I think maybe he had a heart attack—"

"Why would he have a heart attack? He was a young man." Bianca raised her head. Maggie forced herself not to look away. Her mother sat a few feet from her at the end of the table, her back to the fire, close enough for Maggie to hear her breath catching as she inhaled, exhaled.

Bianca's eyes were those of an old woman, sunk deep in her head. "Don't lie to me! He did not die of a heart attack! They came after him, and they killed him!"

Maggie wanted to shake her head, deny what her mother said. This time she looked away.

"I know my son. In spite of what he was, Paolo would not give them what they wanted."

"No. He wouldn't. He was a good son, Mama. He stood up. Papa will be proud of him." Maggie hoped Bianca would not hear the bitterness in her voice. "I saw O'Malley."

"That Irish scum. You went there alone? To his place?" Bianca's voice rose in alarm.

Maggie held on to her patience. She pitched her own voice lower. "He has Jimmy. I heard Jimmy's voice, Mama. On a tape. He was crying, calling for me." It felt as if a roll of barbed wire was unraveling in her chest. She leaned forward, reached a hand across the table, rested it on her mother's arm. Her skin was clammy, her flesh soft and unresistant. "Mama, I need to know where Papa is hiding."

Bianca jerked her arm away. "Why do you need to know this?"

Maggie grasped her mother's icy fingers. Her own were as cold.

"Mama, listen to me. They have my son. Do you hear what I am saying? Your sons grew to be men. James, Paul, they grew up to make their own choices in life. My son is a baby. I am the one who must make the choices for him." Maggie drew a breath, then said, "O'Malley wants to...he wants to meet with Papa. Then he will give Jimmy back to me."

Bianca recoiled. She snatched her hand from Maggie's. "What are you saying? No. No, that man does not want to meet with your papa. He wants to kill him."

Bianca picked up a coffee cup and rose to go over to the coffee machine. She started to pour coffee, but the cup hung from her fingers as if she had not the strength to hold it. She put the cup down before it fell onto the tiled counter. She spoke without turning. "Our people did bad things, Andrea. Yes, I know that, I am not a fool. But they never, never brought families into their business. These people are not men, they are scum."

Maggie stayed where she was at the kitchen table. If she moved, she wasn't sure she could stop herself from shaking her mother until she gave her what she wanted, from screaming at her to remember that her brother Paul had done nothing to find out who had tried to kill her, that it could have been their own people, that she, Bianca's only daughter, had been forced to leave her home, her mother, all that she had held dear to keep on living. And now everything that her new life had given her— her son, her husband—was threatened.

"I know, Mama, but times are different now. These men are different. They'll use what they can—"

"They will not use your father," Bianca said flatly.

"Mom, this is Jimmy's life."

"It is your father's life."

"He made his choices, Mama. Jimmy is a baby."

"No. We must think of something else."

Maggie spoke to her mother's rigid back. "There is nothing else." She heard the rising panic in her voice. "I have to talk to Papa. Where is he?"

"We go to Bobby Patrelli. He's a priest, a negotiator. He'll talk to the Irish. They'll listen to him. He can tell them that Papa is truly dead. He can get the cardinal to tell them—"

"It's too late for that! They know Papa is alive. I don't know how he found out, but O'Malley knows Papa is alive."

"He cannot know that. No one knew, only you and Paolo and me. That's all."

Maggie shook her head. That was not all. The cardinal knew. Bobby Patrelli knew. The doctor who signed the death certificate knew. Even Donnie Provanto, her father's bodyguard, knew Salvatore Bellini's casket had been filled with sand.

Bianca stared at her own reflection in the darkening window. Then she turned. "Aldo Ricci," she said. "The *boccacio!* He talked."

Maggie wanted to scream. *Who cared who talked?* As calmly as she could, she said, "Where is Papa? At least let me go see him. Let me talk to him."

Bianca went on talking as if she had heard nothing Maggie said. "The undertaker. You remember, Aldo Ricci. He took care of my Giacomo.... He prepared Papa's coffin. He weighed out the amount of sand to be correct."

"Mama, it doesn't matter—"

"Yes, listen. Three, four weeks ago, his body was found in his mortuary. In a coffin. His throat was cut and his tongue had been... I heard the white satin was soaked in his blood." Bianca stared at Maggie through stricken eyes. "He was always a drinker. It was getting worse and he was losing business, people talking. Maybe he talked in some bar, made like a big shot, boasted he knew things. They heard, and they came for him and made him talk. Then they killed him. Oh, my God! They did that to Paolo? Cut his throat and his tongue... His poor throat... Oh, my God." Bianca held her arms across her chest, and rocked. "Oh, my Paolo."

Maggie got to her feet, went over to put an arm around her mother's shoulders. She tried to hold her still, fearing she would rock herself into hysteria.

"Mama, stop it!" She softened her tone. Bianca would find

out what had really happened to Paul soon enough. "Please. We have to think of Jimmy now. Please, Mama."

"Andrea, you should go to the FBI."

Maggie stared at her. Never in her wildest imagination had she dreamed Bianca Bellini would suggest such a thing. "I can't do that—"

Bianca's voice cut across Maggie's like a blade. "Why not? You talked to them before."

Maggie stepped back as if she had been struck. "Mama! I didn't talk to them. They followed me." She stopped and took a breath. "They told me Papa was in danger, and they followed me, Mama." The guilt she had fought—still fought—rose in her throat like a poison. How could she have been so stupid on that day of all days? In her panic to find them, Bobby and James and her father, she had disregarded everything James had taught her. Never trust the FBI. If they make an approach, keep silent and always, always, watch for a tail.

"You have friends in the FBI."

"I don't have friends, Mama."

"They put you in Witness Protection."

"Someone tried to shoot me right on the campus of Columbia University, and Paolo didn't do anything. Don't you understand that? Don't you care, Mama? Maybe one of our own tried to kill me—"

"No! Listen to yourself! Our men do not kill families, children. It was the Irish," Bianca said. "Go tell the FBI the Irish scum have your son."

"I can't. O'Malley said he'd..." The words caught in her throat. If she said them, she would see the picture the words painted. "If O'Malley suspected I'd been to the FBI, I'd never see Jimmy again. And there's something else. I called my friend Elle in New Orleans. Her husband's with the police, he used to be Sam's partner. Mama, she said three men were murdered in New Orleans after I left and the FBI says Sam killed them. One was our contact, the U.S. Marshall George Menton. He was already dead when you called him, you were speaking to the FBI. Elle said Sam's disappeared and the FBI has issued a warrant for his arrest. If I get in touch with them, they'll use me somehow to get to Sam."

A moment passed in silence. Bianca stared out at the garden Salvatore Bellini had created, gray and wavering now in the driving rain. The rattling of raindrops on the window was clearly audible, the hiss of the coffee machine a small domestic counterpoint.

When she spoke, Bianca's voice was calm and measured. "Andrea, the FBI will come here now. They will say it is to tell me about my son Paolo, but then they will ask their questions about his business, as if I know or care, or would tell them anything if I did know. But they are dogs with a bone. O'Malley will hear they have come here. He will think you talk to them whether you do or you don't. So, you listen to me." Bianca's face was like a death mask, wiped clean of emotion. "Speak to the FBI now. Tell them what you know. If they want Jimmy's father, if they use you to find him, so be it. At least maybe they can save your son. That is your choice. Not your papa for your son's life, but your husband for your son's life." She stared at Maggie through hard, dark eyes, then crossed the room, lifted the receiver from the phone hanging on the kitchen wall. She held it out to Maggie. "You are still Andrea Bellini, and in spite of everything you have done, your father keeps you in his heart. You call the FBI, you tell them the Irish have your son. And you keep faith with your father. He is dead."

TWENTY-EIGHT

Sam spooned sugar into the cup and stirred. His body was stiff from the pummeling he'd taken, and the skin on his face felt tight from lack of sleep. He took a sip of the brown liquid—it could not be called coffee—and had to work on swallowing. He needed Aunt Pellie and her famous blend. He needed sleep. He needed Maggie and his son. He needed his life back.

Bernie's Luncheonette was busier than he'd seen it, people getting off the street out of the weather. "All You Need Is Love," off the Beatles' *Yellow Submarine* album blasted from behind the counter, and the place was steamy, full of the smell of frying hamburgers, the noise of clattering china and conversation. Sam noticed a glance or two sliding his way and guessed his face was beginning to show some bruising. That, his size, and a two-day stubble, he had to look like a street thug. Not that that would give New Yorkers a ripple, but he'd certainly scared Mrs. Grotka again.

"Father not here," she'd said before he could speak. She'd kept the door open a mere crack, with him standing outside in driving rain. "You go St. Vincent's, *da?* You go there?"

"He left before I could talk to him." He'd turned up the collar on his soaked windbreaker, stepped closer to the door. "Maybe I can wait for him inside."

"*Nyet.* You come back." The door closed and he heard a key turn in the lock.

At Bernie's he'd managed to get a table near the window, but not the one he usually took. He had to crane his neck to see the rectory. No light showed. He glanced at his watch. Five, and already nearly dark. He'd give it until 5:30....

Sam jolted upright, startled by raised voices. Bernie was at the door, wrestling it closed, shoving at a figure encased in a black garbage bag who was trying to enter.

"Get outta here, stinking bum."

"Let me through, you fascist bastard. I got friends eat here."

Sam passed a hand over his face, then got to his feet and went to the door. "Hey, loosen up," he said to the counterman. "It's raining—"

"I got good customers wanna eat in peace, goddamn bum turns their stomachs. He stinks. You get him outta here, or I don't serve you again neither."

Sam took out his wallet, extracted a couple of tens. "Container of milk, a hamburger." He glanced at Yankee. "Better make that two hamburgers, coffee. To go."

Bernie took the bills and jerked his thumb. "You," he said to Yankee, "wait outside."

"He'll wait in the doorway out of the rain while I use your phone, and you get to keep the change." Sam looked at Yankee. "Want anything else?"

"A piece of pie go down great with the coffee, pilgrim."

Sam turned to Bernie. "You heard what the man said."

"Cherry," Yankee said. "Or maybe blueberry. Not apple."

"Outside, you." Bernie opened the door. Yankee hefted his aluminum cans, went through, dropped to his skinny haunches in the entry, his plastic bags spread around him. Bernie turned to Sam. "You think anyone's gonna step over this bum to get in here? I'm gonna lose money, him sitting there, smelling up the place."

"So go get the food. As soon as it comes, we're gone." Tired of the argument, Sam took out a handful of coins from his pocket, counted out what he'd need for the phone. He picked up the receiver hanging on the wall just inside the door, and punched out Petey's home number, hoping to get Petey and not Elle. One ring and a voice said, "Le Pont."

"Pete, it's me. Get anything?"

"Yeah. The Lincoln is registered to the Shamrock Hotel and Casino, Atlantic City. I put a call in to them, NOPD business. Guy manages the carpool, name of...wait a minute, I got it here." Sam heard a rustle of paper. "Yeah, name of Mulrooney, Felix. Says the car is used only for high rollers, pick up at the airport, deliver call girls, you know the drill. But on the date in question, Mulrooney claims it never left the garage. It was in for repairs, and he's got the service vouchers to prove it. Looks like a dead end, buddy."

"Well, that's a bunch of horseshit. That car was armored, Petey. I got off a couple of rounds and they bounced right off the paintwork. Anything else?"

"No record on the Jamaican. We're guessing he was a special order assassin, hires on for a job, then home on the next flight. This time he seriously pissed someone off. Find that someone and you've got a case. Course, officially it's out of our hands, but I'm bound to pick up a word here and there, you know how these things go."

"Yeah, thanks, Pete. Thanks for trying." Sam didn't ask for word on Jimmy, he didn't think he could hear Pete's answer without breaking down. "I'll call you. Take care." He hung up.

The car had been a long shot. He knew that would be too easy. Those guys were professionals. They'd cover their tracks.

He picked up the bag of food Bernie had slammed down on the floor next to him while he was on the phone, shouldered his way out into the rain. He looked down at Yankee.

"You got a dry spot somewhere close by?"

"Got this one. Suits me fine."

"Cops will roust you from here if Bernie doesn't, you know that."

"Yeah, well." Yankee eyed the bag. "That grub for me or you gonna keep it for yourself?"

"Depends. I need some help here."

"What kind of help? I don't do guns or fisticuffs. I saw the action this morning, Southern boy, the guy in the back of that delivery truck had a cannon in his hand. Out of my league."

At a different time, a different place, Sam knew he would have been amused. The old man was probably half in the bag most of the time, and so frail he looked as if a breath would blow him over.

"Nothing like that. The priest, Patrelli, has to come back here and I've got to know when he does. The housekeeper won't let me wait inside. There's a garage off the alley. He could come either way, front or back. I can't be in two places at one time."

The door opened, giving them a blast of warm air filled with the smell of cooking. A man and woman came out and hustled past. Deliberately, the man kicked at the bags surrounding the old man and laughed as the woman remonstrated. Yankee flipped him the bird. The guy lifted his foot, aimed at the old man's chest, and Sam took a step forward.

"Think about it, pal."

The man stared at him and allowed his companion to pull him away. Sam breathed a sigh of relief. He wasn't sure he was up to another round. Yankee rearranged the bags. "So you want me to park in the alley?"

"No, I'll do that, he's probably driving and he'll use the garage. If you know someplace dry where you can watch the front, that'd be a help. If you see him, just come and get me. You up for that?"

The old man thought for a minute then nodded. "Yeah. Now what about that food?"

"Let's get out of this doorway." Sam waited for him to get to his feet, gather his belongings, adjust his black garbage bag poncho. "You know someplace else, somewhere dry?"

"Yeah, guess so. Course, it's only big enough for a cat, but the people I usually doss with will be inside on a night like this, anyway. Down at the Midnight or somewhere. Good thing. Two hamburgers wouldn't go far between a hungry mob."

Yankee started walking down the street toward the river. Carrying the food, Sam fell into step, his head down against the rain. "You been passing that picture around?"

"Yeah. That's what I was coming into Bernie's to tell you. Old gal I know recognized the other guy."

Sam stopped. "Who is he?"

"Keep the feet moving, Southern boy," Yankee said impatiently. "It's raining, or hadn't you noticed?"

Sam resumed walking and the old man said, "She didn't remember his name, but she knew his face all right. Said he used to come here a lot at one time. She doesn't remember when. Of course, she doesn't remember much of anything anymore." A tinge of sadness had entered the old man's voice. Sam had already noticed that occasionally his grammar and diction took on a different tone. Yankee looked up and smiled. "Do I get the bottle of Chivas Royal Salute? The big one?"

"Sure, but I need more information than that. Show her the picture again. And if she remembers him, others might, too. Keep showing the picture, okay?"

"Your dime, pilgrim. And that will be a bottle for the name, right? Two for me for the work, and one for whoever comes up with the identity of the man in question. Chivas, and maybe a Cohiba or two to go with it. Or a Churchill. Love a good cigar."

Sam looked at him. "Who the hell are you?"

"You mean who the hell was I, Southern boy." Yankee smiled again, showing rotten teeth. "I've almost forgotten. Now I'm just a gentleman of the street. Gimme the grub."

TWENTY-NINE

The coffee shop was cheerful and noisy, a completely anonymous HoJo's off the Jersey Turnpike. Maggie scanned the brightly lit restaurant, busy even at this late hour, couples, families with sleepy kids, truckers stoking up for the long night's drive ahead. Her eyes came to rest on a familiar figure in a far booth. He wore civilian clothes, a tweed jacket, jeans. She walked toward him, slid into the booth before he could get to his feet.

"Bobby, thanks for coming."

"No, please. I'm glad to see you." He glanced around at the entrance. "Donnie outside?"

"No. I drove my own car. For some reason, Mom's been keeping it up. She's still got James's Mercedes."

He looked alarmed. "You should have let Donnie drive you."

"No one followed me. I made sure of that. In any case, the FBI probably knows I'm here. I called you from my papa's house."

"My phone isn't tapped, Andrea."

"How do you know? You get the rectory swept, Bobby?"

A hint of a smile touched his lips. "I wasn't at the rectory, I was with my family. My calls are put through automatically when I'm there." The smile deepened slightly. "My dad makes sure his phones are clean."

"The trusted consigliere. Your father still doesn't know about Papa?"

Patrelli shook his head. "No. Anyway, he's retired now."

"Do mobsters ever retire, Bobby?"

"Well, I can only speak for my father. He has."

"What can I get for you folks?"

They both looked up at the waitress, smiling at them, pad in hand.

"Coffee, please," Maggie said.

"Anything else?"

Maggie shook her head.

"When was the last time you ate anything?" Bobby asked. Maggie looked at him. She had no idea. He spoke to the waitress. "Scrambled eggs, hash browns, whole wheat toast for each of us. And bring the coffee now, please.

"You look exhausted," Bobby said as soon as she'd left. "Are you all right?"

"I've seen O'Malley," Maggie said abruptly. "He sent some of his goons to pick me up."

"Did they hurt you?" he asked quickly.

"No. But O'Malley has Jimmy. Bobby, I heard him on a tape crying for me."

"Oh, Andrea...oh, my love..."

Maggie looked at him. He didn't seem to realize what he had said.

"What can I do to help?" he asked.

The waitress arrived to deliver the food and a warning about hot plates, an offer to refill coffee cups. "Anything else. No? Okay, enjoy," she said.

Maggie waited impatiently for her to leave, then leaned forward. "Bobby, I want you to arrange for me to see Papa. If I can talk to him, I can make him understand."

"Understand what? Wait a minute. What are you saying?"

"I'm saying that O'Malley knows Papa is alive, Bobby. Aldo Ricci the undertaker was killed a few weeks ago. My mother thinks he probably boasted in some bar when he was drunk, about knowing things other people would love to know, and she thinks the Butcherboys picked up on it. Ricci was found in a coffin in his own mortuary. His throat had been slashed and his tongue was pulled through."

Patrelli looked stunned. "I hadn't heard that. Ricci was being paid a lot of money for his silence."

"Oh, Bobby, he was a drunk. It had to be him. The only other possible leak would be the doctor who signed the death certificate, and the Bellini family has a lot of dirt on him and both his sons for drug dealing. They're Park Avenue society, and they'd never risk it. It had to be Ricci. Anyway, O'Malley told me he wants to meet with Papa."

Patrelli was shaking his head. "That's not what he wants, Andrea."

"Don't shake your head, Bobby." She plunged on without allowing herself to think of the outcome of what she was asking. "I know Papa, and I know you know where he is."

"No, you're making an assumption—"

"Bobby, stop it. I've thought about it. I know my father. No matter where he is, he would have a confessor. Who else would that be but you?"

Patrelli, his eyes locked on hers, continued to shake his head. "No—"

"Please, don't give me no." She lowered her voice. "The only other priest he would trust, could trust, is Cardinal Matterini and even though they go back to boyhood in Sicily, I can't see His Eminence slinking around wherever it is my father has decided to hole up just to hear his confession. Can you?"

"How can you be sure Salvatore is even in the country? Did you think about that?"

"He's here. He wouldn't leave my mother. I'm sure she still sees him and I know she never leaves the country. Besides, after the Bear Mountain thing the FBI had every airport covered."

"They called off that surveillance as soon as they had the death certificate."

"Bobby, I know he's here. He's still running things through Paul." Fleetingly she realized he did not know Paul was dead, and decided in the same instant that she could not waste her energy on telling him, answering questions, giving explanations. "I know Papa wanted out of the violence of his life. He was getting old and he didn't have the stomach for it anymore. The new men taking over were talking to reporters, the television cameras, making book deals. James was a made man, but Papa wanted him out of the life. That was always a problem between them," she said bitterly. "After James was killed I think Papa just took the chance to get out. But I also think he kept the money laundering part of his business." She glanced at Patrelli, saw the query on his face. "I was in Paul's stockbroking office, Bobby. His desk was empty. No papers, no addresses, no computer. Paul wasn't a stockbroker, he didn't have the smarts to run the operation I saw going on there. He was an elegant, charming front, he could do that well enough, but he certainly wasn't in charge of anything. And there's no shortage of money at my mother's house." She lowered her chin slightly, raised her eyes to his. He always used to melt when she looked at him like that. "Bobby, can you look at me and swear you don't know where my papa is?"

Patrelli refused to meet her eyes. He picked up his fork, jabbed at the mound of cooling scrambled eggs on his plate. "Andrea, please." He put the fork down without eating. "Did you hear any other voices on that tape O'Malley played for you?"

"What difference does that make?"

"Well, you can't be sure O'Malley has Jimmy. You only know O'Malley has a tape of Jimmy's voice—"

"Don't you think I've thought of that? But it's all I've got to go on." A boiling mix of grief and impotence threatened to overflow. "Please. Bobby, please. I just want to talk to my papa." Her voice caught in a sob.

Patrelli got up, came around the table and slid into the booth beside her. He put his arms around her and drew her close. She could feel the heat of his body, the touch of his lips in her hair, hear the murmur of his voice, "Oh, my love, my love." The endearment he had always used with her.

Maggie allowed herself to relax against him. He could tell her what to do, help her shoulder this burden. His body was so familiar, she'd once loved him so much...

But he wasn't Sam, and she was no longer the young girl she had been then. She straightened.

Gently Patrelli pushed the hair from her damp face. He leaned forward to bring his mouth closer to hers and Maggie could feel him trembling. She put a hand against his chest. For the measure of several heartbeats he ignored her resistance, trying to draw her closer.

"Bobby, don't," she said softly. "Please. Don't."

He dropped his arms and stared at her. He looked aimost dazed. He rose, resumed his seat on the other side of the table.

He did not look at her. "Where can I reach you?"

He knew she wasn't coming back to the rectory. "I'll stay with my mother in Port Washington," Maggie said. "We need each other right now. Paul's dead."

"What?"

Quickly she told him what she knew about Paul's death. He listened without asking unnecessary questions as she might have known he would. Once it was thought Bobby would succeed his father, become consigliere to James when James took over as head of the Bellini family, as his father had been consigliere to

Salvatore. But when Bobby chose the priesthood, no one argued. A close member of the family inside the Church of Rome, what could be better? She wasn't sure why he was serving in an impoverished parish, but there had to be a good reason. She was sure of that. She looked at Bobby and suddenly wondered if her father would ever see the result of his princely donations to the church.

"You should come back with me to the rectory," Patrelli said. "With Paul's murder the FBI is going to be all over you out at Port Washington."

"Yes, I know. It will be all right." She picked up her backpack. She had prevailed upon Donnie to give her a replacement for the weapon O'Malley had taken from her, and the weight of the 9mm Smith & Wesson was comforting. She retrieved the envelope she had stowed carefully at the bottom of the bag and placed it on the table in front of him. "Bobby, will you give my papa this letter?"

Patrelli picked up the envelope without speaking. Maggie started to slide out of the booth. "I have to go."

Patrelli looked at her plate of untouched food, then turned to beckon the waitress. "First I want you to eat something." He ordered soup and watched while she ate.

THIRTY

"Hey!" Sam felt the touch of a hand on his shoulder and jerked awake. "Yeah, yeah. What?" He scrambled to his feet. The rain had stopped and a watery moon was making an appearance from behind a scudding cloud cover.

"Mister."

Sam leaned away from the stink of old rags and unwashed flesh. "What do you want?"

The figure moved away a few feet, turned to beckon him. "Gotta come." The voice was that of a woman. Layers of filthy skirts flapped around skinny legs, her feet were lost in enormous sneakers several sizes too large.

Sam reached for his wallet. "Here, you want a crib for the night..." He retrieved a twenty and offered it to her.

The woman shook her head and raised her clenched hand, shaking it at him erratically. He peered at what she held, realized it was one of the photographs he had given Yankee.

"Are you the woman who knows the man in that picture?" He

tried to keep his voice gentle for fear of spooking her. She looked to be on the edge, one of the walking wounded. She ignored his question, if she even heard it. She beckoned again, moving farther away down the alley, looking over her shoulder like a dog wanting him to follow.

"Wait a minute, I can't leave here. You understand?" He glanced at his watch, saw it was three in the morning. Last time he'd looked it had been almost one. In spite of the soaking rain, he'd dozed fitfully, crouched against the wall for over two hours. The old man had no booze with him, Sam thought, he'd made sure of that, so unless Yankee had left to find a way to satisfy his craving, he was still in front of the rectory watching for the no-show priest. He called to the woman, "I can't leave. You come on back here, you can tell me what you want. Don't be frightened, I won't hurt you."

Like a wild animal, she looked poised to flee. It was impossible to tell her age, but the road she'd travelled had been a hard one. "Doc. Doc."

"Doc? What do you mean?"

"Doc," she said again. She waved the photograph clutched in her hand more frantically. "Doc hurt."

She meant Yankee. Sam's heart sank. Old fool must have found a way to get some booze, and he'd fallen, hurt himself. Done it before, he'd do it again. No one's business but his own... Sam brought himself up short. The old man knew this woman, and she knew who it was in that picture.

He glanced at the rectory's garage door. Reluctantly, he asked, "Where is he?" He could see Bellevue in his future, a zoo of an emergency room, a drunken bum, endless forms. As a cop, he'd been down that road more than once.

She beckoned with both hands, agitated now, a rising sound starting from her throat, "Eh, eh, eh, eh..."

Sam raised his hands to soothe her. He spoke in a calm voice. "Okay, it's okay. I'm coming. Where is he?"

She started into a half walk, half run down the alley, looking over her shoulder again to see if Sam was following. When he got too close, her agitation rose, the strange noises starting from her throat, so he dropped back, allowing several yards to remain between them. She set a sharp pace. She was probably not as old as she looked, just buffeted by life. Not too far gone, though, that she couldn't worry about a friend.

Sam followed her out of the alley, south on Pitt, across Delancey. She ducked through a fence, down an embankment, and he realized she was leading him into the darkness beneath the Williamsburg Bridge. He took the Sig from the small of his back, tucked it into his belt in front and felt the reassuring weight of the .22 in the holster on his ankle. Rubble littered the ground: broken bottles, disintegrating cardboard boxes, wheels from God knows what, rusted market baskets, bicycles, remnants of slashed furniture, overturned trash barrels spilling wet ash from ancient fires. Headlights from cars approaching the ramp to the bridge above them reflected off rainwater that had filled the innumerable potholes. The place stank of a stew of garbage and exhaust fumes and moisture.

The woman stopped by a bundle of rags lying in a puddle. This time she stayed where she was until Sam reached her.

A black garbage bag poncho, plastic sacks of aluminum cans. Yankee's precious cargo.

Sam sat on his heels. The old man's watch cap was askew, revealing wispy white hair. Sam put a hand to the stubbled cheek, found the skin cold and clammy. He slipped a hand beneath Yankee's head to feel for a pulse and his fingers slid slickly across the neck. Sam pulled his hand free.

The old man's throat was a gaping wound, the carotid artery severed. Blood had spurted, then pooled darkly, flowing in an uneven pattern around his head.

"Did you see who did this?"

The woman did not answer and Sam looked up. He was alone.

Alone under the Williamsburg Bridge, his hands covered with the blood of a murdered old man whose name he did not know. The woman had brought help as best as she could, then she'd faded back into the terrors that occupied her mind. He wondered if she had witnessed what had happened here.

Careful not to disturb anything—by some remote chance someone might decide to investigate—Sam got to his feet. Without moving he ran his eyes over the immediate area. A headlight swept the scene and he caught a flash of color in the old man's hand. He had fallen onto his side, one arm pinned beneath him. The other was still covered by the garbage bag but the hand was exposed. Sam bent to see what the old man had held on to even in death and realized it was the rich purple of a velvet bag containing a bottle of Chivas Royal Salute. His drink of choice in another life. The big quart size. The bottle Sam had promised to buy him. Tucked into the bag, its edge just showing, was another copy of the photograph Sam had asked him to flash around the neighborhood.

Someone had lured him here, then slit his throat.

Sam raised his head, took a breath of the stinking stagnant air and stared around. What a god-awful place to die. Whoever had done this thought he was safe enough. He'd counted on the fact that no big-city police department had the manpower to waste on solving the murder of one homeless old drunk. Yankee had lived anonymously, and he'd died the same way.

But why? And why now?

Sam looked down at the old man once more, said a silent farewell.

He saw nothing human in the darkness as he left, only the shadow of rats, a few skinny hunting cats. He retraced his steps, ducked through the fence, breathed a sigh of relief when he got into the light and movement of Delancey Street. Outside a market, closed and shuttered against the night, he found a telephone that worked, and dialed 911. While he waited interminably for the operator to answer, he tore the tissues from the small pack in his pocket, worked to clean Yankee's blood from his hands. As soon as he heard a voice, he covered the mouthpiece with the wad of paper and said quickly, "A body under the eastbound ramp to the Williamsburg Bridge."

As he hung up on the operator still asking questions, he realized shreds of tissue were stuck to his skin like soft white feathers. He rubbed them together, rolling the paper into small bloody pellets until they fell away.

Paper was easy, but to clean Yankee's blood off his hands, he would need soap and water—and to catch the old man's killer.

Within minutes Sam was back at Christ the Redeemer. He ran up the front steps of the rectory, rang the bell, banged on the door for emphasis. A light went on in a window above, then another in the foyer.

"What's going on? What's happening?" Father Lachinski, thick white hair standing on end, still tying the belt on a drab plaid robe, peered through a crack between the front door and the frame.

Sam thrust a foot into the space. He felt as if he was seeing the world through a red filter. Blood, rage, fear, exhaustion, he wasn't sure—a combination of them all. "Where's my wife?" As he spoke he knew the words would make no sense to the old priest.

"Your wife? Why would I know that?" Lachinski turned his head to peer down the darkened hall as if Maggie might appear out of the gloom. "She's not here."

"Where's Patrelli?"

"In his bed. In his bed, where else would he be—"

Sam put a shoulder against the door and pushed. "Get him."

"What do you think you're doing? It's the middle of the night. Come back tomorrow."

Sam stepped into the foyer, closed the door behind him. "Get Patrelli out of bed. I want to talk to him."

"I will do no such thing. I'm going to call the police."

"Don't even think about it." Suddenly Sam knew he was losing it. His vision was blurred, his head pounded, the muscles in his belly were in knots. He grabbed Lachinski's arm, dragged the stumbling priest with him as he took the stairs three at a time. He hustled him along the corridor, threw open the first door he came to. A bleak bedroom, icy with disuse. On to the next, the same. Then a room with two votive candles alight in front of a prie-dieu. The bed made up, surfaces dusted. The room had the feeling it had been used recently. A warmth not felt in the previous desolate spaces, maybe a faint perfume, a feminine tinge to the air in a household of celibates. Maybe just his imagination.

Sam stood in the doorway, cut through the incoherent babble of protest pouring from Lachinski's lips. "She was here."

"Well, I told you that. I told you that yesterday, but now I'm telling you that she left."

"Are you alone here?"

Lachinski dropped his glance quickly to Sam's bloodstreaked hands. He started to shake as if buffeted by a high wind. He shook his head. "No. We have a full household."

Sam looked back along the dim corridor. It was cold, lit by forty-watt bulbs. At the far end was a swinging door that looked as if it could lead to another wing of the house. The building was bigger than he'd thought; the church was large and obviously had once been served by more than two priests. Pulling Lachinski with him, he went down the hall, through the swinging door, into a small corridor that felt distinctly warmer than the chilled wing of unused bedrooms they'd just left. At the end a narrow staircase led down, probably into the kitchen area which would account for the warmth.

On his right a door was open. A bedside lamp threw light onto blankets thrown back in haste. Religious pictures hung on every wall, the Black Madonna of Cracow in pride of place. A couple of armchairs, a floor lamp, a table bearing piles of books and magazines, and a telephone half covered by a discarded newspaper.

"That's my room, you have no right to go in there," Lachinski protested. "I just got out of bed to answer the door."

Without releasing his hold on Lachinski's arm, Sam crossed the hall, opened the door of the room diagonally opposite.

It was a monk's cell. Stark-white, a crucifix above a narrow cot. An open breviary, a rosary on a single table beside the bed. No pictures. No furniture. A bare hardwood floor.

"This is Patrelli's room?"

"Yes, of course, but he isn't here." Lachinski sounded astonished.

"I'll wait for him."

"No, you won't. You've got to leave."

Sound drifted faintly up the stairs from the kitchen.

Someone had entered the house from outside. Footsteps crossed a tiled floor, an inside door opened, then closed.

Sam dragged the protesting Lachinski back to his bedroom, crossed the room to a door he'd guessed correctly was a closet, and shoved the struggling priest inside. He turned the old-fashioned key in the lock, dropped the key into his pocket and recrossed the room. He closed the bedroom door behind him, immediately cutting off the frantic drumbeat of the priest's fists against wood.

Sam ran along the corridor, through the swinging doors and took the main stairs down at breakneck speed. Someone had turned off the lights in the foyer. Only the votives in red glass flickered in front of a large Christ figure. A crack of light spilled from beneath a door set in the dark wood paneling.

Sam slammed open the door. Patrelli was leaning over his desk, telephone in hand, saying softly, "Just checking to see you got home—" He turned, shock tightening the muscles around his mouth. He held up a hand as if to stop Sam's advance across the room. His eyes locked on Sam's, he said into the phone, "I've got to go, I have a visitor."

His voice was gentle, reassuring. Not a priest talking to a parishioner. A man talking to a woman.

Maggie. *Maggie.* The name stabbed through Sam's mind like a shooting pain. Son of a bitch was talking to Maggie. *But how could he be? He'd seen Maggie being forced into a car.*

Sam lunged for the phone in Patrelli's hand, but before he could speak, Patrelli put a finger on the rocker and broke the connection. Sam dropped the telephone, grabbed the front of Patrelli's tweed jacket, jerked him forward until the priest's face was inches from his own.

"Where is she?"

Patrelli wrestled at Sam's wrists. "What are you talking about?"

Sam shook him, then drew back his clenched fist. He caught Patrelli's unwavering eyes and suddenly Sam saw himself as if from outside his own body. He topped Patrelli by half a head, outweighed him by forty pounds. He felt like a mastiff shaking the hell out of a terrier. He released his hold, stepped back.

Patrelli moved quickly around his desk out of Sam's range. "Why don't you sit down, Mr. Cady? You look as if you need a drink." He went over to a small discreet bar in the corner of the room. "Scotch okay?"

"Your goombahs have got my wife and my son."

Bottle in hand, Patrelli turned quickly. "No, you're wrong, believe me. The people I know would not harm families. A lot has changed, but not that." He splashed a generous measure of scotch in each of the two glasses, then returned to his desk. He reached across, put a glass in front of Sam. "Water, okay?"

Sam ignored the glass. "So where is she?"

Patrelli sat back in his black leather chair as if exhausted. "I can't tell you that. But I can tell you that she is safe."

"Patrelli, the hell with that. Your goons kidnapped my son, and then they grabbed Andrea Bellini, the woman I know as Maggie Cady, off the street when she came here to negotiate for him. I saw it happen. They certainly don't want ransom money. So you tell me what it is they do want."

"I didn't realize you know who she really is," Patrelli said. "Listen to me. I'm telling you again. This is not a Hollywood movie. The men who took her are not my goombahs, as you call them, and in any case, Andrea is safe. But that's all I can tell you."

Sam took the Sig from the small of his back. He placed both hands on the desk and leaned forward. "Where's my son, Father?"

Patrelli did not look at the gun under Sam's right hand. "I don't know. That's the truth. The people you saw taking Andrea released her a couple of hours later. She's now with her mother. She's safe there."

"*Where,* for God's sake?" Sam raised the Sig, aimed at the middle of Patrelli's forehead.

Patrelli held Sam's eyes. "You're not going to use that on me, Mr. Cady. I know that and you know that. I can't tell you any more."

Sam lowered the weapon. The priest was right, he wasn't going to shoot him. His cop's instinct told him the priest was telling the truth as far as it went. But Patrelli knew more than he was saying. "You have seen her?"

"Yes. She contacted me when she arrived. We grew up as neighbors. I still have connections with certain people, as you saw."

"That was Maggie you were talking to on the phone when I came in." A statement, not a question.

Patrelli stared at him without answering. Sam realized his fingers had tightened around the Sig. He wanted to slam the blank look off the priest's handsome face. "Who were the goons who took her if they weren't your people?"

"An Irish gang, been active in New York for over a hundred years. For the last thirty years they've mainly been into the theft of weapons from the military, selling on the open market. Mostly the IRA, but they deal with anyone who will pay their price."

That explained the car with the New Jersey license plate registered to the Shamrock Corporation. "And they let her go, these thugs? Just like that? Why?"

"I don't know."

"Sure you do. They've got Jimmy and they want something only Maggie can give them. What? What can she deliver to them?"

"I can't tell you any more. Do you understand? Not unless Andrea wants you to know."

"How can she tell me anything if I can't reach her?"

"I don't think she's even aware that you're here in New York."

"I was a cop for twenty years, and she thought I'd stay at home while she went out alone to find our son?" The pain in his gut seemed to deepen as he said the words aloud. Sam reached into a pocket, retrieved the blood-spattered picture he'd taken from Yankee and placed it on the desk. "Who's the man with you?"

Patrelli picked up the picture. "That's Giacomo Bellini."

"Maggie's brother?" The tight fist around Sam's heart loosened its hold. Her brother. Dear God, her brother. Not her lover.

"Called James by everyone but his mother and father. He was my best friend." Patrelli replaced the picture carefully onto the desk.

"He was killed at Bear Mountain Lodge six years ago," Sam said. "As fucked-up an operation as I've ever heard of."

"Yes, that's right. It was. The FBI came in blazing. Of course everyone there was carrying, Irish and Italian, so armed men did what they do when they come under fire. They fired back. A lot of people died that day, including James. Salvatore Bellini died later of wounds. A fuckup, as you say."

"What else do you know? Why was Maggie...Andrea Bellini put into witness protection?"

"You'll have to ask her."

"I'm asking you."

"Someone tried to kill her."

"Who?"

Patrelli shrugged. "The Butcherboys. The Irish. Nothing was ever proved."

"So the FBI stowed her away in witness protection until they could make a case against whoever was left of the Bellini family. Under subpoena she'd be forced to testify when the feds were good and ready."

"That's right. She was on ice until she'd have to testify against her remaining brother, Paul. But that's not going to happen. Paul Bellini's body was discovered yesterday morning. He'd been dead for several days."

"Oh, Jesus," Sam said. "And she's alone out there dealing with these killers?" He felt a kind of fear he'd never experienced before rising in his body. "What do they want?"

"That's what Andrea is trying to find out."

"And you let her? Jesus, man, what's the matter with you? She can't deal with killers. She can't do this alone, she's got to have help. I've got to see her—" He stopped as a thought struck him. The newspaper report he read said the FBI had been refused entry to the Bellini family home in Port Washington. How difficult could that be to find?

"I can tell her that you're here and you want to see her. Let her decide what she wants." Patrelli looked at his watch, then rose to his feet. "I'm sorry, Sam, it's time for the early mass. I must go."

Sam. So now they were pals. Sam said, "Call her now, before you leave."

"Sam, let her rest. Please, it's very early. She hasn't slept since she got here."

How do you know that, buddy? Sam thought. You been sleeping in the same room? He shook his head—God, what was happening to him? He was turning into something he'd never been.

"You're right. I'll be back here." Sam looked at his watch. "Ten, okay? That will give her a few hours' sleep." And time for him to get out to Port Washington. He shoved the Sig into his belt at the small of his back. "Don't disappear again, Bob. Not if you want me to believe we're on the same side."

He opened the door, stood back to allow Patrelli to precede him into the foyer. Patrelli almost stumbled over Mrs. Grotka, the housekeeper, a hand about to knock on the door, tray balanced on a raised knee.

"Father, I thought you might need coffee...." Her voice trailed away as she saw Sam. "Oh, you here."

"Thank you, Mrs. Grotka, but I'm serving mass this morning," Patrelli said.

"But I thought—" Mrs. Grotka started to say at the same time the priest said, "Sam, you want some breakfast before you leave?"

"No, thanks." Suddenly Sam thought of being on the street with Yankee's blood on his hands. "I'd like to use the bathroom, though."

"Mrs. Grotka will show you. I'll see you back here around ten." Patrelli started up the stairs and turned when Sam called to him.

Sam tossed him the key from his pocket. "Check Lachinski's closet. I locked him in. Just make sure he doesn't make any calls."

Alarm flitted across Patrelli's face, but he nodded. "Don't worry." He ran up the stairs, disappeared through the swinging door.

"Come. You eat," Mrs. Grotka said. "I feed old man. I feed you, too."

With an effort Sam smiled at her. "Outside on the steps?"

A lift of the lips that could have been a smile was gone before Sam was sure. "In kitchen."

"Okay, thanks. Maybe some coffee." He looked around. "You got a cloakroom close by?"

Mrs. Grotka pointed to a door, then started down the hall to the kitchen. "You wash face, then eat."

Sam locked the door behind him, then turned on the water, let the faucet run until it was as hot as he could stand it. He held his hands under the flow and watched water pink with Yankee's blood swirl down the drain. A mirror above the sink reflected a face he hardly recognized. Bruised, streaked with dirt, a grizzled stubble. He looked like hell. As soon as the water ran clear, he soaped, cleaned under his nails as best he could, and scrubbed at the blood on the sleeve of his windbreaker, but it was a lost cause, as were his filth-spattered chinos. He soaped his hands again, washed his face, and dried it on shredding paper towels. God, he thought, he was tired. He used the john, washed his hands again, then opened the door. Mrs. Grotka beckoned from the kitchen and Sam went toward her.

She put a plate in front of him loaded with ham, three eggs, a pile of thick slices of fried bread. She poured coffee. "So, you eat."

Her back to him, Mrs. Grotka busied herself at the sink while he ate. The bread had been crisped in bacon fat and was delicious. In a few minutes his plate was empty. He put down his knife and fork and sighed.

Mrs. Grotka turned. She refilled his coffee cup with a brew that was nothing like Aunt Pellie's but nothing like Bernie's, either. "You eat more?" she asked.

Sam held up his hands in surrender. "No, thanks. It was very good, but I've eaten enough for three people already. Thank you."

Mrs. Grotka stood uncertainly. The coffeepot was shaking in her hand. "Your wife," she said.

Sam looked up at her.

"I had daughter before, in my country," Mrs. Grotka said. "Same like your wife. Not now."

Her voice strangled and Sam nodded, giving her a moment to recover.

"I saw your wife through window. Men take her, and she struggle hard. You find her, be good man to her."

Sam felt his eyes start to burn. The pain around his heart where Maggie was began to throb. "Yes, I will."

Mrs. Grotka picked up the plate, and Sam stood. "Thanks."

She nodded and opened the door that led outside to the basement steps where he'd first seen Yankee. He thought about telling her the old man would not be coming around anymore, but knew he couldn't risk it. She'd find that out soon enough.

He climbed the steps slowly, heard the door close as he realized he needed a phone book to find the nearest car rental to get out to Port Washington. He couldn't bring himself to go back and knock again.

The storm that had hovered over the city for the past couple of days had passed, and the air felt fresh and cool. The neon sign over Bernie's had been switched on, and Sam crossed the street, pushed open the door.

He took in the broad figures of two uniformed cops, notebooks in hand, talking to the counterman. Bernie looked up as the door opened and one glance at the man's face told Sam he was going to start yelling.

"There he is. That's the guy. That's the guy left here with him last night."

Sam let go of the door, turned, started back up the street. He felt the weight of the Sig in his belt, the holstered .22 strapped to his ankle.

"Police! Stop right there."

Sam heard pounding feet behind him. For a brief second, he thought of making a run, but knew that would mean certain death from a police bullet. He turned, his hands spread so that the cops could see he was holding them well away from his body.

THIRTY-ONE

Sam watched from beneath his eyelids and kept his back pressed into the corner. At processing they'd taken his watch, as well as everything else, so he wasn't sure how long he'd been there, but certainly long enough for them to have checked his driver's license, pilot's license, credit cards, library card and everything else in his wallet. Long enough to run his weapons through the system. And for sure long enough to have found that he was wanted for the murder of three men in the state of Louisiana.

The muscles in his legs twitched with fatigue, but he couldn't take the chance of squatting on his heels in case he had to come up fast. Four of the five men sharing the cage had been there when he was thrown in with them. They were young, black, tough, bored, and getting jumpy coming down from whatever it was they'd taken to go up. They'd been sliding glances his way for some time, sounding off to each other in a New York version of a Southern accent. Now they'd started to jostle and jive, get in his face.

Pretty soon he'd have to respond or they'd be all over him.

"Hey, peckerwood." The black cop who'd put the cuffs on him outside Bernie's leaned against the bars of the cage. "Get your sorry ass over here."

Relieved, Sam said, "You talking to me?"

The cop made a show of looking around. "You see any other peckerwoods here?"

Sam came off the wall protecting his back and started toward the gate. The gangbangers stood their ground, barring his way, and the cop ran his baton along the bars.

"Back off, scumbags," he said. "Let Mr. Wonderful through here."

"Hey, cappie," one shouted. "What you got this old white man for? Fucking his dead mama?" Everyone laughed, did high and low fives, tapped knuckles.

"Ain't that what we got you for, nigger?" the black cop said. "Back off."

"Hey, who you calling nigger, that's racist shit, man, you got no right—"

"Yeah, so sue the city." The door slid open just wide enough for the cop to grasp Sam's arm and pull him through. The mechanism grabbed and the door slid back into place. The cop gave Sam a push to start him down the corridor.

"You're letting me go, right?" Sam asked. "It was all a mistake."

"You're the mistake, peckerwood. Guys like you give good cops a bad name."

"I'm not a cop."

"Got that right." The man opened a door, shoved Sam through, closed it behind him.

The room was small, empty except for a table, four chairs and a tall figure, who had his back to the room, taking in the view of a parking lot outside the barred window. Without turning, the man said, "Looks like you've got yourself a whole load of trouble here, Sam."

The voice snapped Sam's memory. He stood as if rooted, suddenly sick with a mix of hope and fear. "You've found my son?"

Special Agent Adashek turned. He pulled a chair away from the table. "Sit down."

Somehow Sam reached the chair and sat. He looked at his hands. They were shaking, and he put them on his knees, out of sight. "You've found something about Jimmy?" At least his voice did not waver.

Adashek took a seat with his back to the window. "We're still working on it, Sam. It takes time. Right now you should be looking at your other problems. For a start, you're wanted for killing three men in New Orleans, as I'm sure your friends in the department have told you. Now a harmless old drunk gets his throat cut under the Williamsburg Bridge in New York City. Look at yourself, blood and muck all over, and it turns out you were the man seen with him just a few hours earlier. What the hell is going on?"

"You tell me. I didn't kill the old man, I just found his body, and I sure didn't kill anyone in New Orleans. You already know that."

"How you figure, Sam?"

"Adashek, my son is missing. You think I care about anything else? Who's working that? It's sure not you, is it?"

"Tell me about the killings in New Orleans."

Sam knew it was in his, in Jimmy's, best interest to play along. "What's to tell? Any half-assed scene-of-crime unit could see that the shot that blew George Menton's head apart came through the window from outside. His brains landed up in his bookcase, for God's sake. The crime scene people can also tell you that the other shooter had his head blown off from the street to his left. The casings from my Sig will be found behind the Dumpster halfway up the alley to the parking lot. Whoever capped them did the clerk because he was a witness. My misfortune was to be upstairs talking to George Menton when the shot came through the window."

Adashek's mouth turned down doubtfully. "Sam, you've not

been thinking straight. You dug yourself into a hole when you ran in New Orleans, and dug it deeper when you wouldn't talk to us here in New York. I tried. I sent men to your hotel but you ran again. That sounds to me a whole lot like a man who's got something to hide. Now I could have you shipped back to Louisiana, let you sort it out there. Or..." He let the word hang in the air for a second before continuing. "Or we can talk now."

"Sure, okay, talk," Sam said. "But don't blow smoke, Steve. I've seen the old newspaper reports of the Bellini mess that went down six years ago. I know who Maggie is, and I know you're with the FBI's organized crime unit."

"That's no secret, Sam."

"So how come no one remembered to mention it to me?"

"I just happened to be in New Orleans for a conference, and tagged along to see if I could help out. Do you think that was the time for it? Child gone, parents half out of their minds?"

"If you knew who my wife was, then who else knew? I thought no one could penetrate the witness protection shield. I thought that was the point of it."

"You knew, for one."

"No, I didn't. She kept her secrets from me." Sam wondered if Adashek picked up on the bitterness he felt.

"So how did you arrive at U.S. Marshall George Menton's insurance office, Sam? Don't tell me it was a lucky guess."

"She'd called a number from a phone at the drugstore near our home, I followed that trail." He did not explain how he got the number. Adashek would know that Pete le Pont was his ears and eyes in the department. "It led me to Menton's insurance office. The rest of what I know I found in old newspapers here in New York. You haven't answered my question. Who else knew about Maggie?"

The FBI man held Sam's eyes. "I don't know the answer to that question, and if I did, I wouldn't give it to you. You've been law enforcement, Sam, you know everything's on a need-to-know basis, nothing's sacred. Okay? Now, you want to listen to what I've got to say, or shall I get on with the paperwork that gets you shipped back to New Orleans? That is if the NYPD will let you go after you've been arraigned for the murder of the old man."

Sam took a beat, picturing that desolate scene of loneliness and filth and blood. "You here because he was one of yours?"

"I'm here because you're here."

"An old drunk hangs around a church with a mobbed-up priest then just happens to get his throat cut? What do you think, Steve? Someone knock him off for his fortune in soda cans?"

Adashek shrugged. "The streets are tough."

"I'm guessing he was one of your snitches and it got him killed."

"It's a theory. But I figure he saw something or somebody he shouldn't have."

Sam snorted with impatience. "Where the hell are you guys hiding? Maggie's snatched off the street right in front of the church, an old drunk's killed, and you don't seem to know what the hell's going on."

"What makes you think that?"

Sam shook his head in disbelief. "My wife's dragged into a car at gunpoint, I fire a weapon on a public street, she disappears and I'm left standing there? What does that say?"

"Not what you're hearing. Maggie's carrying the weight here. The last thing she needs is to be distracted by having you in jail for murder. The people who picked her up are extremely dangerous and they've got your son."

Sam wanted to hurl himself across the table, grab the fed by the throat and start shaking. "Well, I figured that out for myself, Adashek. You're the FBI, you're supposed to be on top of this. If you know who they are, where they are, why the hell aren't you out there taking them down?"

"Because we can't afford a mistake. There's a lot more going on here, and like you I can make a lot of wild guesses. I'm close, but I don't know anything for sure. Not yet." Adashek rose to his feet, went over to the window, looked out at the parking lot. He came back, turned his chair around and straddled it. "Let me tell you what I do know. A few weeks ago, a mortician name of Aldo Ricci was found murdered in his own mortuary. Like the old man, his throat was sliced to the bone. But Aldo also had his tongue cut out. Before he was killed." Adashek paused for effect.

Sam stared at him without comment.

"Friend Aldo was the undertaker who took care of the Bellini family, the embalmings, the funerals. Now a couple days ago the only surviving Bellini son, Paolo, was found dead in a love nest he kept on the Upper East Side. He'd been dead for some time and he died hard, Sam. Someone sure as hell wanted to get some information out of him. You see where I'm going here?"

"What makes you think he didn't spill what they, whoever 'they' are, wanted to know?"

"Educated guess. He kept his tongue in his head for a start. Of course, we had to pull his balls out of his mouth to make sure his tongue was still there, but my guess is he was his father's son at the end. Died with his secrets intact. His boyfriend died, too, by the way. Mobsters usually don't approve of gays. Homosexuality offends their moral code."

Sam didn't reply. That wasn't news.

"A woman, who claimed to be Paolo's sister, found the bodies," Adashek said. "Unfortunately, she disappeared before we could talk to her, but the description we got from the doorman of Paul's building fits Andrea Bellini. Your Maggie Cady. And that brings me to the rest of your family, Sam. Specifically, to your father-in-law."

His father-in-law? *His father-in-law?* A light went on. "You think Sal Bellini's still alive," he said slowly.

Adashek made a gun out of the first two fingers of his right hand, pointed at Sam and clicked his tongue.

"You son of a bitch! You're using her for bait!" Sam got to

his feet, circled his chair, grabbed the back of it to prevent himself from jumping at the man on the other side of the table. "You know where the old man's buried. Get an exhumation order."

"The Bellinis would fight it, and they've still got some powerful friends. Besides, it would take too long. No, what we need is someone inside the family working with us."

"What about my son? What about Maggie? Jesus Christ! My family's missing and you're sitting there trying to get me to help you chase down a dead mobster?"

"Oh, he's alive, Sam. You can put money on it." Adashek drummed his fingers quietly on the back of his chair as if considering his next words. "And I'm not sure that he's not behind Jimmy's disappearance."

"Oh, man. Oh, man. Come on."

"Sit down, Sam." Adashek took his time considering his next words, waiting for Sam to sit before he spoke again. "Now, we've got the best team possible trying to find your boy, and of course we'll go on trying, no matter what happens here between us. But some cooperation on your part would sure hurry things along."

The knot in Sam's gut tightened. Every passing hour lessened Jimmy's chances. "Is this a threat, Steve?"

"No. No, of course not. The way I see it, I'm helping you get your priorities straight. Want to hear what I have to say?"

Sam crossed four lanes of traffic on the Long Island Expressway, took the off-ramp, turned onto the highway that would take him to Port Washington. He checked the surrounding traffic by instinct while his thoughts were occupied with the interview with Adashek. Like every FBI agent Sam had ever worked with, the guy held his cards so tight to his vest he could barely see them himself, and then never the full hand. How in God's name could Bellini, if he was alive, be involved in the murder of his own son and the kidnapping of his grandson? And why? Adashek had refused to elaborate. That information was for the organized crime unit only.

Sam found the lane he was looking for, a tunnel of trees turning every shade of yellow, brown, scarlet, russet and smelling of autumn. A neighborhood of high walls and large houses that were occasionally visible at the end of long driveways. Only one parked car, seriously out of place in the carefully natural landscape, its wheels on the grass shoulder so as not to impede traffic. He slowed, keeping his eyes on the rearview mirror when he passed. Two men, front seat. Short hair, dark suits, white shirts, same guys who'd come after him at the hotel. They might just as well have a decal on the side panel: Official FBI Surveillance Vehicle.

He glanced at the address he'd jotted in his notebook in the car rental office, then leaned across the seat to make out the discreet numbers nestled amidst Virginia creepers or hung on fancy iron gates. No curbs here for slapped-on, painted numbers, easy to read. He slowed, turned into the driveway that matched the address in his hand, stopped in front of a pair of closed black metal gates tipped in gold. A keypad was mounted on a stone pillar within arm's reach, and he leaned out of the window of the rented BMW and put a finger on the button marked *Press*.

A buzz of static, then a male voice said, "Yeah?"

"Name's Sam Cady," Sam said. "I'd like to see Maggie Cady, please. Or maybe I should say Andrea Bellini."

A moment of silence, then, "No one here by that name. Beat it." The voice and the static went dead.

Sam jabbed the button three, four times. No one answered. Somewhere on the other side of the wall he could hear dogs. Deep-chested howls sounded as if they came from the hounds of the Baskervilles. He leaned his finger heavily on the word *Press* and kept it there. There was a buzz of static as the line opened. A woman's voice said, "Who are you?"

She had an accent, Italian or Sicilian. He said, "Sam Cady. I'm Maggie Cady's husband. Jimmy Cady's father."

He heard the male voice in the background arguing, then the

mike went dead and the gates started to swing open. He eased the BMW through, the gates closed behind him. Through the open window of the car he could hear the dogs working themselves into some kind of frenzy. That and the caw of crows in the trees that lined the driveway up to the house were the only sounds. A mist was hovering around ground level, and the air smelled as if they were close to open water. He swung into the graveled forecourt and stopped in front of the pale stone two-storey house.

One side of the double front doors was open, a large figure filling the space. Sam got out of the car, walked toward him. When he was within six feet, the man jerked his chin.

"Far enough. Spread 'em."

Sam stopped, legs apart, arms held away from his body.

"I'm not armed," he said. Both his weapons, returned to him by Adashek, were locked in the glove compartment of the BMW. Without answering, the bodyguard ran his hands expertly over Sam's upper body then checked each leg carefully. Satisfied, he stood back. Sam entered the house, taking in the rack of weapons just inside the door.

"Over here." The bodyguard led the way across a foyer—curved stairs to the upper floors to the left—through a pair of doors. The room was large. Sam had the impression everything was pale—furniture, couches, pillows—but his eyes went to the woman standing in front of the fire. *This was how Maggie would look in thirty years.* She had the same dark, almond-shaped eyes, the perfect oval face. Thinner than Maggie and taller, dressed entirely in black, trousers, sweater, loafers. Her only jewelry was the gold in her ears and a gold watch.

"He's clean," the bodyguard said, and Sam was suddenly aware of his disheveled appearance. Unshaven, no shower, the stink of the jailhouse still on him. He needed a toothbrush.

Bianca nodded. She made no apology for the unusual reception. She looked as if she hadn't slept for days.

"Come in, Sam." She did not ask him to sit.

"Thanks for seeing me." He glanced around the room. "Is this room swept?"

Bianca Bellini shrugged, then looked at the man by the door. "Donnie, turn on some music."

Donnie opened a large cabinet revealing a music system. Sound filled the room and Sam moved closer to her so that she could hear him over a soaring orchestra. "Mrs. Bellini. Bianca. You know who I am?"

She nodded and Sam realized she and her daughter had never been out of touch. Another secret Maggie had kept. "Is Andrea here with you?"

She shook her head. "No. She is not here."

"She has been here?"

She stared at him, neither agreeing nor disagreeing, simply waiting for what came next.

"You know that Jimmy, our little boy, was kidnapped on Sunday morning."

The skin around her eyes tightened, but she held the same impassive stare.

"Maggie...Andrea left our home in New Orleans a couple of hours later. She left me a note telling me not to follow her. I realize now that she guessed who had taken our boy and thought it would be safer for everyone if she dealt with them directly. But she's alone and she's dealing with killers. I'm afraid for her. You should be, too." He stopped, considering whether he would gain anything by telling her that the FBI believed her husband was still alive and that Bellini was behind the murder of her son, the kidnapping of her grandson. He said, "I am sorry about your son Paul's death. But if you know anything that can help Andrea, help me, to find our son Jimmy, I beg you to tell me."

Bianca Bellini's voice was low, the accent heavy. "I know nothing. The FBI has been here already. Did they send you here?"

"No. Did they ask you about my son?"

She kept her eyes on him, watchful and steady. "No. How did you know about Paolo?"

"It's in all the newspapers." He hadn't seen the newspapers, but it was a reasonable guess.

"How did you know who we are? Andrea would not tell you this."

"I read the old newspaper accounts of what happened at Bear Mountain Lodge six years ago. That's how I found out my wife Maggie Cady was also Andrea Bellini. The papers said you lived in Port Washington. It wasn't difficult to find you."

"I do not know where my daughter is."

Sam stepped a little closer. "I think you do. Bianca, I know every instinct you have, everything you have learned in your life, warns you not to know anything, not to trust anyone. But I beg you to put that aside. Please. Think of Jimmy now. He's four and he is your grandson, and he's alone somewhere in danger and he's frightened. We have to move fast if we are going to get him back alive. Every day, every hour, lessens his chances of surviving. Please, help me find my wife so I can help her find our son."

She had tensed when Sam said the word *grandson*. The silence in the room throbbed, and Sam allowed it to deepen. He looked through the tall casement window into the garden. The mist was heavier, giving an air of mystery to the faint outline of what looked like a distant boathouse and dock. The garden must end at the water.

"Sam."

He turned back to her.

"I think Andrea fears for you, too. She knows you are wanted for murder." Bianca held her chin high as if challenging him to judge the men of her family. "When she comes back, I will tell her you are here in New York."

"Where is she now? Is she with Father Patrelli?"

"I do not know."

With an effort, Sam kept his voice calm and unthreatening. "Tell her she doesn't need to worry about me. I am not going to be arrested for murder. I can explain everything to her if only I can see her."

Bianca regarded him through dark eyes so much like Maggie's. "You had an appointment with Father Patrelli today. But maybe you had another, more important appointment. Maybe with the FBI."

He wasn't surprised that she knew about his meeting with Patrelli. If he said now that he'd been in jail, she'd know instantly he'd made a deal to get free. "No, not the FBI. I thought I had another lead on finding my wife but I was wrong."

Bianca Bellini shrugged, the expression in her dark eyes showing that she knew he was lying, and said, "Donnie, make sure the dogs are locked up. Sam's leaving. Goodbye, Sam."

"Wait a minute—" Sam started to put a hand in his pocket. Donnie moved faster than his bulk would seem to permit. Sam felt the grip of hard fingers on his elbow, and he froze. The last thing he wanted was violence here, in Maggie's family home. "It's okay, Donnie," he said. "It's a notebook."

Donnie said, "Slowly."

Sam withdrew his hand from his pocket, held up the small pad. "I'll leave my cell phone number with you, Bianca. Talk to Maggie...Andrea and call me. Use it any time." It was the only way she would be able to reach him. Sam scribbled the number, and handed it to her. She nodded, then looked at Donnie. Without a word, Donnie started to herd him to the door. He did not resist.

Outside, the henchman got into the passenger seat of the BMW and Sam said, "No need. I'm really leaving."

"Yeah, you are."

Sam drove down the drive. The gates opened, Donnie got out, waited until Sam drove through and the gates had closed behind him. As Sam turned the car to retrace the route he'd driven from the Expressway, he saw Donnie watching through the bars of the gates to make sure he left.

As soon as the man was out of sight Sam pulled over to the grass shoulder and scanned the road in both directions, but the Official Federal Surveillance Vehicle was gone.

He reached for his mobile, tapped out a number. Time was running out; he no longer had the luxury of being able to race around searching for anonymous pay phones. He had to stay put, gamble that no one would pick up on his call, gamble that Maggie would return home to her mother from wherever she had gone and not back to the rectory. He gave Petey's name to the voice that answered, and waited to be transferred.

"Le Pont," the familiar voice growled in his ear.

"Hey, Pierre," Sam said.

"How you doing, buddy?" Petey's voice was lower, closer to the phone.

Sam waited for him to say he had something on Jimmy. He didn't and the forlorn little hope flickered and died. He thought suddenly his fucking heart was going to break behind all this.

"I've seen Special Agent Adashek," Sam said.

"The hell you did. He see you?"

"He sprung me from jail."

"Jail? What the hell you doing in jail, bubba?"

Quickly he filled Petey in on what had happened. The murder of the old man, his arrest, Adashek's surprise appearance.

"He knows I didn't kill those guys in New Orleans. He doesn't give a shit about a liquor store clerk or George Menton. Adashek's organized crime all the way, Pete. A one-note operator. He thinks Sal Bellini is still alive. He says he thinks Sal may even have ordered Jimmy's kidnapping."

"Christ on a crutch," Petey said. "How'd he get to that?"

Sam gave him a brief rundown of the murders of Aldo Ricci and Paul Bellini, the torture and mutilations.

"So my son is the only male left in the family," he said. "Adashek's a tough operator, and you can bet he knows more than he's telling."

Petey was silent for a moment. Then he said, "Sure sounds like he's got a case for the man being alive. If he's right and he can bring Sal in, the sky's the limit for his career. He'll go straight to the top of the heap. But killing his own son? Even in the mob, that's a stretch."

"No, I can believe it. The guy was gay, lived the life. He had no male heir, no intention of getting one. The old man could have felt it was a stain on his honor or some such old-time bullshit and suddenly decided he couldn't live with it anymore. I don't know, Pete. It's all connected somehow, Jimmy, the killings." He was thinking aloud, tossing out ideas as he and Pete used to do on the cases they worked together to see if anything stuck. "Or maybe the Irish from the Bear Mountain fiasco picked up a rumor and they went after Paul Bellini. He died without giving them anything, so they came for Jimmy."

"Sam, that doesn't hold water, buddy." Petey's voice was unusually gentle, as if talking to a wounded man. "Maggie was in federal protection. No one could find her."

"That's a crock, Petey. The WPP's porous, the FBI can get in there any time they want. Everything's on a need-to-know basis. They're probably listening to this conversation right now. Tap on your phone, mine, who the hell knows?"

"Hey, I'm NOPD." Le Pont sounded outraged.

"Yeah, well, we're talking organized crime here."

The sound of an approaching car caught Sam's attention and he turned. Driving toward him was a Lincoln Town Car, same make, same model as the one used when Maggie was snatched. Petey was still speaking, and Sam said, "Hold on a minute, Pete. I got company."

As the car closed in, he checked the plates, saw that the number was different, but he'd bet it was registered to the Shamrock

Hotel and Casino, Atlantic City. Even though he'd never seen them before, the men inside were familiar. Generic hoods. Both young, slicked hair, open collars spread over leather jackets, stiff faces making a big point of not looking in his direction. Completely out of place in this neighborhood. Sam reached into the glove compartment for the Sig, put it in his lap.

"Same bunch that took Maggie. Petey, are you there?"

"I'm here, buddy. You okay?"

"Yeah, they're driving past." He kept them in sight until they disappeared at the end of the lane, the turn signal blinking as they took a right. "Okay, Pete, they've cruised on down the road."

"Better watch yourself."

"Yeah. It's okay."

"So listen to this," Pete said. "Maggie goes on that retreat alone, twice a year, right? She meets her mother there. Someone follows the mother to the monastery, picks up Maggie."

"Yeah, sounds about right. But remember that FBI situation in Beantown in the eighties? The whole Boston field office was in bed with the Irish mob. If the WPP is open to whoever needs a look, it could be there's a leak from somewhere inside the Bureau, someone who's gotten too chummy with the New York Irish. It's strange that Adashek's always alone when I see him, strictly against FBI regulations, feds move around in pairs. Could be he's shoving Sal in my face because he can't trust his own people."

Petey grunted. "Maybe. He sure didn't spring you out of the goodness of his heart. What's he want?"

"I cooperate from inside the Bellini family, or the team working Jimmy finds its resources limited by other pressures." He kept his eyes on the road as he spoke. A car passed the tee junction at the end of the lane, too far away for him to see what it was. "Maybe O'Malley has done what the feds couldn't do. He discovered Bellini is alive and he's using Jimmy as bait."

"Adashek said that?"

"Not exactly, but that's the message I'm supposed to hear. What he said was he figures with her contacts inside, Maggie's going to find the old man faster than the feds can. I get to Maggie, she tells me where he is, I lead the feds in. Way I figure it, Jimmy's the bait, and Maggie's the hook to bring the old man out. As soon as Adashek gets what he wants, he gives the word and they pour everything they've got into finding Jimmy."

"Son of a bitch!" Petey said. He sounded as if he wanted to start slamming heads.

"They're making sure I'm on target. The only FBI I've seen so far are the guys who tried to take me at the hotel. Today, they're practically waving a flag. Between feds and Irish, they've got their work cut out trying not to bump into each other. All we need is the Italians to show up." Sam turned to examine the street again, but he was still alone. "At least the feds will be keeping a tail on Maggie, as well."

"*Bonne chance.* I guarantee she learned to spot a tail in her baby buggy." There was a breath of silence as if Petey realized what his words implied. Quickly he said, "Hell, man, she'll be out of practice by now, and they'll slap a bug on her car, anyway. Don't worry, the feds won't let anything happen to her."

Sam nodded as if Petey could see him. "Yes, sure. Pete, can you find out if the murder warrants are still out? Adashek said they'd be withdrawn. I want to know if he came through on that." Sam heard himself give voice to his deepest fear. "I've got a pain in my gut tells me things have shifted too far, Pete. This is not about Jimmy anymore. This is mob all the way, and Jimmy's getting lost."

Something Petey had said niggled at him, but he couldn't put his finger on it. It would come back. He said his goodbyes and disconnected.

THIRTY-TWO

Maggie stared at the letter on the kitchen table. Her father had not even opened it. She had driven to the rectory to wait, thinking she would save time when Bobby came to take her to him. She had parked in the alley behind the church but, to avoid running into the other priest, Father Lachinski, she'd entered through the basement door into the kitchen.

"Let me drive you home," Bobby Patrelli said again.

"Just tell me where I can find my father, Bobby. That's all I want from you." Maggie looked at him. "A child of four, or a man with blood on his hands. What makes you so sure of your choice?"

He was silent and Maggie said, "Go away."

"Andrea, please."

Mrs. Grotka murmured in Ukrainian and twitched the shawl she had wrapped around Maggie's shoulders. "Father Bobby, maybe better you go now."

Maggie heard the door close but did not raise her head. The

spasmodic shivering had slowed, and her brain was beginning to function again. *It was 3:30 when Bobby had called to make sure she'd got home to Port Washington safely. Say he slept a few hours until daylight, then delivered the letter and returned to the rectory. It was now eleven. Her father had to be within a two-hour drive from the city, maybe, allowing for traffic, even less.*

Maggie looked around for her backpack, then remembered she had left it in Patrelli's study when she had gone to see if he'd returned. She started to her feet.

Mrs. Grotka put a hand on her shoulder and tried to ease her back into the chair. "What you do? Wait, wait—"

"No, I have to go."

"Your husband, he come for you."

"Oh, God, I wish, Mrs. Grotka. No, he's not here."

"Yes. Yesterday morning. Today, this morning. He is here. Looking for you. You stay now, wait for him, he find you here."

She looked at the housekeeper, stunned. "Sam? Sam's been here? Where did he go?"

Mrs. Grotka shook her head, shrugged helplessly. "He spend time with Father Patrelli, then he eat, here," she gestured to the table, "in this kitchen. Then he leave. Now, you wait. You go walking around, he never find you."

Maggie shook off the shawl, crossed the kitchen, ran along the corridor. She burst into Patrelli's study. It was empty. She stopped for a moment, her eyes on the stylized cross behind the desk, then realized where he had gone. She opened the front door, ran down the steps to the street. The wooden door to the church was unlocked, and Maggie pushed it open.

The interior was dim and cold. She had loved this church. Once it had been richly decorated, a beacon of their faith for immigrants facing an uncertain future, the only sure place in an unknown world. Now the gold was cracked and flaking, the brilliance of the blues and crimsons faded, the stone floors chipped. The last time she had been here, her brother James was alive, and her only fear was that her father would be angry with her for marrying a priest who would refuse his final vows for her sake. How young she had been. She had not even given thought to the enormous donations her father was making to the church, his ambition for Bobby.

The gray stone walls, the roof arching over the icy space threw back the sound of her footsteps as she walked the length of the nave. She stopped, looked down at the silent kneeling figure.

"Why didn't you tell me my husband had been here?" She chose her words deliberately.

Patrelli looked up. He rewound the rosary beads dangling from his fingers, and dropped them into a pocket as he got to his feet. "I'm sorry. I was going to. I knew you would have to go to your father alone and I thought it would be easier for you if I told you after you had seen him."

"Where is Sam now?"

"I don't know. We arranged that he would return this morning but I wasn't here. I was delivering..." He shrugged. "In any case, Mrs. Grotka says he didn't arrive."

"Oh, Bobby. How can you do this?"

He shook his head. His normally vital face had lost all life. "Andrea, I took a vow—"

"The hell with your vows."

She turned, left the church. He did not follow her.

She made her way back to the rectory, the edges of her pain less jagged. Sam was here, looking for her. She murmured a silent prayer for his safety, but she couldn't wait around for him to find her. Not while Jimmy was being held by a monster.

She went back to the questions she had started to ask herself. *Where in the city? Who would know where Salvatore Bellini was hiding?*

Like a flash of lightning splitting the dense night sky, the thought came: *Who else but his* paisano?

The door to Patrelli's study was open as she'd left it, and she went in, picked up her backpack.

She was halfway out of the door when the phone on the desk rang. Her heart pounded. Sam, she thought. She stared at the phone, listened to it ring, then heard Mrs. Grotka's voice answering in the kitchen.

"She is not here—"

Maggie raced back to the desk, snatched up the phone. "Sam?"

"Hey, babe," O'Malley's voice said. "You're still there. Thought you might be home by now."

The room seemed to close in, and Maggie grabbed for the desk to keep her bearings. "Jimmy? Is Jimmy all right? I have to talk to him—"

"Now what kind of greeting is that?" O'Malley interrupted. "How about, 'Hey, Mike, how you doing?' Or 'Hey, Mike, how'd you know I was hanging out with my boyfriend Patrelli?' Or even, 'Hey, Mike, how the fuck's old Tim?' You shot the poor bastard, after all. He could have turned gangrene or something. Gunshot wounds can be fucking dangerous—"

"Please, O'Malley, don't do this. I want to talk to my son—"

"You got any sense, babe, what you want is to give me what I want. How you coming on that little problem?"

"First let me talk to my son."

His voice hardened. "I said, what's happening with Sal?"

"I'm close, really close." Holy Mother, she prayed, let him believe me.

"Not good enough," O'Malley said. "I got a problem here, know what I mean? You've had twenty-four hours and I got zilch. Time's running out, babe, and my fucking patience with it."

"O'Malley—"

"My guy with the chain saw don't like kids much, did I tell

you that? Likes cats, funny how people are. Me, I like dogs. Rott-weilers are good. Hey, that's right, we got that in common. You had a Rottweiler down there in New Orleans. Heard about that." He laughed.

Maggie felt the breath catch noisily in her throat as she stifled a sob of terror.

"Don't start up, you know I fucking hate that crying shit," O'Malley shouted. He blew out a loud breath as if to calm himself. "Tell you what. I'm a father, I know how losing kids can get you upset. I'll give you another twelve hours. It's eleven, now, right? So you got till eleven tonight. Don't worry, we'll start with the little bits, fingers, toes, stuff like that. Bits he won't miss. Tick, tock, honey. Clock's running."

Suddenly, her mind had the sharp uncompromising clarity of an ice field. For a second, she wondered if she would ever be able to get herself back when this was over and Jimmy was safe. Then she said, "I have to have a phone number where I can reach you."

"Okay." He rattled off a number. "Don't bother trying to trace it, you never will. It bounces all over hell and gone, modern military technology, know what I mean? I'll be waiting, so don't disappoint me now. Hey, just a minute, don't hang up. I got something for you." A little voice said, "Mommy, Mommy, I want to go home—" then O'Malley said, "How's that for a bit of good faith?"

"Jimmy? Oh, sweet boy." Maggie held the phone with both hands but she heard no response. "Jimmy? Jimmy? O'Malley, please, let me talk to him." But she realized she was talking to dead air. He was gone.

And she wasn't even sure whether that had been Jimmy, or the recording O'Malley had played before. Or even whether her beautiful boy was still alive.

She paid off the cab outside the cardinal's residence on 54th Street—in case someone still cared about tailing her, she'd left her own car in plain view in the alley behind the rectory—and took a moment to look up at the building that was the beating heart of the enormous political power wielded by the Archdiocese of New York. Then she ran up the steps to the residence, rang the bell. A young priest opened the door. He smiled. "Hello," he said. "What can I do for you?"

"I'd like to see Cardinal Matterini."

"Ah." He nodded, as if strange people ringing the bell demanding to see the cardinal was a daily occurrence. "Do you have an appointment?"

"No, but he'll see me."

"Well, that's not the way it works, I'm afraid." The young man was still smiling. "His Eminence is very busy, so what you have to do is call his office and make an appointment."

"Oh, I see. Is he in now?"

"Well, I'm afraid he's not available—"

Maggie brushed by him, ran up the few inside steps into the foyer. "Tell him Andrea Bellini is here to see him. See what he says."

The young priest no longer looked friendly. He said, "I'm sorry, Miss Bellini. The cardinal is unable to change his schedule at such short notice. I think perhaps you had better—"

"He'll change it for me. Do you recognize the name Salvatore Bellini?"

She could see from the sudden look of alarm that he did. "I'm Salvatore Bellini's daughter. Tell the cardinal that I am here and I must see him."

The young man hesitated. Maggie tightened her grip on the weapon in her pocket. She did not want to threaten, to storm her way in. She hoped it would not come to that.

She said, "Salvatore Bellini was a great benefactor of the church, and a *paisano* of Cardinal Matterini." Deliberately she emphasized the Italian word. "They were born in the same village in Sicily and came here together as boys. His Eminence will at least want to know that his oldest friend's daughter is here. Just tell him, let him decide."

The young man nodded uncertainly, then said, "Wait here, please." He disappeared into the depths of the residence.

Maggie looked up at the series of dark oil paintings mounted on the paneled walls, hardly registering what they portrayed. Old men. Dead old men.

The young priest returned. "His Eminence can give you five minutes."

"Thank you." Maggie released her grip on the gun and followed him into the back of the house. He opened a door. "Ms. Andrea Bellini, Eminence."

A thin cassocked form rose from behind a large desk. He was an elegantly colorful figure; a small red skullcap covered the crown of his head, his well-tailored red cassock was encircled by a rich cerise cummerbund, a gold pectoral cross rested against his chest. He came toward her, a smile of welcome on his face. He did not look stunned at the sight of Andrea Bellini raised from a watery grave in Honduras. A son of the church, a true believer in miracles, Maggie thought. He held out his hand and she bent her head to brush his ring with her lips.

"Andrea, how nice of you to drop by to see an old man." His Sicilian accent was faint, but still there for a listening ear. He nodded a dismissal to the young priest, and Maggie heard the door close. She looked around to make sure they were alone. What she had to say was for his ears only.

The cardinal tapped the chair in front of his desk in passing, and said, "Sit. Would you like something? Coffee, a soft drink?" She shook her head and he resumed his own seat on the other side of the desk. "How is your mother?"

Maggie remained standing. "Eminence, I need your help."

"Ah. Sit down, Andrea. I thought perhaps that was the reason for your visit. Tell me what I can do for you." He leaned back, fingers steepled beneath his chin.

"You can tell me where Salvatore Bellini is hiding."

If he was shocked by her words, he hid it well. Long, ascetic face impassive, he pondered what she said, his dark eyes regarding her over his fingers.

Maggie said, "I have known from the beginning that he was not in that coffin. As you did, Eminence. Now I need to find him."

He leaned forward, narrow hands now clasped in front of him. "Andrea, the Salvatore Bellini you knew is, indeed, dead," he said smoothly. "The man he has now chosen to become must be allowed to keep his peace."

Her eyes holding his, Maggie moved forward until the desk pressed against her thighs. "My brother Paul is dead. Murdered. Aldo Ricci, the undertaker who prepared the coffins for my brother, James, and for my father, is dead, his throat cut. Michael O'Malley kidnapped my son, Jimmy. He is four." She held on to the edge of the desk. *"Where is Salvatore Bellini hiding?"*

"My child! I'm sorry, these are dreadful events you speak of, but they can have nothing to do with your father—"

"Stop it. Stop it. *O'Malley has my son. He is four. He is going to die! Do you hear what I am saying to you? Where is my father?"*

"What do you want with him, your father? How can he help you in this?" The accent was suddenly more pronounced.

"Michael O'Malley wants to meet him. When he does, he'll give my son back to me."

"I know of this O'Malley and his people. They are also Catholic." The cardinal shook his head. "You cannot believe what he says about this. He wants more than to just meet with your father."

"He wants to kill him. But if I can find Salvatore Bellini before O'Malley does, I will be able to arrange protection. Tell me where he is, and I give you my word that I will try to protect him."

"You mean gunmen."

"I mean the real world of Salvatore Bellini," Maggie said. "Not boyhood memories and dinners and charities and hundreds of millions of dollars in donations to the church."

The cardinal looked as if he felt her words like blows to his body. He got to his feet, went over to the window. It faced onto a small garden filled with trees and statuary. After a moment of silent contemplation, he turned.

"Andrea. My child. This is a terrible tragedy. All of it a terrible tragedy. So many lives ruined. But I cannot tell you what you want to know. You must forgive me. In spite of the trappings," he gestured to the large office, the rugs and paintings, the logs flaming in the hearth, "I am a simple priest. In the most humble way, I follow as I can in the shoes of the fisherman. I counsel you to take that path and perhaps you will find some ease for your pain. I can only pray so."

Maggie stared into dark liquid eyes that held hers with a strange intensity, as if he was trying to reach into her soul. She heard the door open behind her. "Eminence," a voice said.

The cardinal closed his eyes slowly as if in prayer, breaking the connection he had created with her. He opened them and said, "Miss Bellini is leaving." He looked at Maggie. "I will pray for you and for your son, Andrea. I will pray for your father and for the soul of your brother, Paul."

Maggie found herself with a large priest on either side of her and knew that before he received her, the cardinal had given orders to the young priest. Five minutes he'd said, and he'd meant five minutes. She fingered the weapon in her pocket, but realized that would only bring the police.

"Andrea," the cardinal said as she reached the door. "Father Roberto Patrelli. I know of your past relationship with him. He is a good priest, a good man. Trust him."

As she left, she heard him pick up the phone.

THIRTY-THREE

At the sound of an engine disturbing the tranquility of the lane, Sam glanced in the rearview mirror, expecting the Lincoln. But it was a dark blue Mercedes, driven too fast, barreling down on him. It roared past, the driver swerving at the last moment to avoid Sam's BMW without taking her eyes from the road.

Sam turned on the ignition, pulled out into the lane to follow. His gamble had paid off. He'd found her. His Maggie. The daughter of the don. Whoever she was.

The Mercedes turned into the entrance to the driveway and disappeared from sight and Sam gunned the engine, just managing to scrape through the pair of gold-tipped gates before they closed. When he got to the house, the Mercedes had already skidded to a stop, leaving in its wake a long wound in the pale gravel of the forecourt.

Sam parked beside the Mercedes and got out. He crossed to the house, and banged on the fancy front door with his fist.

The door was flung open, a furious voice asked, "How the hell you get in here?"

Donnie Provanto stepped outside, slammed a ham-sized hand against Sam's shoulder. Sam staggered, recovered fast and drove his fist into Provanto's diaphragm. Air left the henchman's lungs, bending him double as he struggled to regain his breath.

Sam grabbed him, held him upright. "Someone should teach you some manners," he said into the man's ear. He supported the wheezing Provanto back into the house, kicked the door closed, then shoved Provanto against the rack of weapons. "Where is she?"

"What you talking about?" Provanto tried to breathe.

"It's all right, Donnie."

It was the voice that had the power to break his heart. Sam dropped his hands from Provanto's shoulders and turned. Maggie came down the curved stairs to the foyer. Even from twenty feet away he imagined he could smell her scent.

"How did you find me?"

"You want to tell me what's going on?"

Maggie glanced at the bodyguard. "Donnie, why don't you go get some coffee? Sam's my husband, he's not here to harm me." She crossed the entry, entered the room where he'd talked to Bianca, leaving one of the tall double doors open. Sam followed her, and closed the door behind him. She was standing by the fire facing him, her small form straight and tense, her hands by her side, but he noticed they were clenched into fists, the knuckles white.

"Are you all right?" Sam said. "Did they hurt you?"

"Who?"

"The guys who picked you up in front of the church. Did they hurt you?"

"Oh." She shook her head, gave a small sharp exhalation of breath. "No, they didn't hurt me. Sam—"

"Why didn't you tell me you were an expert with weapons?"

"I'm not."

"Could have fooled me. The woman I saw knew exactly what she was doing."

"I don't know what you mean."

"I mean I was the patsy in the middle of the street shooting at the car, trying to stop it."

"Oh. I thought—" She stopped. "Sam, you know I hate guns."

"No, I don't. I thought I did, but I don't. I don't know who the hell you are."

"I'm sorry. Sam, I'm so sorry..."

Sam put steel in his voice. "Sorry won't cut it, Andrea, Maggie...whatever your name is. Where is my son?"

Maggie drew a breath that caught in her chest. Sam could see the jerking movement of her throat as she swallowed and had to stop himself from going to her, holding her close to him. She owed him more than an explanation. She owed him his son.

"I don't know where he is. I just know who has him."

"That's a start. Why don't you try something new now, like maybe the truth about all this? You've fed me just about all the lies I've got the stomach for."

"Michael O'Malley has him. He's the boss of an Irish mob who call themselves the Butcherboys. They're a sort of updated version of the old Westies, an Irish gang—"

Sam cut in. "I don't need the history lesson. I know who they are. So why did they come after our son?"

Maggie held his eyes and said, "Salvatore Bellini is my father."

"Ah. The truth must choke in your throat, trained by a family that kills or corrupts everything it touches." He saw her wince and hated himself. "I know all about Bellini. I went to the public library and read the old newspapers. So now start telling something I don't know."

"Sam, please." Her eyes filled with tears. "You were police when we met. What did you want me to say? Oh, hi, Sergeant. I'm Andrea Bellini, the daughter of the notorious Salvatore Bellini, but I'm in the federal witness protection program, so you'd better call me Margaret Jameson. And by the way, I'm really one of the good guys?"

"No, that's not what I think you should have said. But wasn't there one minute in the five years we've had when you knew you could trust me with who you are?" That was it, he thought. It always came back to that. All the sweet intimate hours when she could have let him into her life. Loved him as he loved her. Trusted him as he trusted her.

Maggie was shaking her head slowly from side to side as he spoke. "Sam, Jimmy was born eleven months after we were married. I was terrified from the beginning."

"I would have protected you and Jimmy. But you took that job on yourself, so you didn't need me. I'd have laid my life down to protect you."

"I did need you. I do." Her voice was cracking. "But I love you, Sam, I didn't want you to have to lay down your life. I didn't want you worrying every day, watching me to see if I was a fit mother for Jimmy. I wanted us to be a family like other people, with a house and friends and a dog. I thought I could take care of it myself."

"You didn't think I had the right to know my son was the only male left in the Bellini crime family? You think I don't know what that means?"

Her body seemed to fold in on itself. "We had Max, and a house in a cul-de-sac. I thought I could protect him."

"Sure, why not? You are what your blood says you are. We know all about blood ties in New Orleans. You are your father's daughter, that's what counts with you, right? Your bloodline." He intended to hurt and he saw that he had. It made him feel worse.

Maggie lifted her chin. "Yes, I am my father's daughter. Just listen to yourself, Sam. This is exactly what I feared would happen when I lay awake at night while you were flying that damned helicopter you loved so much."

"I flew nights to provide for you and Jimmy."

"You flew at night because you love it. You love the danger, the challenge. We didn't need more money. We needed you at home—"

"So why didn't you say so? Why suffer in silence?" He slapped his forehead. "Oh, of course. *Omerta.* Isn't that what it's called in your family. *Omerta?*"

"You want truth? Is that it? Try this. My father's coffin in our family crypt is filled with sand. Yes, that's right. Salvatore Bellini is alive and in hiding. O'Malley found out. He wants my father in exchange for our son."

My God, he thought. Adashek is right. "Who else knows your father's alive?"

She seemed not to notice he wasn't surprised. "It doesn't matter. Everyone who knew is already dead."

"The priest, Father Patrelli, is not dead." He saw from her face that he'd scored. "So he knows. Who else?"

"What does it matter who knows?"

"It matters. Who else knows Sal Bellini is alive?"

"My mother. Cardinal Matterini. Donnie Provanto. That's all. Oh, and O'Malley."

"You're sure. No more lies, Andrea."

"Don't call me that. I don't think anyone else knows, but I can't swear to it if that's what you want."

"I want the rest, everything you know."

"I don't know anything. That's just it. O'Malley wants me to bring my father out of hiding for a meeting. But I can't find him. Bobby Patrelli says he can't tell me anything, my mother won't tell me where he is because she knows O'Malley's going to kill him. And the awful thing is I understand how she feels, how they all feel. What would I do if someone wanted to kill you like that? She wants me to go to the FBI, but I can't, O'Malley will kill Jimmy if the FBI is brought in." Maggie was stumbling over the words that were pouring out as if an infected wound in her very being had been lanced. "I went to see Cardinal Matterini, he and my papa were born in the same village in Sicily, they came here together as young boys, but he says he doesn't know where my papa is. That's *la legge del'omerta,* Sam. That's what it does. That's what silence is. Nobody... A little boy..." Maggie put her hands over her face. "I heard Jimmy's voice. O'Malley played it for me. He was crying." She started to cry herself.

Sam fumbled in his pockets for a tissue, but came up empty-handed. He went to her, pulled her to him, held her head against his shoulder while she wept. She was feverish, her body shaking.

Minutes passed in silence except for the sound of Maggie's sobs. Slowly they diminished enough for her to speak. "I was so frightened I'd lose you, Sam, but I shouldn't have left without telling you about this."

"You're right, you shouldn't," Sam said. "But we're going to work this out somehow. First we'll get Jimmy back, then we'll go home. It's going to be okay."

She hadn't lifted her head, and he knew what she was waiting for. He put a hand on each side of her head, tipped up her face, and looked into her dark eyes. They were huge, suffused with pain. He passed his thumb carefully over the soft bruised-looking skin under each eye, smearing the tears.

"I love you, Mags. You are everything to me." Somehow, maybe, it could be that way again, the trust and love rebuilt. "You and Jimmy, you're all that counts for me. We'll get through this, okay? We'll get our son back."

"Yes. Okay. What are we going to do, Sam? I spoke to O'Malley. He says we have until eleven tonight and then he's going to..." She stumbled again over her words. "He says he'll start hurting Jimmy and send... Sam, he say he'll cut..." Her words strangled in her throat.

"It's all right. That's not going to happen." Somehow he would get the information he needed from Bianca. The henchman might prove difficult, but he'd manage that as he came to it.

Maggie said, "You look exhausted."

"No, I'm all right. I need a shower, that's all." He could smell his own sweat. "Then we'll talk to Bianca again. We'll start there." He glanced at his watch. It was already two hours past noon.

"You take a shower and I'll get you something to eat." She took his hand, led him toward the bathroom. "Elle said there was a warrant out for your arrest for the murder of three men in New Orleans."

"I didn't do it. NOPD knows that."

"You'd better stay out of sight, anyway, the FBI will be all over the place. They've been here once already to see my mother. My brother Paul was killed."

"I read about it. Don't worry about the FBI, they're not going to find me. Let me clean up, then I'll talk to Bianca. She'll understand what she has to do."

Maggie could hear the sound of running water. He'd been in there long enough for her to run down to tell her mother that he was here, but Bianca had already heard it from Donnie Provanto. They'd exchanged few words. Bianca looked even more tense than before, her face tight, her movements jerky as she went about the kitchen. She was bracing herself, Maggie thought. She knew she was going to get pressure from Sam to tell him what she knew. But she'd put together some sandwiches and filled a thermos jug with the coffee that was always ready in the kitchen.

Maggie put the tray on the table in the corner of her bedroom, recrossed the room to look out of the window overlooking the forecourt. The damage she had done would not be easy to repair—she had felt the depth of Sam's pain, his reluctance to tell her that he loved her. All she could do now was cling to what they'd had between them, the passion that was still there. Later, maybe that could be the foundation on which to rebuild the trust she had destroyed. And they had Jimmy, their precious boy... Please God, please Holy Mother...

She went back again over the words Cardinal Matterini had spoken. It seemed as if he'd meant to trigger some memory, something she already knew, something that hovered on the edge of her mind. St. Peter. Why St. Peter? Why the fisherman?

Suddenly, like a bolt thrown from heaven, she knew. She knew where her father was. She started toward the bathroom to tell Sam, then stopped in the middle of the room.

If she told him, he would insist on coming with her. But if she was right and her father was where she thought he was, he might not be alone. Someone had tried to kill her before, maybe O'Malley's people. Maybe their own. But she couldn't just leave, not again, not without telling him. Not if they were to have a life together if she did get back...

She went into the bathroom, pulled open the door of the shower. Sam was propped against the clear glass wall, eyes closed, water pounding his shoulders. Through the steam she could see the scar from the wound he had taken in the crash of his chopper six years ago writhing from his back, around his side, to his belly.

"Sam, I know where he is."

"Jimmy?" Sam struggled to turn off the water, swearing when the hot water became hotter as he fumbled with the unfamiliar taps.

"No, my father."

"Where?"

"About an hour from here. I'm going now to see him."

Sam left the water running and stepped out of the shower. "I'll take you."

She leaned in, turned off the water. "Sam, listen a minute. I got Bobby Patrelli to give him a letter and he sent it back unopened. If I'm right, and he is where I think he is, he'll refuse to see me if I'm not alone. He may refuse, anyway, but if anyone is with me, I know he won't see me."

"I'll drive you there, I'll stay out of sight, he'll never know."

"There is no way he couldn't know, Sam. He'll know. This is a onetime shot, there won't be another."

Sam grabbed a towel and looked around. "Where are my clothes?"

"Sam, my father is a very dangerous man. I know what he can do, I've seen photographs...." She tried to keep her voice calm and reasonable, but her body was shaking with tension. Time was racing and she had to get there, talk to him. If she could persuade him to meet O'Malley, they'd have to put protection in place. She had to get back, contact O'Malley. All in nine hours. "There's no time for argument. You said I was part of the Bellini family, and you're right. That's why I have to go alone. He'd kill anyone else who discovers where he is. And someone has to be here for Jimmy, Sam, think about that. Jimmy is all that's important." Maggie reached up, pulled his head down so that she could kiss him. His face was rough with stubble.

He jerked his head back. "This is bullshit. You're not making any sense. If he's that dangerous, you can't go alone."

"No, I'll be okay. He's my father, he loves me. He won't harm me, but he wouldn't hesitate to kill you. Sam, listen," she stumbled through the words, "if you have to, call the FBI. If I don't get back, and you think—"

"Christ, Maggie, don't do this. Get me my clothes. Goddam it, you can't do this."

Maggie left the bathroom, closed the bedroom door behind her, cutting off the sound of Sam cursing. She ran down the stairs, avoided her mother in the kitchen by going through the service porch, out into the vegetable garden. She kept to the edge of the shrubbery and ran down to the dock, listening to the guard dogs barking in their kennels.

Both boats were in their slips inside the boathouse that was open to the Long Island Sound, the cabin cruiser used for family outings, and the swift, racy, flat-bottomed Boston Whaler, old now but the most recent of the many her father had owned. The wooden deck of the boathouse was slippery from the slapping tide, and she had to be careful where she placed her feet as she ran along the water-soaked boards to the storage room at the rear. It never used to be locked, no one would have the nerve to steal from Don Salvatore Bellini, but times had changed. She let out a breath of relief when the door opened easily as she twisted the knob. For a moment the smell from her childhood took her breath away. Salt and tar and engine oil, life jackets, fishing tackle, anchors, bouys, a cold northern smell so different from the sun-warmed scents of the Gulf.

Maggie picked her way through the piled equipment, opened a shallow cupboard on the rear wall and unhooked the key hanging beneath the words *Bellissima Bianca*—like all the others, it had been named for her mother. She removed the other keys and dropped them into the water on her way back to the Whaler.

Within seconds she was on board, untying the small craft. The highwayman's hitch gave way instantly and she dropped the rope onto the deck, then went back to the cockpit, turned on the engine and sent mental thanks to Donnie Provanto when it caught on the first try—he had a way with engines. Part of his job had been to keep everything in running order. She gave it some throttle, getting the feel—it had been six years since she had handled this boat—and backed out of the boathouse without incident.

She turned into the Sound, narrowly avoiding another powerboat that chose that precise moment to cross her heading. Then, knees flexed against the pounding water, she opened up the ninety-five horsepower Mercury engine and did not look back.

Barefoot, dressed only in the towel around his waist, Sam ran down the stairs, following the sound of voices. He burst through the door to the kitchen.

"What have you done with my clothes?"

Donnie Provanto moved to stand protectively at Bianca's side. She stared at Sam in astonishment. "They are still washing. Andrea put them into the machine. Here's your cell phone, she took it out of your pocket—"

"Maggie...damn it, Andrea's gone. Just get me my clothes. I don't care if they are wet."

"No, no, you can't put them on, they're not—"

Sam went into the service area where the machine was chugging along, Bianca hard on his heels. "You can't put them on, they're washing in soap. Wait, I'll get you something. Giacomo, he always kept some things here, even after he had his own place. You're about the same size. Come, I show you."

"You be okay, Mrs. B?" Provanto had followed them into the service area. He jerked his head at Sam. "Maybe you want I should take him up to Giacomo's room?"

"Goddamn it, this is not a discussion." Sam said. "Bianca, I want to talk to you. You," he looked at Provanto, "stay put. I might need you."

Provanto opened his mouth, then shut it without speaking.

Bianca led the way quickly through the kitchen and dining room to the foyer then up the stairs, Sam on her heels. Bianca crossed the upper gallery and opened a door. "This is my son's room. His things are hanging up in his closet over there."

Sam pulled her inside the room, closed the door. "Bianca, did you hear what I said? Maggie's gone to see her father. She did not use her car, it's still outside. How is she getting there?"

Bianca put her hands to her face. The blood had drained from her face, leaving her olive skin a sickly gray. "My God. My God. She knows."

"Wait, don't move." Sam opened the door to which Bianca had pointed. He found himself in a walk-in closet that was larger than his bedroom had been when he was a kid. He grabbed a pair of jeans folded on a shelf, opened drawers until he found underwear, socks, a white T-shirt. He dressed, shoved his feet into his own well-used sneakers, pulled a suede windbreaker from its hanger as he passed, shoved the cell phone in an inside pocket. In the bedroom Bianca was where he had left her.

"Where has she gone?"

"It doesn't matter, you can't follow her, you can only get there by boat. There's no way—"

"Do you have more than one?"

She stared at him as if not understanding.

"Do you have more than one boat?"

"We have a cabin cruiser, but Donnie's working on it, the engine, it's broken."

"Jesus. Wait. Wait. Is there an airport close by, a small field?"

"No, nothing like that. What do you want with an airport?"

"I want a helicopter."

"Well, the country club. They have helicopters, people use them to get—"

"Okay. Listen. Call them..." He stopped. "Do they know you?"

"Yes, we belong. Sal liked that we belonged to the country club, for the children, you know, and now I take Jolie, my son Paolo's daughter."

"Okay. Call them, have them get a chopper ready. I want it fueled, warmed up, ready to go when I get there. Got that? Okay. Now listen. Where has she gone, Bianca?"

"Sam, let her go alone. She's going to see her papa. She will be safe with him."

"She won't be alone, Bianca. There are people watching for her."

Alarmed Bianca said, "The FBI? They follow her?"

"Probably, and whoever else is after your husband. I don't know, but I don't want her alone out there on open water. Do you understand? She's in danger, and I don't know where it's going to come from. Come with me."

Sam ran back down the stairs to the kitchen. Donnie Provanto was leaning against the counter drinking coffee, staring out of the window at the garden.

"You got a map of the area?" Sam asked.

"What you looking for?"

"A map of the Sound. Come on, come on. Do you, don't you? A map!"

"Mrs. B, what's happening here?" Donnie looked over Sam's shoulder. "Where did Andrea go?"

"She's looking for her son," Bianca said from the doorway.

"She found him?"

"Maybe," Sam said. "I think so."

Donnie put the cup down. "You want I should get some of the guys? We got people we can call on—"

Sam shook his head. "No. I want a map."

"I don't know about no maps."

"Donnie," Bianca said.

"She took the Whaler, Mrs. B.," Donnie said. "I heard it start up. Only one place she's going by boat." Provanto reached for the wall phone.

"No calls, Donnie," Bianca said. "Anything my husband finds out now he gets from his daughter."

She'd come through! Sam felt for her hand, found it icy, although her skin was damp. He squeezed her fingers gently, hoping she'd feel his gratitude. Without looking at him, Bianca disengaged from his grasp, the small gesture all revealing. She was giving up her husband, the father of her children, the head of her family, an action contrary to every belief that generations of her people had held sacred. The conflict and pain had to be tearing her apart.

Donnie said, "Mrs. B—"

Bianca cut him off. "No more. Andrea is the only one who can tell her papa what has happened to her son. She needs her papa's help now. I want you to get Sam what he needs." She gave no further explanation.

The bodyguard hesitated then jerked his head, gesturing to Sam to follow. He went through the service area, opened a door, turned on the light in a garage filled with cars. At a quick glance maybe six, a couple of motorcycles, a number of golf carts. Paintwork gleamed, light bounced back from metal hand-rubbed to brilliance. Sam turned his attention to Donnie, riffling through the maps racked above a fitted workbench. He picked one out, spread it over the hood of a large black Mercedes.

Sam beckoned to Bianca. "Show me."

Bianca put a finger on a small group of islands, mere specks in Long Island Sound northeast of Whortleberry Island. Sam leaned over to read the name: Pestilence Islands. Below the name, tiny lettering said: Landing forbidden. He looked at Bianca. "She's going there? What pestilence?"

"You can't land a helicopter, just boats."

"I don't want to land. I just want see to it that she does. What pestilence?"

"Leprosy."

Sam stared at her, aghast. It took a moment, then he said, "Make that call."

Ten minutes later Sam turned into the discreet gates of the Point Sandspit Yacht and Country Club. The gateman stepped in front on his car and Sam slowed, said one word: "Bellini." The guard touched his cap, waved him through.

A Robinson 22 stood on a pad some distance from the clubhouse, its blades turning slowly, a mechanic leaning inside the cockpit. Sam slammed the BMW to a stop, ran across the grass.

The man straightened. "Mr. Bellini?"

"That's me." Sam grabbed the sides of the chopper, hauled himself aboard.

"Mr. Bellini, sorry, sir, you have to go to the clubhouse first. The pilot's waiting, and you have to fill in some forms—"

Sam slid the door closed. He pointed upward, then increased the rotation of the blades. The mechanic's eyes widened, Sam saw his mouth move, "Aw, shit!" before he dropped to the ground, tucked his head to his knees, covered up with his arms.

Sam threw a glance at the gauges. No warning lights. Good enough. He settled the earphones, grabbed the collective. The bird lifted sweetly, and Sam swung toward the gray silver-streaked cumulus obliterating the sun.

Below him, the Sound buzzed with traffic, pleasure craft of

all sizes, both sail and power, more commercial vessels than he'd expected, their wakes opening dirty white seams in the choppy texture of the water. Rain hazed the Plexiglas bubble surrounding him, and Sam realized he was looking for a marine version of the proverbial needle. At fifty feet the turbulence caused by the blades was swamping some of the smaller craft below him. Boats rode the chop hard and he could see the outrage on the faces turned up to him and not a few heavy-weather gear-clad figures pumped their arms angrily, waving him off.

He climbed to five hundred feet to get a line of sight, and headed northwest. She'd had maybe half an hour's head start in a craft with a maximum speed of forty-five knots. In a chopper flying at eighty he would close the gap in minutes. Sooner or later he'd spot her. Just the same, he cursed himself for not bringing binoculars.

The line of waves washing onto the beaches of Long Island dropped away, and the marine traffic below eased. Most of the pleasure boats stayed closer to the shore, expecting heavier weather, so what remained was mainly the larger commercial vessels.

Then he saw what he was searching for. A Boston Whaler moving in the same direction he was headed, one small figure in the cockpit.

One hundred yards behind her was a larger power craft, carefully staying back, not crowding, maintaining distance.

THIRTY-FOUR

Maggie found herself suddenly struggling to keep the Whaler on course against an increasingly hard chop. The pounding of rotors overrode the noise of the engine, and even before she looked up to search the sky, she knew Sam had found the only way possible to come after her.

Inside the bubble of the chopper hovering over her head, Sam waved one hand in a circle, then pointed back. Keeping course, Maggie turned to see what he meant and saw the large power craft—a Seacrest 500—behind her. The roar of the Whaler's engine and the cry of the wind had drowned out every sound, but clearly the boat was riding too close to be out for a casual afternoon's pleasure cruise.

Her heart lurched unsteadily, and a scalding mix of emotion boiled up: frustration, guilt, rage. A killing rage. It had happened again. She had almost led them—O'Malley, the FBI, whoever they were—right to him. And in doing so, she had lost the only chance she had of talking to him...of getting Jimmy home. The truth pounded home with the single voice of the powerful engines surrounding her, beneath her feet and overhead and following. Jimmy was a pawn in a bigger game, a hostage. If O'Malley got Sal Bellini first, he'd have every reason to kill her child, dump his little body—

She could feel her own screams burning her throat as she swung the Whaler into a close turn. She crossed the wake of her pursuers, flexing her knees to take the shock as the flat bottom slammed against water that felt like concrete. She came up behind the Seacrest, the lust to ram it, to kill the two men, all-consuming. She had to cling to the wheel, buffeted by the speed of the Whaler and the violence in the air overhead, and realized that Sam had brought the chopper down and was staying with her. In a flash of sanity she knew he was telling her there had to be another way, that Jimmy's only chance at life was if she stayed alive, got to her father. At the last minute she wrenched at the wheel. The Whaler turned, its gunwales slicing the sea.

She had missed them by feet.

Sam stayed with the Whaler until Maggie looked up. He waved, then made his own sharp turn. Salt spray mingled with the rain on the Plexiglas as he skimmed the waves and headed straight at Maggie's pursuers. One struggled with the wheel. It was the other guy that grabbed Sam's attention. He was steadying himself with a hand on the windshield. With the other he was aiming at the Robinson with a weapon the size of a cannon.

Even with the threat facing the country, the FBI would not shoot a chopper out of the sky and ask questions later. In any case, he had no choice.

He roared down on them, close enough to see the blossoming terror on their faces before he brought the chopper up ten feet, flew over them and turned. He lined the chopper up, held course, lower now, until he could almost hear the screams coming from their open mouths. Then he gave the Robinson lift, and they were behind him.

He came up beside Maggie, pacing her as she headed away from her original course. She looked up, and Sam gestured toward the northwest. Holding the wheel with both hands as she rode the turbulent sea, she shook her head, took one hand off the wheel long enough to point east. Sam circled an eye with one hand, hoping she understood he was asking her to watch, then peeled off, came up again behind her pursuers, keeping steady at five feet. The men in the cockpit threw themselves down, the craft decelerated and yawed dangerously as the wheel spun. In the instant before impact, Sam brought the chopper up, and went after Maggie.

She looked up, nodded vehemently that she'd seen and understood he would keep her pursuers busy, and managed to wave as she took the Whaler back to the northwest and opened it up.

The Seacrest had lost way, and Sam dropped the Robinson into the space that had opened up between the two boats. Like a collie herding sheep, he put the chopper straight at the Seacrest, holding steady, his skids only feet from the bow. One of the men had grabbed the wheel and the craft was making some headway, but he was losing the battle to maintain control in the waves kicked up by the chopper's blades. Sam could see the recoil from the gunman's weapon, but in that kind of turbulence, the shots were going wild. He took the Robinson up to twenty feet, flying a tight circle to keep the seawater slopping inboard, then realized that both men were firing now, filling the air around the chopper with semiautomatic rounds. One lucky shot, and they'd bring him down.

He reached behind his seat for the distress flare, loaded the canister, slid open his side panel. Holding steady, he aimed at the Seacrest.

The men below dived overboard an instant before the vessel exploded. The Robinson rocked from the blast even as Sam gained altitude. Wreckage settled, a column of black smoke rose from the burning hull. Sam searched the sea for Maggie but the Whaler had long gone, fading like a mirage into the increasing squall.

Arms flailing, both men had regained the surface, floating amid the debris. Sam looked again, realized they were not flailing. They were treading water and signaling. He scanned the area, spotted what they had already seen—a Coast Guard cutter emerging from the mist, its teeth bared and ready for action. The .50 caliber on the bow was uncovered, manned and trained on the Robinson.

Sam searched the horizon. Visibility was closing in, he could take a chance they wouldn't open fire. He started his turn, south away from Maggie. In the same instant he heard the sound of rotors above him, heavier and stronger than the Robinson's blades. He looked up. Twenty yards above his port side was the lethal giant known to the army as a Blackhawk, called by the Coast Guard the Jayhawk. By either name, he knew it was time to call it off.

He turned on the radio, tuned in to 123.025l, the air-to-air frequency, for Coast Guard instructions.

THIRTY-FIVE

Maggie heard the explosion, and for a brief instant she considered returning. With the next breath she knew Sam would not want her help, that Jimmy was their priority. She sent up a small prayer for his safety and held her course.

Eventually, the series of rocks she was looking for appeared out of the gloom of the squall like the ridged back of an ancient sea monster. Somewhere in the center of these uninhabited specks of land was the island she sought. Maggie cut the power until she had just enough leeway to steer the Whaler and started to thread carefully through the maze of islets.

She had been twelve the last time he'd brought her here, but she could almost feel her father behind her, his arms encircling her, his strong hands covering hers on the wheel, as if she were back in one of the early *Bellissima Biancas*. Bringing them in had been her special treat.

Their visits had been a secret they had shared since he'd brought her for the first time when she was eight. Then somehow Bianca had found out. Submissive wife though she was, Bianca had thrown a fit. Maggie remembered her father laughing at her mother's fears, but if his sons were his, his daughter's upbringing was her mother's business. He had agreed not to repeat the offense. In spite of her pleas, he'd kept his word.

Brush-covered isles pressed in, forcing her to make a hard turn to starboard, almost immediately another turn to port, making it through with a few feet of clearance on either side. If the fog were less dense, it would be easier, she'd have a frame of reference. As it was, she was beginning to feel as if she could go on forever, moving among these ghostly islands like the Ancient Mariner.

But the water finally opened up where she thought it would and a larger body of land rose in front of her. Slowly she cruised along the rocky shoreline, the engine barely turning over, looking for the small declivity she remembered, more indentation than bay. There should be a floating dock, and if she was right about the elliptical message Cardinal Matterini had given her, it would still be there, although no one was allowed to land except the monks who lived and prayed at St. Peter's Monastery. No one but Cardinal Matterini, whose special refuge it was, a place for him to be a simple monk for a few hours. A place for him to sit with his *paisano* at the end of the dock, their fishing lines in the sea, while they talked of their childhood and their village in the mountains of their distant homeland.

The Whaler was barely moving, the engine just puttering along. Maggie forced down a rising panic. She could not be wrong. Where better for a fugitive to hide than the old leper colony for immigrants who had brought with them to the New World the most dreaded disease of the old? She remembered being told the story of the Dominicans who had built the chapel and infirmary and the other buildings, whose outlines she could see drifting eerily in and out of the sea fog covering the island, how they'd served the lepers for more than a hundred years, until leprosy became known as Hansen's disease and was treated in hospitals.

The monastery still had to be here and in use....

Then slowly, the outline of a figure emerged, his lower body obscured by the sea mist so that he looked as if he was hovering on the water. She nosed the Whaler toward him. Gradually he took on shape and substance.

She had found him.

She'd half expected the cowl and brown robes, the sandaled feet of the Dominicans, but he wore boots, a windbreaker with the collar turned up against the weather. A dark blue knitted cap covered his hair.

The Whaler nudged the dock beside two other tethered boats, rising and falling with the waves, jostling bumpers made of old tires. Salvatore Bellini bent to hold the small craft steady and Maggie threw the line. He caught it, threaded it through a ring set in the sea-sodden wood, and tied a highwayman's hitch.

"How did you know I was coming?" she called.

"Does your mother know you're here?"

The first words he had spoken to her in six years. His voice sounded exactly as it always had.

"I don't know," she answered. "Maybe by now. Who told you I'd be here?"

"Why did you come?"

Just like her father, never answering a direct question. "I have to talk to you."

He held out his hand, and Maggie said, "I thought females were not allowed here except those already dead. Maybe you'd better come aboard."

"A special dispensation was always made for you, Andrea. You remember that. Come."

Maggie grasped the proffered hand. It was warm, the palm hard and calloused and unfamiliar. Not her father's hand as she remembered it. That one had been soft, a stranger to physical labor. The floating dock moved beneath her feet as she jumped ashore.

"How are you, Papa?"

"In body, I am well. In my heart?" He shrugged.

"Paolo is dead," she said abruptly. "He was murdered."

"Yes, I know of this."

"Mama told you?"

"No. Come." He took her by the elbow, ushered her from the dock onto the land. He took a path that led them away from the buildings, the chapel and infirmary, the monks' cells, the kitchen and refectory, leading her instead through a grove of towering ash trees. Maggie remembered that they had been donated by charity, planted as saplings in the waning years of the nineteenth century. Now, in autumn, their fallen leaves provided a carpet of yellow that absorbed the sound of footsteps. Mist drifted around the enormous trunks, reaching like fingers into the canopy of bare limbs overhead.

Even in her misery, half consumed by fear for Sam and her son, Maggie found herself waiting for her father to speak first. Minutes passed in silence as they walked through the grove. The trees thinned, and they were at the edge of the cemetery, rows of small headstones on a hillside that led down to the sea.

"They put the graveyard here so that the people would be in sight of their heart's desire for all eternity. I don't know whether that is a comfort, or a cruelty. What do you think, being so close to what you want, and yet knowing you will never get it?"

"I don't know and I don't care about dead people. I care about the living, about my son."

"Tell me what it is you want of me."

Instead of answering his question, she found herself saying, "Papa, I did not lead the FBI to you at Bear Mountain."

Salvatore Bellini waved a hand in dismissal, but Maggie ignored him. Something in her demanded that he understand the past before she told him why she had come. "No. You have to listen. The FBI was waiting for me when I came out of class at Columbia." She had been a graduate student in early childhood education. "Special Agent Adashek from the organized crime unit. He told me the FBI knew you were meeting with O'Malley. They knew it was to be at Bear Mountain, but they didn't know when."

Salvatore Bellini grimaced and put up a hand to stop her, but she shook her head. "No, you listen, Papa. You have blamed me and you have refused to let me speak. Now you listen."

Bellini turned away and started to walk away from her. The path was close to the edge of the bluff and the sound of waves washing onto the rocky shore below, the lonely calls of gulls flying over the rows of tiny white headstones deepened the sense of desolation. Maggie shivered. Mist beaded in her hair and clung to her eyelashes. She blinked the moisture away and hurried after him, keeping pace, refusing to be silenced.

"The FBI had a man undercover and he got close to O'Malley. They knew you wanted to get O'Malley's support to stop the Russians in Brighton Beach from becoming too strong. Agent Adashek played a tape for me, O'Malley talking with two men, Russians. Orloff. And Kariakin, I think, something like that. They were making plans, Papa. They were planning to kill you and James and Bobby Patrelli and his father. All our people. The FBI wanted to be there to stop it. That's what Agent Adashek said. It would be a bloodbath and the FBI had to stop it." With an effort she kept her voice strong and steady. He hadn't stopped her but if she showed weakness, he would dismiss her. Salvatore Bellini hated weakness in anyone, male or female.

"He showed me pictures, Papa. Terrible pictures. The FBI man's body. He was young and he had been mutilated, his genitals gone, his throat cut and his tongue pulled through the wound." She thought of Paolo and his lover, and Aldo Ricci in his blood-soaked coffin. "He had been thrown out of a car in front of the Federal Building. Agent Adashek said you had done that to him. I knew you hadn't. I knew you couldn't do that. I knew that it had to be O'Malley or the Russians." She waited for Bellini to say something, to say that he had not done such a thing, nor ordered it to be done. But he remained silent. She moved in front of her father, forcing him to stop and look at her. "It was O'Malley's people who did that to him, not you, Papa. You didn't do that."

Salvatore Bellini shook his head. "No. Of course not. We are not the Butcherboys."

She searched his face. His dark eyes were fixed on hers and she knew she would never really know the truth. How young she had been then. Young and naive—but it had been the naiveté of desperation. She had believed in her father. But why was he the one in hiding while O'Malley walked the streets a free man?

"I tried to find you, and James and Bobby but I was too late, you were gone, and I guessed where. I had been planning to go up to the lodge at Bear Mountain with..." She stopped. He did not need to know that it was with Bobby, that he had called and left a message telling her to stay home with her mother. That, furious, she had told James that she was going to find Bobby and make him tell her why.

"James made me promise not to go up that weekend. He said I had to stay home with Mama, that I could go the following week. When he'd left I realized where he was going. I knew the meeting was going to be at Bear Mountain Lodge. So I drove up there to warn you. The FBI followed me, Papa. They stopped me on the road, and kept me there until it was over. Then they drove me home, and everything was confusion. James was dead, and Bobby had been hurt, and his father was trying to keep things going because you were hurt, too." It had been chaos, Bobby lying downstairs, her father upstairs in his room, Donnie Provanto guarding the door, armed men at the gates, doctors and lawyers coming and going. "That's what happened. I did not talk to the FBI, Papa. I wouldn't do that."

Salvatore Bellini stopped some feet from the edge of the cliff and stared out at the bank of fog that hung like a shroud over the sea. "I know all of this. Your mother has talked to me." He glanced at her. "She has the same friend that you have so she is able to visit me here. Andrea, I have listened and now you listen to me. I am of the old stock, not like these...these...*disgraziato* who run things today. Men who cannot keep their tongues quiet. You understand? I would rather you die, your brothers die, even your mother, than have you talk to people who would pry into our family business. So." He raised both hands in dismissal. "These events are in the past. Leave them there. I ask you again, today. *What is it you want of me?*"

Maggie took a breath. "O'Malley knows you are alive. He came last Sunday and took my son from his bed. He has killed Paolo to find out where you are hiding. He wants to meet with you, Papa. He wants to talk about the deaths of his brothers—" She stopped herself. "No. He wants to kill you. If I arrange the meeting, he will give me back my son. That is what I want of you. I want you to meet O'Malley, and give me back my son."

He stared at her for a moment, then nodded. "Good. That is good. You should have been a son. You have the courage for the truth."

Maggie put a hand in her pocket, took out the photograph she had kept for this moment. She held it out. "His name is James Cady. I named him for Giacomo. He is four."

Salvatore Bellini held the picture. He took a first casual glance, then looked closer. His hand started to shake. His voice was hoarse when he said, "He could be Giacomo at that age."

"Yes, Mama says that, too."

Bellini's face creased. Stunned, Maggie watched him struggle to maintain control. Never in her life had she seen her father show what he felt.

"Papa—" Maggie took a tentative step toward him.

He jerked his hand up to stop her. Clutching the photograph, he turned away, took a few stumbling steps. A large piece of the bluff gave way beneath his feet, falling to the rocky sea below. The edge of the cliff was perilously close. He stood still, staring down at the waves crashing against the shoreline. Maggie feared to move—all it would take was for him to take one step away from her and it would be into the void at his feet. She held her breath. He spoke without turning.

"I caused his death."

For one horrified moment, she thought he meant the mutilated FBI man.

"My Giacomo. My son. I might just as well have pulled the trigger myself." He glanced at the picture in his hand. "I came here to die, because I could no longer live. But I did not die. I lived to hide. From that world. From myself." He shrugged. "Paolo was killed, it changed nothing. But I cannot feel peace. I already know of what you speak and I went down to the dock to think. How could it be that you came out of the fog in that moment? Now you tell me that I do not have the right to hide. I think...I think it is time that I must listen to you."

Maggie rubbed a hand over her eyes, tried to take in what she had just heard. Her father, an old-time Mafioso, "a man of honor," had attempted to explain himself to her, even suggested that his way was not the only way. She was stunned. It was a concept that once he would never even have comprehended.

"Papa, we haven't got much time. O'Malley called me and said he would start to...to...harm Jimmy. A man with a chain saw..." She could not go on. She brushed the rain and tears from her face.

Salvatore Bellini turned back to stare at the sea. Moments passed, then he said, "This will not happen. You understand? You will see your son today."

Her legs were suddenly weak with relief. A flood of guilt followed. Her father was going to die. She cared about that, but she cared more for the life of her son. "We need to get Donnie Provanto to line up some people, and there isn't much time. We have to hurry."

Bellini stepped back from the edge of the cliff. "There will be time. Now, come, let us walk back to the chapel."

He took her arm, started back through the grove of ash trees.

"Papa, you must call Donnie Provanto. He can get some of our people—" Not *our* people, she thought, panicked. Where had that come from? His people. She was Maggie Cady.

Bellini shook his head to silence her. "Andrea, it has been a long time. You were always the child of my heart, gentle, uncomplicated. Let us walk here as father and daughter. We'll talk for a while of Giacomo and Paolo and Andrea, when you were all just my children."

His words showed how much he had seen the daughter he wanted, not the child or woman she really had been. In the few minutes it took them to get back to the chapel he spoke of the long-gone years of childhood. Maggie forced herself to listen, but her thoughts were of James, dead of gunshot wounds, and Paul, murdered because of her father's life, her mother scarred forever, her own child kidnapped. She kept silent and held on to his arm. He did not ask about Sam, and she volunteered nothing. This was truly the end of the life she had once known. Sam did not belong here.

The night was closing in when Salvatore Bellini took the path that led to the tiny gray stone church facing the sea.

Maggie held back. "Papa, please, we must go. It's getting late, we have to call Donnie—"

"We have time. There is someone here I must talk to."

He opened the weathered door. The interior was a study in black shadow and bleak whitewashed walls, illuminated only by the lights above each of the twelve stations of the cross, six on either side of the church. Even in her pain, Maggie was riveted.

The central figure in the paintings stumbled along the *via dolorosa,* the street of tears, face bloody from the crown of thorns jammed upon His head, His back bent under the burden of the cross. Although the flesh tones were bleached out now, blue eyes faded, the robes a grubby white, the figure was clearly intended to be the focus of the painting, the only one with any vestige of color. But it was the people pressing in around Him that drew the eye. Clad in drab grays and browns, each bore the signs of leprosy: faces without lips or nose, blinded eyes, hands with no fingers, crippled limbs that ended in bandages where hands and feet should be. Even more dismaying were those that were cowled, their disfigurement left to the imagination of the beholder.

Filled with disquiet, she looked away from the strange paintings. At first glance the chapel seemed to be empty, but as her eyes adjusted to the gloom of the interior, she saw a tall thin priest kneeling at the altar rail.

Bellini started along the aisle toward him. "Vittorio, forgive the interruption. My daughter is here. We have spoken together. I have changed my mind. I will meet with O'Malley as you ask."

The priest's shoulders sagged as if in relief. He bent his head briefly, then rose to his feet and turned toward them.

"Andrea," Cardinal Matterini said. "I think God has spoken through you today." He beckoned and Maggie, too shocked to speak, followed her father to the front of the little church. "I did not have the words to convince him—"

"Vittorio, old friend," Bellini interrupted. "You tried hard enough. But look at this." He held out the photograph of Jimmy. "He could be Giacomo, don't you think?"

The cardinal looked at the picture and nodded. "Yes, there is a great likeness." He gestured to the wooden pew and Maggie slid in, her father beside her.

Salvatore Bellini said, "So now we must decide how to accomplish what we want."

The cardinal looked at Maggie, then back to Salvatore. "I spoke personally with Michael O'Malley on the telephone."

Maggie found her voice. "Why didn't you just tell me that my father was here?" she asked the cardinal. "Why this...this charade, making me guess what you meant?"

"I had to tell you something, but without seeing your father first, to get his permission, how could I break his silence?" Shaking his head, he shrugged, a very Italian gesture, coming from somewhere deep in his childhood. "Had you not understood, I intended to call you. But I had to give myself time to come here first to discuss matters in person. This is not a thing for the telephone." The cardinal glanced at his watch. "But I did take the liberty of starting some arrangements. Father Patrelli is on his way to meet with O'Malley now. As soon as he has seen Jimmy and has assured himself that your son is unharmed, he will call me here." The cardinal held up a mobile phone. "Then we will take the next steps."

"Good, Vittorio. Good. Bobby Patrelli is a man like his father. He can speak for me," Bellini said. "Now, this is what I want done. We decide on a place to meet and a time. Bobby will take charge of my grandson. He will drive to the meeting place with Michael O'Malley and will remain with little Giacomo during the exchange."

"Salvatore, there will be no exchange. I will speak with O'Malley—"

"Don't trust him," Maggie said to the cardinal. "O'Malley wants only to kill my father."

"Well, that will not happen. I will myself be there to mediate. When Michael realizes that I am there, what will he do? Kill a prince of his church?" The cardinal shook his head, smiling. "I think not."

For the first time Maggie allowed herself to feel hope. This could work. The presence of the cardinal had changed everything. "No, I don't think even O'Malley would do that."

The phone buzzed and Cardinal Matterini answered quickly. "Yes?" He nodded as he listened, and a smile crossed his face. He looked at Maggie. "Your son is unharmed—"

Maggie was on her feet, reaching for the phone. "Let me talk to him."

"He is not there, you must wait. But he is safe," the cardinal said. Then into the phone, "You have seen him yourself, Father Roberto? Good. Yes, I am listening. Yes, do as the man asks. Just be sure the child remains close to you so you can protect him. Is O'Malley there now?" He kept his eyes on Bellini, nodding as he listened. "Let me speak to him... Ah, Michael. What is it you propose?" He listened, then said, "Now, this is what I propose. Bring the child to St. Patrick's Cathedral. Salvatore Bellini will be there."

From where she sat, Maggie could hear Michael O'Malley laughing. The cardinal held the phone against his chest. "He says you are wanted as a fugitive, he has a kidnapped child. The meeting must be in a place that is far from prying eyes. His words. He says it must be Wharf F, Hoboken. 1:00 a.m."

Salvatore Bellini thought for a moment, then nodded. The cardinal lifted the phone to his ear and said, "Michael, Salvatore Bellini will be there. Now, there will be no weapons, you understand me, Michael? I give you my solemn word that Bellini will be unarmed, and I want your solemn word in return. No weapons, you understand? Good. God bless you, my son." He broke the connection and looked at Bellini. "It is settled then. He will come unarmed. One a.m. Wharf F, Hoboken. You know it?"

Salvatore Bellini nodded. "Yes. It's derelict, an area controlled by the Irish but one place is like any other. Thank you, Vittorio."

Maggie shot him a glance. "No, this is not good."

"Andrea, it will be all right," Bellini said. He smiled. "The cardinal will be there. What can happen?"

"I must call Sam," Maggie said. "Eminence, may I use your phone? He'll be at the house with Mama."

The cardinal shook his head. "No, that would not be wise, Andrea. The fewer people who know this, the safer it will be. We cannot afford an error, too much is at stake. We must keep this between ourselves. Only a few more hours and you will be reunited with your husband and your son. Salvatore, you agree?"

"Of course. Father, I would like to make my confession." He smiled at his daughter. "It will be short, don't worry. There is not much opportunity for sin here and it has been only a week since my last confession."

"Bobby Patrelli is not your confessor?" Maggie asked.

"Bobby?" Salvatore said. "No, of course not. Father Matterini has always been my priest. He comes here every couple of weeks."

"What about the letter I asked Bobby to deliver to you?"

"What letter? I know of no letter. What do you mean?"

A moment passed, then Cardinal Matterini looked at Bellini. "Father Patrelli brought me a letter Andrea had written to you. To my shame, I sent it back without mentioning it."

"You had no right to do that," Maggie said.

Cardinal Matterini stiffened, suddenly very much a prince of the church, unused to challenge. "My concern was for an immortal soul. My friend Salvatore has been in seclusion for six years. I believe he is returning to God in a most profound way. I did not want that seclusion disturbed."

Maggie looked at her father. There was no change of expression on his face. But she knew. He had continued to run the money laundering through Paul and he had kept that part of his life from his confessor. *Omerta.*

Bellini said, "With respect, Father, that was not your decision to make."

A flush passed over the cardinal's thin face. For a breath a charged silence sparked between them, then he said, "I am painfully aware that I must continue to struggle with the sins of pride and arrogance. I ask for your forgiveness."

Bellini edged off the seat onto one knee. He reached for the cardinal's hand and pressed his lips to the ring. Matterini rested the other hand on his head, his lips moved in prayer, then he bent to raise Bellini to his feet. The two men started toward the tiny confessional at the back of the church.

"Eminence," Maggie called.

The cardinal turned.

"So Bobby Patrelli never knew where my father was?"

"No. Only I knew. And your mother, of course. Have faith, Andrea. Everything will be all right."

"Yes, I think it will. Thank you, Father Vittorio," she said. It was the form of address she had used when she was a child and a smile softened the cardinal's austere face.

Whatever he had done, Cardinal Matterini's presence on that wharf tonight would ensure the safety of both her son and her father. She just had to have the faith that Sam, too, was safe.

THIRTY-SIX

"You've got a death wish, Cady, you know that?" FBI Special Agent Adashek braced himself on the scarred table, his arms shaking, either from taking his weight, or from rage. It was hard to tell, the man had iron control.

They were in the police building at JFK, where the Coast Guard had forced Sam to land the Robinson 22—now being dismantled and searched. Sam had told every officer who'd tried to interrogate him—Coast Guard, customs, NYPD, resident FBI agents, other unnamed hard-faced men—that he was willing to talk, but only to Special Agent Adashek of the organized crime unit. They'd run him through the system and come up with Adashek's flag against his name. Someone had made the call.

"Thanks for the character assessment, Adashek. Those hoods were shooting at me and I defended myself. They're the guys who've got Jimmy. Go talk to them." Sam got to his feet. "Better yet, let me talk to them."

"Sit down. We don't need your help. What the hell were you doing out there?"

"I told you. Defending myself."

"You just happened to be out joyriding in a chopper owned by some fancy country club and these guys opened fire. I'm supposed to believe that?"

Sam regarded him silently.

Adashek snorted. "If you'd done what you agreed and called us regularly from the house at Port Washington, kept us in the loop, you would have saved everyone, mostly yourself, a lot of grief. We were cruising the neighborhood, trying to keep out of your way."

"Yeah, like the three blind mice. You did see O'Malley's thugs, I suppose?"

"Oh, give it up, Cady," Adashek said wearily. "What do you think?"

Before Sam could tell him, the door opened, two men entered. Sam recognized them instantly. Younger than he'd thought, early to mid-thirties, though their tight-assed ways made it hard to tell with the FBI, and he hadn't exactly taken the time to stop and study them. But definitely the guys from the hotel, the same two who had been in the car outside the house at Port Washington.

"Cady," one said to him. "Just tell me how you managed to disappear on 53rd and Madison. I was right behind you, and then you were gone." He was smiling, friendly, interested. The good cop.

"This is Agent Brad Steers," Adashek introduced them. "And Agent Zig Warchawski."

"Both organized crime, I suppose," Sam said. "Neither looking for my son."

"You're wrong, Cady," Adashek said. "No thanks to you, we think we've got something."

Sam leaned forward. "What?"

"Too early to assess, but—"

"Adashek, this is my boy. Come on, man, what have you got?"

"I'm waiting for a call. If it comes, I'll know more."

Adashek looked at his watch. "It's after ten. If something's going down, I'll know about it pretty soon."

As if on cue, a phone buzzed and Adashek reached into an inner pocket, retrieved his mobile. He got to his feet, turned his back. "Yeah." Without another word, he crossed to the door, went out, pulling it closed behind him.

"What's going on?" Sam asked. He addressed the room in general, but neither agent responded so he looked directly at Steers. "Who's he talking to?"

"Sam, it's okay." Warchawski answered for his colleague. "Steve knows what he's doing. He's been working on this for a long time."

"My boy's been gone three days."

"Yeah, we know," Brad Steers said. "There are other issues here but your boy has not been lost in the shuffle. I know that's what you think, but you're wrong. Steve understands what it is to—"

"Okay, Brad," Warchawski interrupted. "No need to give the store away."

Steers shrugged, folded his arms across his chest, propped up the wall. Sam slid his eyes from one to the other. Something here wasn't sitting right. A cold finger of anxiety stirred in his bowels.

Adashek came back into the room. At first glance he showed no emotion, another look and the area around his mouth was white with tension.

The man was under serious strain.

"Okay, time to roll."

Sam grabbed his jacket—Giacomo Bellini's jacket—from the back of his chair. "What's happening?" That question seemed to be his mantra these days.

"There's going to be an exchange. Your boy's fine. If Salvatore Bellini turns up as he says he will, you're home free."

"And Maggie?"

Adashek frowned. "You mean Andrea. Yes. She's okay."

"Where's it happening, Steve?" Warchawski asked.

"Wharf F, Hoboken. I want to be in place by midnight."

The same FBI chopper that had brought the three agents to JFK was waiting to take them back to the city. The site of the attack on Manhattan was a gaping hole in the brilliance of the lighted buildings, but apart from that, the view was phenomenal. When this was over, Sam promised himself, he and Jimmy would take the same helicopter trip together. The FBI would surely do that for a little guy...so small and defenseless...

He took several deep breaths.

The chopper put down on the helipad that topped the Federal Plaza building on the edge of Chinatown, and they took the elevator down to the underground parking garage.

Sam looked around expecting to see a hive of activity. An organized crime figure was going down, a kidnapped child retrieved, but at eleven at night, the garage was quiet. Only the three FBI agents and one very anxious husband and father.

Warchawski slid behind the wheel of a black four-door sedan, Steers took the shotgun seat. Adashek opened a back door.

"Wait a minute," Sam said. "Who else is going along here? Not just the four of us."

"We don't leave anything to chance. Teams are already getting into place," Adashek replied. "Now get in, or get out of the way, Cady. There's no time to horse around here."

Sam got into the back without more argument. His position was not strong and he knew it. In spite of television police dramas, it was damn near unheard-of for a civilian, even an ex-cop, to be allowed along on a law enforcement action, particularly one run by the FBI.

They took the Holland Tunnel to Jersey, turned north on Washington Boulevard, then penetrated Hoboken's bleakly industrial wharf district. No one spoke, but the tension in the car was palpable. The buildings were dark, punctuated by the flickering neon of a few saloons, the steamy windows of the occasional diner. Sam watched the passing streets, expecting to see federal agents in the same dark cars converging on the designated wharf, but if they were there, they kept their distance, and their radios were silent.

Adashek leaned forward to speak in Warchawski's ear. "Take the next turn. Keep it down."

The well-tuned engine turned over slowly, making little sound. Warchawski nosed the car over a chain-link fence that had long since been knocked adrift from the decrepit gateposts. Overhead, the weathered lettering on the wooden sign spanning the gates was indecipherable. They rumbled over metal tracks, and Warchawski cut the speed even more. At Adashek's instruction he took several more turns, until the car was inching along a tunnel created by two dark, decaying warehouses. The tunnel ended at a sharp left turn, and before them there were the skyscrapers of Manhattan putting on a misty magical light show on the far side of the fog-shrouded East River. Warchawski eased the sedan along until the black oil-slick water became visible and with it a couple of derelict barges leaning drunkenly at their moorings, some overturned trash barrels, a few bits of rusty equipment too far gone to be of use or even sell for scrap.

"This is good," Adashek said. "Stop here."

"Where are your people?" Sam looked around. "No one's here."

"Don't worry, Sam, we've got enough people here," Adashek

said. "If you could see them they wouldn't be much good, right?"

The mobile in Sam's pocket buzzed, and the three agents' heads turned his way. Quickly he retrieved the phone, holding it out of Adashek's reach as the FBI man grabbed for it.

"For God's sake! Not now, Cady."

Warchawski half turned to look a silent question at Adashek in the seat directly behind him and Adashek shook his head.

"It'll be Bianca Bellini, and I have to talk to her," Sam said. "I left my number and told her to call if she heard from my wife." He turned away, lowered his voice. "Yes?"

"Sam, listen to this," Petey Le Pont's voice said.

"It'll have to be later, buddy. You've got me at a bad time," Sam said softly.

"No, wait, I'll make it fast, you gotta hear this. I've been nosing around here a bit, had a few drinks with Wilson out of the New Orleans field office. He tells me Adashek's only son was undercover. And get this. The kid was killed by the mob a week before that fuckup at Bear Mountain. Sam, according to Wilson, the FBI went in there blazing, Adashek and some of the kid's pals, no intention of taking anyone in. It's the old story, the feds protect their own, so it's no harm, no foul, no court, no convictions. The junior men got transferred out of OCU. Adashek was too big a dog, but he's been locked to a desk ever since. The guy doesn't do fieldwork, Sam, his latest gig is twenty-four seven tracing Al Qaeda money. So what the hell is he doing, getting you out of jail, making propositions like that?"

Sam felt the blood draining from his face. The niggle in the back of his mind jumped into focus. For the last year, the FBI had eased off on the mob, and Adashek was too close to retirement age for this to be a career advancement play, as Petey had suggested. Plus, until tonight, Adashek had always turned up alone, contrary to Bureau policy. This was personal.

"Got it. Thanks," Sam said. He replaced the phone in his pocket.

"Who was it?" Adashek asked.

"Petey Le Pont in New Orleans."

"This time of night? What did he want?"

"Just tipping me off the FBI knows I'm in New York."

Adashek grunted. "Good to have friends—"

"Here they come," Steers whispered.

From their spot between the two buildings they had a wide view of the loading area bordering the river. A dark Lincoln Town Car, its lights off, inched into view. It stopped, looking like a cardboard cutout against the Manhattan skyline.

"Who is it?" Steers asked.

"O'Malley. He's early," Adashek answered. "It's half past midnight. The meet was set for one."

The silence inside the sedan deepened. Sam could feel the sweat running down inside his T-shirt. Where was Adashek getting his information? Come to that, when had the calls been made to put FBI teams in place around the wharf?

The Sig was in his belt in back, but Sam was pressed against the leather seat and couldn't get to it without bringing attention to himself. Slowly, he reached down to loosen the .22 tucked into his ankle holster. The weapons had been returned to him again on Adashek's order. He'd wondered about that at the time. Now he knew why he'd been allowed to come along. He was not intended to get out of this alive. If he were armed, law enforcement would claim a righteous kill, the internal investigation would be a walk-through.

"Heads up," Warchawski said softly. "Here we go."

A second car came into view, headlights on, making no effort at stealth. The car was a dark Mercedes. The last time Sam had seen it had been in the garage at Port Washington. The car made a turn until it faced the Lincoln, leaving a distance of twenty feet between them.

The Lincoln turned on its lights. The back door opened and a man got out.

"It's going down," Steers said. He pumped the sawed-off shotgun he retrieved from beneath his seat. Then, "Hey, that's a priest. What in hell's going on?"

"It's Bobby Patrelli. He's a mob mediator," Adashek said. "His father, Benito, was Sal's consigliere."

"So what's he doing with O'Malley? Did you know about this?" Steers asked. "Steve, I thought this was going to be a straight hit on—"

"Shut up, Brad," Warchawski said. "The guy's a mobster in a dog collar. Don't sweat it."

Sam palmed the .22 and kept his eyes on the Lincoln. No matter what happened here, there was a chance that Jimmy was inside that Town Car. He felt for the door handle.

A man emerged from the Mercedes, and Sam took his eyes from the Lincoln long enough to get a bearing on him. Tall, thin, white haired. Another priest, his hand in front of his face to protect his eyes from the blinding glare of the Lincoln's headlights. He walked toward the Town Car.

"Hey, wait a minute," Steers said. "Wait a minute. That's another priest. Jesus, it's Cardinal Matterini. Oh, Christ! No one said anything about killing a cardinal. I'm a Catholic, I can't kill a cardinal—"

"Hey, Steve," Warchawski turned to look at Adashek. "I'm with Brad on this. We can't do a—"

Sam had a glimpse of the silencer on the pistol in Adashek's hand in the same instant he heard the hiss of the compressed gas, the double thuds as Steers's head exploded, then Warchawski's.

Sam wrenched at the door handle and fell out as Adashek swung the weapon toward him. The hiss of the third shot was the last thing he heard.

* * *

"I can't see Jimmy," Maggie said. The windows of the Lincoln were dark. Provanto, behind the wheel of the Mercedes, leaned aside to give her a better view through the windshield. She could see Bobby Patrelli standing by the open back door of the Lincoln, Cardinal Matterini walking slowly toward him, one hand to his eyes. Suddenly she realized what an old man the cardinal was. "Is he there? Is Jimmy there in the back seat? Can you see him, Donnie?"

Provanto shook his head. "No, I can't see nothing."

"Vittorio will check. As soon as he has seen Giacomo and spoken to O'Malley, he will signal and I will get out," Sal Bellini said. "We will talk and O'Malley will see that we were all the targets of the FBI. They set us up. His brothers, my son, the others. We will settle this thing." He took Maggie's hand. "This man you married, this policeman. He is a good man?"

Maggie's eyes were locked on the Lincoln. She didn't answer.

"Andrea, look at me," Bellini said. "Your husband. Is he a good man, a good father?"

Maggie tore her eyes away, turned to face him. "Yes, Papa. He is. A good husband, a good father."

Bellini nodded. He leaned forward, touched his lips to her forehead. "Your mother always said you have been the child of my heart since you were born." He laughed softly. "A cop. Well, you have my blessing for this marriage to your policeman."

Maggie started to respond, but her attention was caught by the two priests. They turned sharply toward the dark warehouses to the side and behind them. Patrelli started to run back to the Lincoln.

"What's the matter? What's happening?" Maggie asked in alarm. "They've heard something. Oh my God, Jimmy... What are they doing?"

The doors of the Lincoln slammed open. Two men scrambled out, weapons trained on the alley between the buildings.

"Fuck!" Provanto grabbed the semiautomatic from under his seat and opened his door.

Maggie fumbled in her backpack for the .38 Donnie had given her—she had dismissed the cardinal's naive talk about weapons. Too much was at stake for her to trust reassurances made by O'Malley. She knew her father felt the same. She slipped the .38 into her pocket and looked at her father. He caught her glance and opened his coat so that she could see the butt of the gun under his arm.

O'Malley was out of the front seat of the Lincoln. "Hey, Sal, long time no see," he shouted toward the Mercedes. "Come on, man, get out here. I got something here for you."

"Salvatore, wait there," Cardinal Matterini called. "Michael, you gave me your word. Have these men put their guns away. There will be no shooting here tonight."

O'Malley turned to his men. "What's the matter with you guys? Don't you know it's uncouth to shoot people in front of a cardinal?" He grinned at Matterini, spread his arms helplessly, his own weapon dangling from his right hand. "Hey, what am I gonna do, Father? They're not going to listen to me. The nuns did their best to whack good manners into us Micks, but it didn't take." He tapped the gun against his forehead. "Thick Irish skulls, Father, know what I mean?" He stopped smiling, turned his head. "Tim, get the kid."

Bobby Patrelli stood in front of the back door of the Lincoln. "Leave him where he is. You don't need him here."

Tim swung the gun in his hand against Patrelli's head, and he staggered away from the door long enough for Tim to drag a small figure out of the Lincoln. Patrelli recovered, lunged forward, wrapped his arms around both figures. The men swayed, struggling, the child caught between them.

"Jimmy!" Maggie scrambled across her father to reach the door. Salvatore Bellini grappled with her, trying to hold her back. He opened the door and got out, Maggie right after him. Sal kept a strong grip on her arm to restrain her.

"Stop it," Bellini said. "Wait, Andrea. Wait. You want Jimmy in the middle of a bloodbath?"

Maggie heard the urgency in his voice. She looked across at the Lincoln. O'Malley's other gunman had knocked Bobby Patrelli to his knees and was holding a gun to his head. Tim held Jimmy in front of him, exposed, vulnerable, the man's hands gripping the boy's fragile shoulders.

Maggie stopped struggling. "Jimmy, sweetheart," she called. "It's Mommy, sugar. Jimmy, it's okay, sweet boy, Mommy's here. Just stay still for a few minutes, then I'll come get you. Stay very still, honey."

Jimmy was crying but he did not struggle. "Mommy. Mommy. I want to go home."

O'Malley laughed. "Gets you in the heart, right, Sal? Your grandson, how about that? Hey, Andrea, how you doing, babe? Come on, now. All you gotta do is send old Sal over here and you get your kid."

Cardinal Matterini put a hand on O'Malley's arm. "Wait, Michael, this is not the way." O'Malley pushed him away.

"Stay here, Andrea. Don't move," Bellini murmured. "Tell your mother I have always loved her." He turned suddenly, held her in a fierce embrace. "Forgive me for the years of silence." He released her and walked toward the Lincoln, his arms held away from his body. "Vittorio, take my grandson."

"Papa, wait." Maggie started after him.

"Salvatore! Stay where you are," Cardinal Matterini shouted.

Sam opened his eyes, the sound of voices penetrating the buzz in his ears. He raised himself onto an elbow. What remained of Steers's head rested amid the blood and brain matter draining down the passenger door window. The other fed, Warshawski, was slumped over the wheel. Sam put his hand up, felt his own blood still oozing. He'd taken a head shot from a crack marksman and lived, but scalp wounds bled like crazy. His skull seemed filled with static, but gradually the voices became clearer. Sam inched his way around the car. Adashek was a black outline crouched against the denser black of the warehouse. Beyond him in the glare of the headlights Sam could see the Lincoln, its doors open, Jimmy held in front of a gunman, Bobby Patrelli on his knees with a gun to his head.

Carefully Sam grabbed the door of the sedan, dragged himself to his feet, then heard Maggie's frightened voice, "Papa, wait," and another, a man's, shouting for Salvatore not to move.

Adashek raised the weapon in his hand.

"Maggie," Sam shouted. "Maggie, get down."

At the sound of his voice, Adashek turned and loosed a stream of fire toward the sedan, then stepped out into the open.

"Bellini," he shouted. "Remember my son? Jason Adashek of the FBI. You killed him. Are you watching, Sal?" Adashek swung the weapon toward Jimmy. "This is for him."

Jesus God, Sam screamed in his head. It wasn't Bellini he wanted. *It was Jimmy.*

Sam grabbed the Sig from his belt and fired, his vision obscured by the blood from the wound in his head. Adashek staggered, then dropped to his knees, struggling to hold up the weapon in both hands, to keep it trained on Jimmy.

Sam ran forward, his finger locked around the trigger of the Sig. Adashek jerked with the impact of each bullet. He fell forward, braced himself on his hands. He lifted his head, rocked with the effort to stay upright, then slowly crumpled to his side.

Sam shoved the Sig to his temple. Adashek's eyes were open, but he was dead. The last thing he must have seen was Sal Bellini, alive and running toward his grandson.

Gunfire seemed to be coming from all directions. A voice shouted, "Vittorio, get down!"

Sam jumped over Adashek to get to his son, but it was over in seconds. The scene played out like an old black-and-white movie, flickering light and shadow: Bellini firing at the gunman holding Jimmy; the man collapsing; Patrelli grabbing up the child, throwing him halfway into the Lincoln then covering Jimmy with his own body; Maggie, a shadowy figure running in the dark on the other side of the headlights, reaching her son, straddling Jimmy and the priest, her left hand cupping the right, the gun in her hand steady; Provanto dropping the other gun-man, then trying to take down O'Malley crouched on the other side of the Lincoln; and Salvatore Bellini taking round after round from O'Malley, yet still somehow staying on his feet, stumbling toward his daughter and grandson.

Maggie screamed, "Papa!" She swung her weapon toward O'Malley. O'Malley turned to look at her. His mouth opened in astonishment as she fired. Life had already left his body when it hit the filthy cracked paving stones of the loading dock.

The sudden silence was a shock.

The Sig heavy in his hand, Sam walked to where Maggie sat on the wet ground holding their son, her back against the back wheel of the Lincoln, her hand spread against Jimmy's head, pressing his face into her shoulder. Patrelli was on his knees, his arms around them both.

As if feeling Sam's presence, Patrelli raised his head and met Sam's gaze. He hesitated, then ran his hand over Maggie's hair, the caress lingering as if he could not bear to end it. He stood. Silently, the two men looked at each other, then Patrelli said, "Are you all right, Sam?"

"Yeah." He glanced at Maggie and his son, then looked back at the priest. "Thank you."

Patrelli nodded then went to the body of Michael O'Malley.

He dropped to his knees and started the ritual words of the last rites of the Roman Catholic Church. Cardinal Matterini, with a bloody and weeping Donnie Provanto at his side, was already praying over the lifeless body of his *paisano,* Salvatore Bellini.

Maggie stroked Jimmy's hair. "Daddy's here, sweetheart, it's okay," she whispered. She looked up, then stared at the body of her father. Her face was creased into lines of grief. "He tried to get to us, Sam."

"I know, Mags. I saw him."

Suddenly Sam's legs lost the last vestige of strength. He dropped to his knees, wrapped his arms around his wife and son.

"We're going home now, Jimmy. It's okay now, son. Mommy and I are taking you home, honey."

THIRTY-SEVEN

"So when are you and Maggie going to give Jimmy a sister?" Petey Le Pont asked. He'd changed from the well-tailored blue suit he'd worn for the christening of his daughter and now wore a T-shirt emblazoned with the logo from Chef T-Paul's Louisiana Kitchen.

"We've talked about it, but we think it's too soon," Sam answered. He and Maggie had just stood as godparents for two-month-old Camille Margaretta Le Pont. "Jimmy still needs to know he's really safe, that everyone's in their place. We don't want to make any changes."

On the other side of the Le Pont's garden, Deke Washington looked up from where he was cruising the buffet table set up under the arbor and caught Sam's eye. Eyebrows raised, Washington shook his head slowly from side to side, a slight smile of wry bemusement around his lips. He lifted his glass in salute, and Sam grinned at him as he raised his own glass.

Petey said, "How's it feel to have a grande dame of the old-time Mafia as a mother-in-law?"

Sam looked over at Bianca Bellini, hovering with Maggie over Elle and her new daughter. "Getting used to it. Maggie's happy and that makes me happy."

Petey grinned. "You always were crazy about that woman."

"Yeah, well, Jimmy's got grandparents now, my dad and Bianca. We're a family. It's a bit awkward sometimes but we're working on it. That's a lovely little girl you got there, Pierre."

Pete kept his eyes on Elle, glowing with pleasure as people admired her daughter. "Yeah. Looks just like her mother."

"Lucky for her she doesn't look like you."

Petey raised his long neck in mock salute. "Friends like you, who needs the FB and I? How's Jimmy doing? He looks pretty good."

Jimmy was hunkered down with Petey's son, Yves, in the shade of a mimosa tree, digging a hole with the help of a half-grown Rottweiler pup. Maggie was laughing and chatting with other women, very deliberately keeping out of Jimmy's way but making sure she was always visible to him.

"He's doing all right," Sam answered. "Still gets nightmares, but the dog's been a godsend. Thanks for bringing him over." He and Maggie had been uncertain at first when Petey had put the puppy in Jimmy's lap, fearing it would reopen the wound of losing Max. But the reverse had happened, and the two dogs seemed to have fused into one in Jimmy's mind. "He feels safe with Max in his room."

"Thought he would. Next thing is to pry him loose from his mama and take the boys fishing."

"Well, maybe. We'll give it another couple months." He looked at Pete. "Agent Wilson called me yesterday, laid out the whole story. It seems Adashek had it planned down to the last detail. He hired the Jamaican through contacts in the island, nothing anyone can take to a court of law, but Wilson says the source is kosher. He killed Menton and the Jamaican and the kid in the liquor store. He had help with Ricci and Paul Bellini."

"What about the old man, the old drunk, what's his name?"

"Yankee. I don't know his real name." He'd thought about trying to trace Yankee's identity, but decided against it. Nothing to be gained by keeping the past alive. "Adashek killed him to get extra leverage with me. He knew I'd be arrested and was waiting for me. Anyway, the investigation has been wound up."

"Yeah? So when's the trial?"

"What trial? Who? The whole thing was limited to the three FBI men."

"All conveniently dead, and no more embarrassment to the Bureau," Petey said.

"Man, you're a cynic," Sam said. "Brad Steers and Zig Warchawski went through Quantico with Jason Adashek. They were all three on the fast track and pretty tight, but the Bear Mountain shoot-out ruined their careers. Jason's killing had all the earmarks of the mob, it wasn't hard for Steve Adashek to enlist them. The way Wilson tells it, Adashek kept a watch on Bianca, followed her to the monastery, picked up Maggie that way, like you said. They found a set of plans of our house in his office at Quantico. They'd been stolen from the architect who did the remodel. The guy didn't even notice they were gone until he was asked to look. Wilson claims the Federal Witness Protection Program is watertight."

"Yeah, and I got a nice piece of land down in the swamp I'd like to sell him."

"Well, that's what the man said. Anyway, seems Adashek had spent some time smoothing paths for the Shamrock Corporation, gambling, prostitution, gunrunning. They had no trouble providing a plane, no questions asked. Adashek played O'Malley like a violin. It wasn't difficult to enlist him. You know the Irish, they love a blood feud as much as the Sicilians."

"Now there's a complex character."

"Mick? Yes, he really liked kids." O'Malley had kept Jimmy in his home with his own children. It was not clear whether he knew Adashek's plan had been to kill Jimmy in front of Salvatore Bellini. "His wife took it all in her stride. I don't think she knew who was there and who wasn't. Not that she'd ever cross Mick, he'd loosened her teeth more than once."

Maggie looked up, caught Sam looking at her. She wore a pale filmy-type dress, and Sam's heart lurched in the old familiar way as she half turned her head and smiled at him.

Petey followed his eyes and said, "That poor bastard still holed up on the island, praying for his immortal soul?"

Sam did not have to ask what poor bastard. "Last I heard. On permanent retreat in the monastery there."

"Jesus, that gives me the creeps," Petey said. "Can you imagine, spending your life in a place called Pestilence, struggling between God and the flesh like that?"

Sam looked at him and grinned. "Man, that's a very deep thought."

Petey shrugged. "Yeah, well, I'm a deep kind of guy."

The Cajun band Petey had hired for the christening party swung into "Jolie Blonde," to the whooping appreciation of the guests, mostly NOPD cops and their wives.

Petey draped a beefy arm over Sam's shoulder. "Come on, bubba. Let's go dance with our ladies."